Anthony Gilbert and The Murder Room

>>> This title is part of The Murder Room, our series dedicated to making available out-of-print or hard-to-find titles by classic crime writers.

Crime fiction has always held up a mirror to society. The Victorians were fascinated by sensational murder and the emerging science of detection; now we are obsessed with the forensic detail of violent death. And no other genre has so captivated and enthralled readers.

Vast troves of classic crime writing have for a long time been unavailable to all but the most dedicated frequenters of second-hand bookshops. The advent of digital publishing means that we are now able to bring you the backlists of a huge range of titles by classic and contemporary crime writers, some of which have been out of print for decades.

From the genteel amateur private eyes of the Golden Age and the femmes fatales of pulp fiction, to the morally ambiguous hard-boiled detectives of mid twentieth-century America and their descendants who walk our twenty-first century streets, The Murder Room has it all. **>>>**

The Murder Room
Where Criminal Minds Meet

themurderroom.com

T0352387

Anthony Gilbert (1899–1973)

Anthony Gilbert was the pen name of Lucy Beatrice Malleson. Born in London, she spent all her life there, and her affection for the city is clear from the strong sense of character and place in evidence in her work. She published 69 crime novels, 51 of which featured her best known character, Arthur Crook, a vulgar London lawyer totally (and deliberately) unlike the aristocratic detectives, such as Lord Peter Wimsey, who dominated the mystery field at the time. She also wrote more than 25 radio plays, which were broadcast in Great Britain and overseas. Her thriller *The Woman in Red* (1941) was broadcast in the United States by CBS and made into a film in 1945 under the title *My Name is Julia Ross*. She was an early member of the British Detection Club, which, along with Dorothy L. Sayers, she prevented from disintegrating during World War II. Malleson published her autobiography, *Three-a-Penny*, in 1940, and wrote numerous short stories, which were published in several anthologies and in such periodicals as *Ellery Queen's Mystery Magazine* and *The Saint*. The short story 'You Can't Hang Twice' received a Queens award in 1946. She never married, and evidence of her feminism is elegantly expressed in much of her work.

By Anthony Gilbert

Scott Egerton series
Tragedy at Freyne (1927)
The Murder of Mrs
  Davenport (1928)
Death at Four Corners (1929)
The Mystery of the Open
  Window (1929)
The Night of the Fog (1930)
The Body on the Beam (1932)
The Long Shadow (1932)
The Musical Comedy
  Crime (1933)
An Old Lady Dies (1934)
The Man Who Was Too
  Clever (1935)

Mr Crook Murder
  Mystery series
Murder by Experts (1936)
The Man Who Wasn't
  There (1937)
Murder Has No Tongue (1937)
Treason in My Breast (1938)
The Bell of Death (1939)
Dear Dead Woman (1940)
  aka *Death Takes a Redhead*
The Vanishing Corpse (1941)
  aka *She Vanished in the Dawn*
The Woman in Red (1941)
  aka *The Mystery of the
  Woman in Red*

Death in the Blackout (1942)
  aka *The Case of the Tea-
  Cosy's Aunt*
Something Nasty in the
  Woodshed (1942)
  aka *Mystery in the Woodshed*
The Mouse Who Wouldn't
  Play Ball (1943)
  aka *30 Days to Live*
He Came by Night (1944)
  aka *Death at the Door*
The Scarlet Button (1944)
  aka *Murder Is Cheap*
A Spy for Mr Crook (1944)
The Black Stage (1945)
  aka *Murder Cheats the Bride*
Don't Open the Door (1945)
  aka *Death Lifts the Latch*
Lift Up the Lid (1945)
  aka *The Innocent Bottle*
The Spinster's Secret (1946)
  aka *By Hook or by Crook*
Death in the Wrong Room
  (1947)
Die in the Dark (1947)
  aka *The Missing Widow*
Death Knocks Three Times
  (1949)
Murder Comes Home (1950)
A Nice Cup of Tea (1950)
  aka *The Wrong Body*

Lady-Killer (1951)

Miss Pinnegar Disappears (1952)
aka *A Case for Mr Crook*

Footsteps Behind Me (1953)
aka *Black Death*

Snake in the Grass (1954)
aka *Death Won't Wait*

Is She Dead Too? (1955)
aka *A Question of Murder*

And Death Came Too (1956)

Riddle of a Lady (1956)

Give Death a Name (1957)

Death Against the Clock (1958)

Death Takes a Wife (1959)
aka *Death Casts a Long Shadow*

Third Crime Lucky (1959)
aka *Prelude to Murder*

Out for the Kill (1960)

She Shall Die (1961)
aka *After the Verdict*

Uncertain Death (1961)

No Dust in the Attic (1962)

Ring for a Noose (1963)

The Fingerprint (1964)

The Voice (1964)
aka *Knock, Knock! Who's There?*

Passenger to Nowhere (1965)

The Looking Glass Murder (1966)

The Visitor (1967)

Night Encounter (1968)
aka *Murder Anonymous*

Missing from Her Home (1969)

Death Wears a Mask (1970)
aka *Mr Crook Lifts the Mask*

Murder is a Waiting Game (1972)

Tenant for the Tomb (1971)

A Nice Little Killing (1974)

Standalone Novels

The Case Against Andrew Fane (1931)

Death in Fancy Dress (1933)

The Man in the Button Boots (1934)

Courtier to Death (1936)
aka *The Dover Train Mystery*

The Clock in the Hatbox (1939)

Death Takes a Wife

Anthony Gilbert

An Orion book

Copyright © Lucy Beatrice Malleson 1959

The right of Lucy Beatrice Malleson to be identified as the author of this work has been asserted in accordance with the Copyright, Designs and Patents Act 1988.

This edition published by
The Orion Publishing Group Ltd
Orion House
5 Upper St Martin's Lane
London WC2H 9EA

An Hachette UK company
A CIP catalogue record for this book is available from the British Library

ISBN 978 1 4719 1014 2

www.orionbooks.co.uk

CHAPTER ONE

'IN THE MIDST of life we are in death,' intoned Dr. MacIntyre genially. 'Now, Nurse, there's no need for you to look so disturbed. You did everything you could. Even if Miss Turton's sister is inclined to think we should have worked a miracle, well, we know what the laity are like.'

But the girl to whom these encouraging words were addressed continued to look pale and apprehensive.

'Why exactly did she die?' she asked.

Dr. MacIntyre looked disapproving. 'Because she had pneumonia. She was only two years from her allotted span, pneumonia is particularly dangerous at that age. Now, you'll let Mrs. Esdaile know what's happened, and, take my advice, Nurse, try and get a couple of days off. You've had a lot of hard cases lately, and I can't have my favourite nurse getting peaked. Now, I must just have a word with the sister . . .' and off he bounced, as jaunty as Santa Claus.

Miles Gordon, the young architect who had surprised everyone, except himself, by winning the County competition for a new Masonic Hall at West Barsley, was driving

1

past in his ramshackle car when the door of The Firs opened and Nurse Wayland appeared. She was still in uniform and carried a small case.

Her expression bothered him. They had known one another for two years or so, ever since she had nursed his aunt through a nasty attack of gastro-enteritis. He stopped the car.

'Helen!'

She came out of the gate without apparently seeing him. He tooted the horn and she looked up. He swung open the door.

'Get in.'

She hesitated. 'Mrs. Esdaile doesn't like us accepting lifts when we're in uniform,' she murmured.

'She'll like it even less if you're brought in on a stretcher!'

He reached over and took the little case.

'I could sleep for a hundred years,' said Helen unexpectedly, collapsing in the seat beside him.

He put the car in motion. 'Old Murdering Mac been at it again?'

'Miles!'

'Oh come, you must have heard that before. You know as well as I do the old boy hasn't opened a textbook since he graduated forty years ago. Talk about getting away with murder. Who was it this time?'

'Ellen Turton. But . . .'

'Look!' He took one hand off the wheel and put it momentarily over hers. 'Don't fly off the handle but take the advice of a well-wisher. Get Ma Esdaile to hire you out to some other doctor, one whose patients don't invariably hand in their checks. It's not doing you any good, you know.'

'I don't know what you mean.' Her voice was breathless.

Staring straight ahead Miles began to chant:

'Have you ever wondered why
All Nurse Wayland's patients die?
Other doctors feel as you do.
Poor Nurse Wayland, she's a hoodoo.'

'That's sheer nonsense. Just because you've an aptitude for these silly rhymes . . .'

'I didn't write it.'

'Oh!' That brought her up short. 'But people can't actually think . . .'

'I can only assure you that Dr. Hawke wanted someone for a child case some time back and Ma Esdaile offered him you—he told me this himself—and he said he'd prefer someone whose patients occasionally survived. Not knocking you, mind, but truth's what the other chap believes, and it's going the rounds that you—well, that you are a hoodoo.'

'You can't be serious.' But her voice was uncertain. She was remembering another incident a month or so previously that seemed to bear out Miles's contention.

'I know all about hoodoos,' Miles went on. 'My father was one. A stockbroker. He only had to invest half a crown in a prosperous gold mine, say, for the vein to dry up overnight. Why, he once wrote a cracking good letter to *The Times* and they didn't dare print it for fear they might cease publication at the week-end.'

She laughed unexpectedly. With the cloud momentarily lifted from her face you saw what an attractive creature she could be, with her bright smooth hair and blue-grey eyes, and the mouth that, too large for perfect beauty, gave character and charm to the face.

'Here we are,' said Miles, drawing up a few doors away from Mrs. Esdaile's famous nursing home. ('Get one of the Esdaile's nurses if you can,' doctors told their patients' families. 'If anyone can cheat death they can.') 'Now, if the old girl's propped at the window, she'll see you stepping in on your own feet. And don't forget what I said. You're getting too many notches on your stick and that's a fact.'

Mrs. Esdaile stared at Helen. 'Gone? Well, that's a surprise. Still, there's never any knowing. You look as if you could do with a change.'

'So I could,' said Helen. 'Of course, I know Dr. MacIntyre's patients are all elderly and so more prone to qualify for a death certificate, but do you think next time I might go to a case with some prospects of survival?'

Mrs. Esdaile's dark pug face sharpened. So she'd been hearing the whispers, too. No wonder Mac always asked for her, the type of girl to rouse confidence in the most cynical breast. But it was hardly fair to her. She, too, remembered Dr. Hawke's swift denial.

'All right,' she said. 'It's time you had a break.'

So you might say it was due to Miles Gordon that Helen ever met Paul French.

* * *

It was Paul's wife, Blanche, who was her prospective patient. Blanche's father had been 'Midas' Mullins, for whom everything he touched turned to gold and who expected, as indeed she did also, to find that money could buy him his heart's desire. So it was a shock when the confidently anticipated son turned out to be a girl. Being a rich man's daughter proved no advantage to Blanche, who grew up with a sense of inferiority and secret resentment against Providence. Her father warned her that the world was full of fortune-hunters aching to be a rich man's son-in-law, and took care to see that no poor young man ever crossed his threshold.

'I haven't worked like a Trojan all these years to see my money chucked away by some young spendthrift,' he said.

By the time she was thirty Blanche was aware of her reputation as 'that dull Mullins girl.' She played a fair game of golf and drove a handsome car all over the county; she presided at the head of her father's table when he entertained his business associates, she knew their wives were sorry for her, and that she could look forward to nothing but being an even richer middle-aged woman in due course. She didn't have to earn a living and her father wouldn't have heard of her trying; she learned to paint on china, which she didn't do very well. That was all 'Midas' Mullins's money had done for her.

And then she met Paul French.

It was the chanciest of meetings. Paul was employed by a lawyer called Jayne, he was twenty-one, had neither money nor influence, but great ambition, drive, and a firm intention to climb to the top of the tree the hard way if there was no other. His parents had been killed by one of the German bombs in 1944 when he was eighteen and just due to join up. After the war he found himself without money and, not caring for the plans a parental Government was making for him, found himself a job with Stanley, Jayne and Stanley.

Mrs. Jayne was giving a dinner-party and at the eleventh hour one of the guests cracked his ankle and couldn't attend. Mrs. Jayne rang her husband.

'Bill Wallace has let me down,' she said. 'I can't find another man at this stage, bring someone from your office, anyone will do who won't get drunk and possesses a dinner-jacket. He can go down with that Mullins girl. It doesn't matter much who she has, she'll sit like an idol right through the meal.'

Mr. Jayne looked about him desperately; most of his staff were married men who couldn't be asked out at short notice without their wives. Then his glance fell on Paul. A nice-looking boy, he thought, a good worker, a good-looker, too, though that hadn't struck him before, not likely to have any very important engagement for to-night and probably tickled pink to be asked to dinner with the boss. Only thing was he probably hadn't got a dinner-jacket.

'Dinner-jacket, sir?' said Paul, looking surprised. (It was typical of Jayne that he asked about the dinner-jacket before finding out if his clerk was free that evening.) 'Why, yes, sir.'

'Good. Give you a chance to air it. My wife wants me to bring an extra man to dinner. Not doing anything to-night, I suppose?' he added, as an afterthought.

'Nothing I can't put off,' said Paul, promptly. He didn't imagine there'd be much sparkle to an evening dominated by the Jaynes, but a young man with his way to make has to take the rough with the smooth. So far Jayne had scarcely noticed his existence. If he could make him think, 'Why, there's more to the chap than I dreamed,' that meant one more step up the ladder.

As soon as Mr. Jayne had departed, leaving his clerk to close the office, Paul snatched up his hat and went along to see a friend who might be persuaded to lend him a dinner-jacket. That was the kind of man he was.

Blanche was far less of a fool than her father supposed. She saw in a flash what had happened. Someone had fallen out and the obvious substitute was being wished on to her. He was a young man who couldn't conceivably be interested in anything she had to say, probably thought thirty was as old as the hills.

Within ten minutes of the start of dinner she was astounded to find she was enjoying herself and, what was more, carrying on an easy conversation with her partner.

Paul had no inhibitions. He talked frankly about himself. Oh yes, he was going to be a lawyer, that's why he'd taken this job with old Jayne. True, he was only a hewer of wood and drawer of water at the moment, but he believed firmly—didn't she?—that if you wanted a thing badly enough you invariably got it.

'I'd like to,' Blanche admitted.

'What do you want most out of life?' No one had ever asked her that before. No one had cared enough. It wasn't surprising that his gay attentions went to her head. She was startled to find her tongue unlocked, her laughter coming spontaneously, if a little rustily, like water from a tap that hasn't been used for a long time. She asked him if he ever played golf; he said he could handle a club but that was about all. She asked him if he'd play a round with her the following Sunday, she'd pick him up about ten.

That was how it started.

It had been going on some time when the whispers reached Edgar Mullins's ears. 'What's all this nonsense about you and that boy from Jayne's office?' he asked his daughter.

'I don't know what you've heard,' said Blanche, her heart going like a piston.

'He's been playing golf with you.'

She nodded. (She didn't know till long afterwards that he'd hired his first set of clubs before he'd saved enough to buy them for himself. The dinner-jacket came first. He had the good sense to see things in perspective.) 'He plays a very good game. I tell him he should join your club.'

'You're making yourself conspicuous,' Edgar snapped. 'He's nobody.'

'He will be. If he'd had a little money everyone would have heard of him.'

'I don't choose to have my daughter a subject for gossip,' he snapped.

'Pity they've nothing better to talk about,' said Blanche airily, and then the telephone rang and she went to answer it and didn't come back.

* * *

When a bit later she told her father she was going to marry Paul French he didn't believe it. Then he said cruelly, 'Does he know?'

'It's not official yet; he has to pass his law exams. and of course he can only work in his spare time. I help him,' she added.

Edgar guffawed. 'You're dumber than I thought if you swallow that. Can't you see he's out to be a rich man's son-in-law?'

'If so,' said Blanche outrageously, 'he's in the minority. There hasn't been exactly a competition.'

'I'll have a word with the young man,' promised Edgar grimly.

He expected Paul to be overwhelmed, but he appeared sunnily calm. 'I quite see how it must appear to you, sir,' he acknowledged. 'Hanging up my hat on a golden hook. But it's not like that at all.'

'I take it you've no objection to living on your wife's money.' It was infernally unreasonable of his wife to have left her small fortune to her daughter. Women shouldn't be independent. It's against Nature. 'I understand you propose to give up working after your marriage.'

'Blanche can't have made the situation clear,' said Paul. 'I shan't stop work, I shall only stop being paid for it. In fact, I shall be working harder than ever.'

'And while you're climbing?' asked Edgar. 'Who pays the bills?'

'You wouldn't object to your daughter investing in a gold mine, say,' Paul suggested. 'Can't you look at it like that? Give me a year or two and the investment will start paying dividends. And they won't be small ones.'

Edgar gasped. 'I must say you know how to sell yourself,' he admitted. 'Have you persuaded yourself you're in love with her?'

'We're excellent friends,' said Paul. 'Love? I don't know much about it. I've been in love in one way and another ever since I was seventeen. I think it will work,' he added soberly. 'I shall do everything I can to make it.'

Edgar Mullins had an uncomfortable feeling that the young chap was getting the better of him. A likely-looking lad, good presence, a hard worker—all the same . . .

'The fact remains you've got nothing to offer,' he insisted.

'The future,' said Paul. 'And that's what counts. Her future and mine.'

'By God,' said Edgar, and no one was more surprised than he to hear his own words, 'I wish I had a son like you.'

*　　*　　*

The gossips waited to see the marriage crack; at the end of five years they were less certain. Marriage had worked wonders in Blanche. Paul had passed his exams and been persuaded to let his wife buy him a partnership in Nunn, Nunn and Norris. 'Call it a wedding-present,' she pleaded. 'Old Nunn has retired and Norris will follow his example in about ten years. Then the whole business will be yours. And he's anxious to have you. He made that perfectly clear.'

Norris wasn't the only lawyer willing to give the young man a chance and Paul was proving the investment Blanche had foreseen. Before Edgar died of an aneurism he was generous enough to admit that his daughter had more sense than he'd ever realised. Paul had the power to encourage confidence, really cared about his clients, while, so far as time was concerned, clocks need never have been invented for him. Blanche sometimes complained she saw far too little of him. 'You have a wife as well as an office,' she used to remind him, half-laughing.

In the eighth year of the marriage, however, the laughter had died out of her voice. She had the uncomfortable knowledge that her money now made precious little difference to him. He was doing well and could have supported a wife without her fortune. And he was popular. Sometimes he was asked out without her.

'Of course you won't go,' she said.

'Of course I shall. This isn't a wives' party. And I can't afford to refuse.' He found it difficult to persuade her that a man wants to be something besides a rich woman's husband.

Blanche became increasingly exacting; she had nothing but her money—in spite of all her hopes she hadn't been able to give him children—and she didn't want him to forget it. When he bought himself his first car she asked, 'What on earth made you buy a Morris? A man in your position should drive a Bentley.'

'I can't afford a Bentley, not yet,' said Paul cheerfully.

'You could afford a Rolls if you fancied one,' she said sharply, and while he was away she arranged to have the car exchanged. That was their first serious row. The following summer he arranged their holiday abroad, insisting on paying for every detail. When Blanche found they had a room without a private bath she stormed down to the office and had it changed.

She had passed her fortieth year when she slipped on the stairs in her own house and fractured her leg. Paul wanted to send her to hospital but she refused outright.

'Hospitals are for people without homes of their own,' she said. 'I shall be able to run the house from my bed. I'll have a nurse, of course . . .'

She rang up Mrs. Esdaile and asked for Nurse Chesterton, who had come to them once before when she had a bad bout of 'flu and ran a high temperature.

'Nurse Chesterton is engaged,' said Mrs. Esdaile smoothly, 'but I'll send you

someone else.'
And she sent her Helen.

CHAPTER TWO

THE INSTANT he set eyes on the new nurse Paul French knew he was done for. During nearly ten years of marriage to a woman whose sense of insecurity had gradually built up a wall between them he had known an occasional flutter of the heart, but this was something as definite as a thunderclap, as loud as a pealing bell. Indeed, the silence that followed her entrance amazed him; he could only suppose that his own ears were sealed to all sound.

In a matter of seconds he had crossed from the world inhabited by normal people into the country that only lovers know. Good sense deserted him, he never thought, 'This is a nurse, my wife's nurse, not a woman but a symbol.' He didn't think, 'How will Blanche like having this lovely creature in the house?' because you might as well ask how people liked seeing a rainbow after a storm. He thought: 'Here she is, here she is.' The whole of his past life with Blanche closed up behind him like one of those vanishing roads in the ancient fairy tale. Turn your head and there's nothing to be seen. Not darkness, not shadows even, just nothing, because until now nothing real has existed. Blanche didn't exist any more, not in any personal relationship, someone for whom he had accepted responsibility and to whom he had made vows. The world comprised only two people, and if an earthquake had swallowed up all the rest it wouldn't have surprised him at all; he wouldn't even have missed them.

As for Blanche, she was furious. 'That woman's a fool,' she snapped when Helen had gone to her room to change. 'I asked for Nurse Chesterton. If she couldn't switch her' (and her voice said it was ridiculous that she couldn't have worked the change) 'at least she needn't have sent me a girl like that.'

Paul found his voice. 'What's wrong with her?'

'You don't seriously suppose she's going to settle quietly into our sort of household? It wouldn't be natural. It's dull here, how dull you've no notion. You're out all day. And I wanted someone who could give me a little companionship as well as nursing. I'm going to be stuck up here for weeks. Besides, Mrs. Hoggett won't like her.'

'What on earth has Mrs. Hoggett got to do with it?'

Blanche made a gesture of exasperation. 'That's exactly like you, Paul. You imagine households run themselves. Let me tell you, it would be a great deal easier to get a fresh nurse than to find another house-keeper. They always detest nurses, anyhow. She was bad enough about Chesterton.'

'Why should you suppose she'll be any worse with this one?'

'Because she's young. This isn't a suitable house for young people. She'll get bored, want to be slipping out to meet boy-friends— Chesterton was past all that. She used to go to the Bickwell Zoo in her spare time.'

'To visit her relatives, I don't doubt,' agreed Paul, unguardedly. 'She looked like an elephant, she walked like an elephant, she trumpeted like an elephant. It's my fervent belief that in a previous incarnation she *was* an elephant.'

Then Helen came back, wearing her uniform. She had a bandbox neatness, looked as fresh as if she had been new-minted that morning. She went over to the bed and began automatically making her patient more comfortable. She didn't even seem to notice Paul's existence; and he saw, with shock and outrage, that to her he was simply a husband, as impersonal as the dressing-table or the bed.

*   *   *

Mrs. Hoggett was the Frenchs' housekeeper, a squat sallow woman with a face like a toad. Her first name was Ruby.

'What on earth possessed anyone to call her that?' Blanche would demand, and Paul, coming in on his cue, would say, 'A jewel of a woman, my dear, that's why.' Mrs. Hoggett had made it clear from the start that she was not to be asked to wait on the sickroom or the sickroom attendant. It was her experience that you were taken advantage of left right and centre if you didn't look after your own interests. She resented the fact that nurses could not be asked to eat in the kitchen, but must either have their meals with the family or on a tray in their own rooms. She made it abundantly clear that she should only be asked to bring meals upstairs on the nurse's night off and only answer bells that evening in the unlikely event of there being no one else in the house. She came into the sick-room on Helen's first day on a pretext of asking Blanche something about the dinner.

'I suppose Nurse will be having hers with Mr. French like Nurse Chesterton did?' she stated baldly.

'Unless she prefers a tray in her own room.'

'I'm afraid I couldn't do extra trays,' announced Mrs. Hoggett.

So, naturally, it was arranged to suit her.

★   ★   ★

Helen was meeting Miles Gordon on her afternoon off.

'What's it like at the Dene?' he inquired. She had been with Blanche French almost two months; even Blanche found no fault with her, punctual, competent, well-mannered. She even rubbed along all right with Mrs. Hoggett.

'Mrs. F. would never be my favourite patient,' Helen now admitted, guardedly. 'She's got a "Why-me?" complex. There are times when I'm tempted to remind her it's only her leg and that's getting on quite well. I found her hobbling round her room, with a stick, the other day when I went in unexpectedly. She said I'd forgotten to give her something and she wanted to see how much she could do. She wants to start coming down, but Dr. Kemp won't let her.'

'You're wasting your time there, my girl,' said Miles.

'There's no pleasing some people. You were on at me when I was working for Dr. MacIntyre, now I'm with a safe case you don't think that's satisfactory either. One thing I can promise you, we shan't lose this patient through death, unless she gets so tired of bed she throws herself out of the window. Sometimes she has me so bewildered I feel she'll be dancing at my funeral. She has the idea that when you're paying people they should never sit down.'

Inevitably he asked, 'How about French?'

'She's silly about him, I think. Harries him all the time. Must you go out? Who are you going to see? Who's that letter from? Who rang up? Why do you have to go through papers to-night? I didn't marry to lie by myself evening after evening. It's beginning to run him ragged.'

'It's worth remembering that people don't change overnight,' said Miles, dryly. 'She's presumably been harrying him for years and he seems to have borne up remarkably well.'

'There's always the last straw,' said Helen vaguely.

'Meaning?'

'Well, the one word too many. Miles, do be careful, you're beginning to get like her. This is my time off. I want to enjoy myself. I know Mrs. Esdaile says it's not a hard case, and in the sense of sitting up at night and that sort of thing it isn't—nothing to Miss Turton—but if I could have pulled one of them through it wouldn't have been Mrs. French.'

Inconveniently Miles remembered that when the theme of Blanche French's appalling death became the talk of the county.

★　　　★　　　★

It appears inconceivable that all this time Blanche had no inkling of her husband's feelings. Mind you, she'd always been a jealous wife, making excuses to visit his office whenever he changed his secretary; had kicked up the father and mother of a row when once he had taken a client out to dinner.

'The girl was catching a late train,' Paul urged. 'She couldn't be left to starve. She's a client.'

'She could have got a meal at the White Hart,' said Blanche resentfully.

'Besides, she wanted to talk to me about her fiancé. I'm her lawyer, which is on a par with being a doctor. I've been fixing up her affairs—a case of a will...' But he wouldn't give her the details. Clients didn't expect their affairs to be discussed, not even with a wife.

Helen in that household was pure dynamite; Mrs. Hoggett saw which way the wind was blowing long before Blanche noticed it had even changed; but she didn't suppose anything would come of it. You didn't throw away a rich wife for a girl who had her own living to get. Blanche would have been furious to know that her mind and her housekeeper's ran on parallel lines.

*   *   *

In the evenings, except on Wednesdays when she had the afternoon off, Helen had dinner with her patient's husband in the room beneath Blanche's. If it sometimes seemed to her that during the meal she was summoned to the sick-room rather more often than was reasonable she didn't let it trouble her. Blanche hated her own weakness, resented other people's mobility. Paul was the most entertaining of companions. Blanche would writhe to hear the laughter coming up through the boards. She counted the days to Wednesday, when Mrs. Hoggett grudgingly served dinner for the two of them in the sick-room.

'It won't be for much longer,' Blanche assured her. 'I'm beginning to get about the room on sticks.' She sat up at the table now. 'Dr. Kemp won't let me attempt stairs yet. I had thought of having my bed put downstairs, but . . .' She looked round at the large lovely room. 'I don't much like the idea of sleeping on the ground-floor,' she confessed. 'Anyone could come through the garden.'

'Cat got your tongue?' she asked Paul on another occasion.

Paul looked surprised. 'I hadn't anything special to say,' he confessed.

'You seem to have plenty of conversation on tap other nights,' she taunted him. 'I hear you, laughing away with that girl like mad. It's not very amusing for me.'

Even though she knew she was crazy to do it she couldn't stop nagging him; she hated him to enjoy himself with anyone away from her.

Some said later that, even if he was responsible for her death, and as to that opinion remained mixed to the end, it was really a case of indirect suicide.

'Helen,' said Mrs. Esdaile, 'how's your patient getting on?'

'Raring to go,' said Helen. 'She'll undo all the work of past weeks if she can't sustain her patience a little longer; she will go around with sticks on that polished floor when I'm not there. One slip and she's back where she started.'

'You've been there a long time,' said Mrs. Esdaile. 'I can't afford to have one of my best nurses acting as a lapdog to a spoilt woman. All she really needs now is a nurse-companion, not a highly-trained girl like yourself. I'll have a word with Dr. Kemp, and if he thinks you can be spared I shall tell Mrs. French myself.'

She was sorting through some cards in her card-index, so she missed Helen's expression of blank dismay. It was like a thunderbolt, the realisation that she wouldn't be seeing Paul

24

French any more. She couldn't put her finger on the moment when she'd stopped thinking of him as Blanche's husband.

'I'm out of my mind,' she told herself candidly. 'Falling in love with a married man . . .'

There had been one or two cases in Bryan Mouncey in the past three years, girls losing their heads—and it had always implied the end of their career so far as Mrs. Esdaile was concerned.

'I wonder if I've given myself away to everyone,' she tormented herself. 'I wonder if he guesses.'

Next day she knew. Blanche had sent her into the garden to pick some flowers for her room. Someone was coming to tea. Helen picked them casually, thinking about Paul, muttering his name. And suddenly he was there, he had his arms about her, his mouth was on hers, it was all unreal, a fantasy . . . Suddenly she came to her senses.

'No, no.' She pushed him away from her.

'Don't worry,' said Paul, 'it was bound to happen. Fire either spreads or extinguishes itself.'

'Then you . . .?'

'From the very first minute. You didn't guess?'

She shook her head. 'No. Why, I only

realised myself a few days ago when first Mrs. Esdaile and then your wife spoke of my work here being done. It goes to prove what happens when you try to lift yourself out of a rut,' she added, uncontrollably. 'I asked Mrs. Esdaile to take me off Dr. MacIntyre's list for a time, I'd had so many old people who died and I didn't want to get taped—and she had to send me here.'

'Well, of course she had to.' Paul sounded surprised. 'We had to meet somewhere, didn't we?'

'I ought to have left the minute I knew, but I thought—It's only a little longer, and Mrs. Esdaile's so sharp, if I'd made a point of it . . .'

'Stop bothering about Mrs. Esdaile. She's bound to know along with everyone else before many more moons are past.'

Helen wrenched herself free of his detaining hand. 'What do you mean, know? Of course she can't. This can't go any further.'

'You talk as though love's like a tap to be turned on and off at will. You're wrong. It's on and it's flowing like Niagara, and it's going to sweep us both over the edge. It's no use fighting fate.'

Helen struggled against the tide that threatened to overwhelm her.

'On the contrary, we spend half our lives doing that very thing.'

'And look at the result. Anyway, even if you can fight fate you can't fight me; and don't get any melodramatic ideas about breaking up a happy home. Blanche and I have been washed up for some time. It only needed the last straw...'

She remembered her own words to Miles Gordon. But she had never identified herself with the straw...

Mrs. Hoggett's voice broke suddenly into their absorption. 'Nurse, Nurse,' she called.

'Don't let her see you,' breathed Helen. She snatched up her few flowers and hurried up the garden. Mrs. Hoggett stood at the head of the path.

'Mrs. French has been ringing like mad these past five minutes,' Mrs. Hoggett told her, surveying with a crafty, knowing gaze the roughened hair, the brilliant colour in the cheeks and sparkle in the eye.

'How unreasonable!' snapped Helen. 'She sent me to pick some flowers...'

Mrs. Hoggett's gaze moved to Helen's meagre harvest. 'Storm must have knocked them about worse than Mrs. French guessed,' she hazarded. 'As for reason, well, we know sick folk, don't we, Nurse?'

There was a wealth of meaning in her voice. Helen pushed past. 'I must take these up.'

'I knew you were in the garden,' Mrs.

Hoggett's voice called after her. 'I could hear you talking to yourself. She must be in love, I said.' She followed the girl into the house, with her usual clumping step that Paul had said made you think of clods being dropped on to a closed coffin. Her wide toad's mouth was set in a knowing grin.

*　　　*　　　*

By Wednesday Helen's mind was made up. She would ask for a transfer immediately, try for something outside the neighbourhood. Sometimes doctors asked for nurses to accompany invalids to the seaside. She might be lucky . . .

She and Paul had been very circumspect since that morning. On Sunday he had been playing golf all day and he and Blanche had supper together, Mrs. Hoggett being out. On Monday and Tuesday they kept up appearances. It was a good thing, she thought, that it wouldn't go on much longer. Now that the truth was out in the open it seemed that it must be obvious to everyone, even to Blanche. But fate seemed against her. When she reached the Nurses' Home on Wednesday, which was her afternoon off, she learned that Mrs. Esdaile had been sent for on account of an accident, feared to be fatal, to her sister in

London. She never delegated her duties; any decisions must await her return. If nurses were wanted—well, she had no one free at the moment and by the end of the week at the latest she would be home.

There was an air of relaxation about the Home. 'When the cat's away,' quoted Katie Cameron, tucking her arm into Helen's. 'Mind you, I'm as sorry as anyone about the accident—the one person on earth Ma Esdaile cares about is the sister—but there's no doubt about it, there's not much chance to come up for air when she's on the premises. You look washed out, darling. Your treasure being more of a hell-cat than usual?'

'Mrs. Esdaile was speaking of a transfer,' said Helen vaguely.

'I suppose you're the only one of us who'd have stuck her so long,' said Katie, in her cheerful outspoken fashion. 'How long have you been there? Still, poor old Paul French has had to cope with her for ten years. I suppose it's all a matter of habit. They say there's an African tribe that lives solely on earth, because it's never learnt to cook.' Fortunately she never paused for an answer to her questions. 'Look,' she ran on, 'seeing you can't beard the dragon in her den this evening, come to the pictures. It's Jack Hawkins. I do wonder what it would be like to be married to a famous film star. One imagines it would be Glamour Inc. but of course the glamour might incorporate too many other accommodating females.'

Helen began to laugh. Her intention to ask for a transfer was unchanged, but to-night she could relax. They ate at the Home—it wasn't specially good but it was cheap and, as Katie Cameron said, at least you knew the stuff hadn't come out of a trap. The film was absorbing. Jack Hawkins was playing a policeman and inevitably Katie began to wonder what it would be like to be a policeman's wife.

'A detective-inspector at least,' she insisted. 'What comes after that? A superintendent? I never can remember . . .' She chattered away like Lord Tennyson's brook that went on for ever. She was always on the lookout for a husband, complained that bachelors seemed to like going into hospital instead of having someone to cosset them in their own homes.

'Bachelors don't have homes,' Helen reminded her.

'P'rhaps they're lucky. Some of the wives we see . . .'

That reminded Helen again of Blanche and she was suddenly quiet.

'I must get out,' she cried like Sterne's

starling, not guessing that already it was too late.

CHAPTER THREE

WEDNESDAY EVENINGS were the highlight of Blanche's week and it was understood that Paul should make no engagements for that night. So it was unfortunate that on this particular Wednesday he found himself compelled to dine with a new and important client, called Roberts. This man was leaving the country by the night plane which involved catching a ten o'clock train from West Barsley, and had certain dispositions to make before his departure.

'Surely Blanche will be reasonable for once,' Paul reflected. He had been out when the staccato message came through and his secretary had made the appointment. He paused to telephone Roberts's house to confirm the arrangement, then went up to explain to his wife. He found her in one of her least accommodating moods. She had had a long empty afternoon. Mrs. Hoggett had brought up her tea-tray at 4.15 and removed it smartly at five. No one had come in, no one had telephoned, her library book was boring to a degree. She nourished herself on the thought of dinner with Paul. And then when he did come in it was to tell her that he had to leave again within the hour.

'Nonsense,' she said flatly. 'I don't know what your engagement is but it can't take precedence over our permanent arrangement. Goodness knows, it's deadly enough lying here all day—and this is Helen's evening off, or had you forgotten?'

'Of course I hadn't forgotten, Blanche, but this is something I can't postpone. Roberts has to catch the late train to town . . .'

'He should have considered that before. You're not an office boy to fetch and carry . . .'

He passed his hand over his face. 'I could do with a shave,' he said vaguely. 'It's no good, of course I must go. It was quite a feather in my cap to get Roberts's business. All the local lawyers wanted to handle it. It could be one of those really big things . . .'

'Then *let* one of the others handle it,' she snapped. 'It's different for them. They're dependent on their earnings and can't afford to let chances slip. But you can pick and choose . . .'

In his impatience he said an unfortunate thing. 'Can't you understand I don't want to be Mr. Blanche Mullins all my life?'

Her face turned a hideous plum colour; for a moment she looked as though she might actually break a blood-vessel.

'That's a charming thing to say to your wife,' she cried. 'There was a time when it didn't stick in your throat to use my help ... Don't forget that if it wasn't for me you'd still be somebody's clerk, and your wonderful Mr. Roberts would never have heard of you, unless you'd been asked to whistle him up a taxi.'

He said scornfully, 'That's not true and you know it. Oh, I don't mean to sound ungrateful; without your interest, your help, I should have taken longer to climb the ladder, but I should have climbed it in any case.'

'How?' she demanded.

'Oh, I might have attracted attention in another quarter, like Scholes and old Barton. Or I might have backed a winner or pulled a millionaire from under the wheels of a car—anything.'

'But, of course, it was safer marrying a rich woman.'

He said quietly, (and here she should have been warned, since quiet anger is a terrible thing) 'Are you never proud that your investment turned out as well as it has? Your father was generous enough to admit before he died ...'

'My father warned me before we were married that this would happen. He said if I supposed you were marrying me for anything but the money ...'

34

'He may have thought so then. He didn't believe it five years later.'

'Then you fooled him as well as me. That's a feather in your cap, if you like. Not many people fooled "Midas" Mullins. Why can't Mr. Norris have dinner with your precious Roberts?'

'Because he's my client.'

'I thought you were partners.'

'Dr. Kemp and Dr. Lawrence are partners, but you wouldn't be particularly pleased to see Lawrence in Kemp's place.'

'It would depend. If it was urgent and Dr. Kemp was unavoidably detained . . .'

'The key word is unavoidably.'

Then she said it. Jealousy raked her from head to toe. 'If it weren't a Wednesday, if it were a day when Helen Wayland was at home, we might hear less of the importance of your new client.'

She looked across the room as she spoke and she saw his face in a glass hanging on the wall. She had spoken in fury and spite, not believing her own words. Then the truth flashed into her mind and she went a yet deeper shade of purple; her voice choked as though she were suffocating.

'You—you—no, I won't believe it. Not in my own house, you and a servant . . .'

Paul caught the infection of her mood.

'Don't speak of Helen like that.'

'Don't dare dictate to me. I shall say what I please. The girl's no better than a...' instinctively he put his hand over her mouth to stop her utterance; furiously she struck it down. 'How long has it been going on? I suppose everyone knows except myself. How much did you pay Mrs. Hoggett to keep her mouth shut? It's no wonder you chose that little room at the end of the passage—Then I shan't disturb you, you said. And all these weeks...' Now that she had begun she seemed unable to stop. The words, bitter, revengeful, abhorrent, poured from her lips like pus from a wound. 'But I'll put a stop to it,' she shouted, gasping for breath, her hand grabbing for the telephone. 'I'll let Mrs. Esdaile and everyone know what she really is. She'll be drummed out of the place, ruined. . . .'

He put out his hand to stop her, then realised it was no good; she would telephone the instant he had gone if he prevented her now, and surely Mrs. Esdaile, that sane woman, would recognise hysteria when she heard it. An instant later he understood, with relief, that Mrs. Esdaile had been called away and was not expected back till the end of the week.

Blanche turned back to him. 'I'll ask you

one question,' she said. 'Are you in love with the girl?'

'Yes,' he said quietly. 'I am. But, you can believe this or not as you please, we've given you no grounds for divorce. As soon as she realised the position, and this was only a few days ago, Helen said she must ask for an immediate transfer.'

'Indeed? And you?'

He said fervently, 'I can't live without her. If I'd had any preparation—but to come in and find her here, the one I was meant to love . . . Blanche, can't you accept the fact that this has happened to scores of other people besides ourselves?'

'Which means that I drop out of the picture and she takes my place? Of course, you're a successful lawyer now, aren't you? You can support a wife. Well, you needn't build up any false hopes. I shall never divorce you, and however fond of this girl you may be, I think you're just a little fonder of your own career. You won't jeopardise that by running off with her. The whole neighbourhood would talk.'

'I'm not bound to Bryan Mouncey for the rest of my days,' he said, more coolly than he felt. 'Look, we can't discuss this any more now. It's come as a greater shock to you than I anticipated. It didn't seem possible that you shouldn't know, I felt everyone must know . . .'

She said again, 'I dare say they do. They say the wife's always the last to hear. It won't look well, you know, intriguing under my roof when I'm a sick woman. That's not the sort of thing that recommends lawyers to influential clients.'

'Be quiet!' he ordered, now at the end of his tether. 'That's how women get themselves murdered.'

She was beside herself with passion. 'It's a pity I haven't a witness. That was a threat if ever I heard one.'

'A warning. But, of course, that wasn't intended to be taken seriously. Only—I never knew a man could feel like this about another human being . . .'

'Didn't you? I knew—ten years ago. Do you think I didn't put up with a good deal of mockery when our engagement was announced? Cradle-snatching, someone called it. Buying a husband. I didn't go through all that to let you go to the first girl who takes your fancy. Paul.' Suddenly she put out her hand. 'You're not yourself to-night, this has come on you as a shock, knocked you off your balance. When you've had time to see the situation more coolly you'll realise that what you suggest is absurd. I shan't divorce you. I shan't change about that. But—let the girl go, and I won't say a word to Mrs. Esdaile. Kemp thinks I should be able to go for convalescence soon; you could get away for a few days, we'll escape from this atmosphere. Oh, it'll be painful for a time, but presently you'll get over it, because anything that's starved is bound to die. And—they've not been so bad, have they, the years we've shared together? I did help you to start with, I can help you again. And, if you won't think of me, think of her. Life isn't very kind to a woman living with a man she can't marry—and I could go on living for twenty or thirty years. Believe me, you'd sicken of your situation long before then.'

Her last words moved him as none of her fury had had power to do. For the first time he saw her as a middle-aged woman facing emptiness. But, logically, he saw no sense in three lives being ruined, when two might be salvaged. All the same his voice was quieter, more friendly as he replied, 'It's no good, Blanche. You can't put the clock back. The mischief's done. Helen's in my blood, she'll never be out of it.'

She saw then that she had lost, and she said something so unpardonable that he winced away from her.

But before he could reply there was a sound in the shadows behind them—the huge room

ANTHONY GILBERT

was lit only by the circle of light thrown by the bedside lamp—and Mrs. Hoggett's voice said, 'Excuse me interrupting, Madam, but when would you like me to serve dinner?'

'Dinner?' repeated Blanche vaguely.

Paul glanced at his watch. 'Good heavens, I'm late. I hadn't realised the time.'

'I did come up a little while ago,' said Mrs. Hoggett demurely, 'but you were talking and I didn't like to interrupt you.'

'Probably had her ear to the keyhole for the past twenty minutes,' thought Paul bitterly. Still, it wasn't of such great importance. Everyone was going to know the truth soon enough.

'I shan't be in to dinner,' he said. 'I told Roberts I'd be there at seven. It's nearly that now.'

'Telephone and explain you've been detained,' said Blanche. 'Go on. Use my extension.' He realised that she now had doubts of the man's existence, probably thought he was meeting Helen somewhere to spend the evening together.

Furiously he snatched the receiver from its hook. He heard the bell ringing away at the other end, then Roberts's voice spoke as clearly as though he were in the next room. Paul explained his delay.

'Well, make it as soon as you can,' said

40

Roberts, crisply. 'Time's short. I've got everything laid on.'

'What did that mean?' demanded Blanche. 'It's all right, Mrs. Hoggett. I shan't want any dinner. I'm not feeling very well. And, as you know, Nurse is out.'

'Quite so, madam. Then I'll bring dinner in about fifteen minutes?'

'Just an omelette. I couldn't eat anything else.'

'It was lamb cutlets you ordered. You'll find them very tasty.' She made it clear that she had no intention of putting herself out by so much as beating up an omelette. 'I'll bring the tray,' she added, looking at Paul's back, where he was still speaking to Roberts.

'What did he mean by everything laid on?' Blanche asked again as the door closed behind the woman. 'It sounds like a party.'

'He probably means something in a bottle. I've told you, he has to be at the Air Terminal in Cromwell Road by ten o'clock. It's gone seven now. I can't wait.'

'It would help if you could manage to be civil to me in front of my servants,' Blanche pointed out. 'She's the kind that would love to spread mischief. I wonder,' she added reflectively, 'how much she heard to-night.'

'It simply doesn't matter,' said Paul, and at the moment that seemed to be true. 'When the balloon goes up . . .'

'What balloon?'

He said desperately, 'I can't start the argument all over again, not now. You heard for yourself what Roberts said. But don't imagine or persuade yourself that I didn't mean what I was saying. Things can't go on like this.'

'How convenient it would be,' she gibed softly, 'if you could induce a haemorrhage or a fatal seizure. Solve all your problems.' She began to laugh, caught her breath and started to cough heartrendingly. His gesture to restore her was automatic, but she pushed him away as soon as she had partially recovered, crying, 'If I'm going to suffocate I can do it without your help. And if you see Nurse by any chance when you're out,' she added elaborately in a rather wheezing voice, 'you can tell her I don't want to see her again this evening.'

*   *   *

As they emerged from the cinema the two nurses ran into Miles Gordon and a friend and the four of them went into the Live and Let Live for a glass of beer 'to round off the evening.'

'Anyone could tell Ma's away,' said Miles,

candidly. 'You wouldn't dare go back reeking of drink if she were there.'

Katie tossed her head. 'What we do in our spare time's our own affair, isn't it, Helen?'

They lingered for about twenty minutes, then Helen said she must get back. She had left her bicycle in the shed at the Nurses' Home, and as she wheeled it out the rain started. She tied a blue plastic hood over her bright hair, buttoned up her mackintosh and set off for The Dene. She rode the machine as far as she could up Lurchers Hill—there was a perpetual competition between the nurses as to who could get farthest before being compelled to dismount, and no one had ever ridden right to the top—then wheeled the bicycle the rest of the way, and prepared for the long swooping freewheel ride down almost to the gates of The Dene, Blanche French's handsome house. Everyone spoke of it as hers, even now.

Her foot was actually on the pedal when in the shadowy hedge beside her something stirred, a voice called her name. Instantly her heart rocketed. She thought if he walked past her grave and said 'Helen' above the stone she would hear in the dust and answer.

'Paul.'

He came out of the shadows, laid hold of her bicycle and pulled it into the ditch, almost concealed by the brown stalks of giant cow parsley.

'I was afraid I'd missed you. Roberts ran it so fine I had to warn him he wouldn't make the train . . .'

She shook her head and some cool diamond drops fell against his cheek.

'I don't know what you're talking about.'

'It doesn't matter. Helen, don't go near Blanche to-night after you get in.'

'But—she may ring.' She sounded dismayed.

'It's her wish. As well as mine. Frankly, I don't believe it would be safe. You see, she knows about us.'

He felt her stiffen under his hand and automatically his arms went round her. 'But there's nothing to know,' Helen said at last.

'Of course not. Only that we are in love. Doesn't that seem important to you any more?'

She sounded aghast. 'You didn't tell her . . .'

'I didn't need to. She knew it. I suppose women do when they're affected personally. Stop shivering, Helen. She had to know sooner or later.'

'I was going away—I told you—oh, couldn't you have prevented this?'

'You know I couldn't. And you couldn't

have gone so far I shouldn't have found you.'

'You don't know what you're saying. You've got your own life . . .'

'You are my life. You can't put love on a leash like a pet dog. It's like a prairie fire. It consumes everything.'

'Including Blanche—and your career—?'

'I can get a living anywhere. I'm not afraid of the future.'

'I am.'

'That isn't like you.'

She said desperately, 'I'm a nurse, not a secretary or a—a companion. It implies obligations . . .'

'You can't put your profession before me.'

'I shouldn't be much of a creature if I was prepared to steal a patient's husband. Why, no wife would feel safe.'

'I never heard that life offered anyone complete security. It's the chance you take. Blanche took it ten years ago. Now it's your turn. We can't know how it will turn out, but we can't deny it . . .' Suddenly he, too, stiffened, drawing her farther into the shadows, casting an anxious glance at the bicycle lying in the shelter of the hedge. 'Take care, someone's coming.'

Through a gate in the wall on the farther side of the lane, a wall enclosing woodlands free to the public, a dumpy cloaked figure

45

emerged, carrying something square and white. The two in the hedgerow stood rigid, as though even their careful breathing might betray them. The authorities had put a pillar-box on the crest of the hill for the benefit of cottagers living on the height; the figure plodded across, hesitated a moment, then shot a letter through the box's mouth. Then it turned and stood leisurely looking around. It was impossible to tell how much was visible beneath that cloudy sky with the rain spitting and snarling all about them. After a minute it turned again and disappeared through the gate.

'Well.' Paul released Helen with a sound that was almost a laugh. 'I never thought to see Mrs. Tiggy Winkle in the flesh.'

The girl was whiter than cloud. 'Why did you stop me? I must go back at once. Suppose Blanche rings?'

'She's said already she didn't want to see you again to-night. Anyway, the Jewel's there.'

'That's just what I think she isn't. Paul, do you suppose Blanche could have set her on to spy on us? Or has she somehow recognised that we're in love and . . .'

'You mean that was Mrs. Hoggett? Helen, are you sure?' But as he spoke he remembered a familiar aspect to the intruder—a toad really, rather than Beatrix Potter's amiable hedgehog . . .

'She was there to-night,' he allowed slowly. 'I don't know how long, I don't know how much she heard, but . . . all the same, she couldn't know I should see you this evening. I didn't know myself.'

'She knew I was bound to come back this way, there's no other if you're cycling.'

'Why shouldn't she simply have slipped out to post a letter?' Paul argued. 'Blanche sleeps a good deal in the evening—of course, she shouldn't have taken the chance . . .'

'It doesn't make sense. The post went out ages ago, and the man would have collected the letter when he brought the mail in the morning. There was no need for her to trudge through the woodland on a damp night.'

'Then perhaps she doesn't want anyone to know who she's writing to,' Paul persisted.

'It's not good enough,' insisted Helen. 'Paul, could she possibly have heard anything between you and Blanche this evening?'

He had a lightning vision of her, standing so demurely, so hatefully, on the threshold, saying, 'I did come up before, but you were talking . . .' Of course, she'd been eavesdropping. He had never had a doubt.

He didn't answer the question. 'We don't even know she saw us,' he argued. 'She wouldn't be looking, and in this light . . .'

'She stood there quite a minute, looking about her. We could see her. Paul, I don't like it.'

'She couldn't recognise us,' he insisted.

'She could make a good guess, and we could scarcely deny it.'

'Deny it? To whom? After all, it's no crime to exchange a few words with your friend . . .'

'She could hear if she couldn't see. We weren't whispering. Paul, I'm going back. I want to get there before she has a chance of rushing up to Blanche . . .'

He said dryly, 'As you've just pointed out, it's too late to alter facts.'

'If I'm there first I shall catch her coming in. That will put her in the wrong. She knows she's no right to leave Blanche.'

He would not voice his ugly suspicion that Blanche was not above putting a servant to spy. But he could find no words to detain his love, who remounted her machine and, an instant later, was flying down the slope towards The Dene. Involuntarily he shuddered, as though she were being carried out of his reach. Then, reliving the night's occasions, first with Blanche and then with Helen, he retraced his steps towards the corner where he had left his car.

CHAPTER FOUR

MRS. HOGGETT hurried back through the trees. She thought it unlikely that the engrossed couple on the hill had recognised her, though she had no doubt at all about their identity. Nor did it occur to her that the meeting was anything but pre-arranged. It was even possible this fellow, Roberts, was in the plot. Men all stood together when it came to something nasty, was her experience. Take Sam now . . . Sam was Mr. Hoggett, who had vanished out of her life early in the war. Got himself a job of national importance at Bristol, while she stayed in London, and after that not so much as a postcard. Mind you, he hadn't been much of a catch storming in at night worse for the drink as often as not, smashing her precious china vases after calling them your Aunt Lilian's bloody sacrifices—as if anyone didn't know how much store Aunt Lil had set on them. And then waltzing away as though she didn't exist, imagining he was shot of her for the rest of his days.

It had been a bit of luck, spotting him on the parade at Brighton with that girl on his arm, looking lost to the world. Disgusting really, seeing she was about five-and-twenty years his junior. Regular married look they'd had. That had given her an idea, and she could hardly wait for the returning char-à-banc to test it. Straight to Somerset House she'd gone next day and there it was in black-and-white. Samuel Obadiah Hoggett—she should have known better than to marry a man with a name like that—widower—(the sauce of it, with her working her fingers to the bone and him going round spending his wages on that—doxy) to Catherine Green... Presently, when her temper had cooled, she'd begun to see the information as a weapon in her hand. Sam looked prosperous these days, with money in his pocket. All she had to do was find out where he was now and put the screw on. They'd been married in Bristol after the war, but there was no trace of him there. She'd tried Brighton, but so far without success and of course he could just have been down for the day. She'd been on a bus, and by the time it reached the next stop and she had got off and retraced her steps there was no sign of either of them. Still, he was alive and married—or that's what he called it. Sooner or later she'd pick him up. She had just answered an advert. from a man who called himself a private investigator. 'Missing relatives traced' it said. Wanted a pretty penny, no doubt, but don't worry, it 'ud all come out of Sam's pocket in the end.

As to Paul French, anyone with half an eye could see which way that wind was blowing. Ever since the start he'd been knocked endways by that nurse. Not that Ruby had anything special against Helen Wayland. A bit of a fusspot the way nurses were, but then she liked things clean and tidy herself; and she didn't try coming the Madam over the housekeeper like some of them did. Came down for her own trays and brought them back, too. Altogether a much sweeter cup of tea than Blanche. Still, right's right and nobody made him marry her, and it wasn't fair—Mrs. Hoggett had quite a fellow-feeling for Blanche, having been slighted herself for a younger woman—that he should haul himself up by her bootstraps and then move on when the fancy took him.

'Not that I can stop him,' she confessed frankly, only—people had to pay for their fancies. It was a bit of luck seeing those two on the hill, silent as one shadow they were; and remembering what had taken place in Madam's room this evening—the little shop on which Mrs. Hoggett had set her heart came appreciably nearer.

The house, when she returned to it, was as still as a grave. Mrs. Hoggett scuttled up to her room to put away her hat and coat and change her big clumping shoes. It was muddy coming through the woods, she'd have to brush that off as soon as it was dry. She did wonder if either of them had recognised her identity, but, if so, they wouldn't dare speak.

'Conspiracy of silence,' grinned Mrs. Hoggett, coming back past Blanche's door, that was as dark as the rest. Lucky thing Madam asked for that sleeping-tablet. Not likely to wake for hours yet, not unless something happened to disturb her.

She was coming along the passage when she heard the gate clang, and then the sound of tyres being wheeled up the path.

Nurse, thought Mrs. Hoggett, falling downstairs like a sack of coals, but reaching the hall in time to nip into the kitchen before Helen had her key in the front door.

As the girl came in the housekeeper moved to meet her. 'You've had a nasty night for your ride, Nurse,' she said in a sympathetic voice.

'Some fool had left a broken bottle on the road,' returned Helen caustically. 'I ran straight into it in the dark, three punctures at least. I didn't dare ride the machine home on the rim . . .'

'No hurry,' said Mrs. Hoggett smoothly. 'There hasn't been a sound from Mrs. French's room, and if there had been I was here.'

She turned her bland sallow face in the girl's direction. Helen knew a sudden surge of rage. On an impulse she exclaimed, 'It's a funny thing, I thought for a moment I saw you on the way as I cycled back.'

'Really, Nurse?' There wasn't a shadow of unease about the woman's heavily jocular manner. 'Isn't there a proverb about all cats in the dark looking grey?'

'Naturally, I didn't see how it could be you,' Helen agreed, sweetly. 'Not when Mr. French was out of the house.'

Instantly she saw the dark coarse eyebrows lift, and realised with a stab of horror how utterly she had betrayed them both. For the arrangement with Roberts had only been made at the eleventh hour, long after she herself had left the house, so how did she know anything about it? There was only one answer, and you could be sure Mrs. Hoggett would supply it.

'Is he back yet?' she added, as carelessly as she could, doing her best to patch up the situation.

'I couldn't say, Nurse, I'm sure. I've been in my kitchen all the evening.'

Helen walked past her and opened the study door; of course, the room was in darkness.

'No. How has Mrs. French been?' she asked.

'She did ask for her sleeping-tablets. Last time I went past the light was out, so let's hope for all our sakes she's quieted down.'

Mrs. Hoggett had always made it clear that she regarded herself, the permanent controller of the household, as superior to a nurse who was only temporary and could be exchanged at practically any minute; now she did not even pretend to her normal surface courtesy.

'I'm sorry if she wasn't well,' said Helen evenly. 'Perhaps I'd better just look in on my way up.'

'You don't want to rouse her,' said Mrs. Hoggett, in vigorous tones. 'You know what that'll mean, pots of tea and arguments—she and Mr. French did have a few words,' she added in a calm voice.

'What Mrs. French says to her husband is nothing to do with either of us,' said Helen more crushingly than she had intended.

'Well—' Mrs. Hoggett rubbed a big broad finger over her lips, 'I wouldn't be too sure. I believe I did hear your name.'

'Unless she said something to you—' Helen began.

'Well, no. Mrs. French isn't one for confiding in those she doesn't think are her equals. You must have noticed that yourself, Nurse.'

Helen let that go.

'She was probably telling Mr. French that I'm expecting to be relieved here very shortly,' she returned. 'Mrs. French has made excellent progress, and Mrs. Esdaile wants me for another more complicated case.'

'More complicated,' echoed Mrs. Hoggett meaningly. 'Well, Nurse, I'm sure you'll be greatly missed. Quite like one of the family you've become, haven't you? Somehow Mr. French never seemed to take to Nurse Chesterton, though I'm sure she was conscientious enough . . .'

'Don't stay up if you want to get to bed,' Helen cut in unceremoniously. 'I'm going up myself. Mr. French will lock up when he comes in.'

'I dare say he won't be long,' insinuated Mrs. Hoggett.

'I wouldn't know. It depends on his engagement, I suppose.'

'The gentleman was catching the ten o'clock train.' The housekeeper looked at her watch. 'Why, it's nearly a quarter to eleven. How the time does fly when you—have things to do.'

Her manner was greasy with triumph. But she's cooked her own goose, thought Helen, mounting the stairs. She can't say now that she saw us together, because she's just assured me she didn't leave the house.

She sucked what dubious comfort she could out of that. But already she had begun to understand the corrupting influence of a clandestine relationship, with its inevitable tarnishing of love.

At Blanche's door she paused, then opened it a crack. Only darkness met her eyes, there was no sound from within. She stole along to her own room, walking with conscious care, as though an unguarded step might bring the whole house crashing about her. She had a vague feeling that she ought to remain awake, warn Paul—but against what? She undressed quickly, folding and hanging her garments, leaving the place as neat as the proverbial new pin. She heard movements below and then the sound of Mrs. Hoggett's heavy feet on the stairs and a clink of china. She was taking her tea-tray up with her. She always made tea last thing at night.

'I could do with a cup myself,' she reflected, uncorking a little phial and pouring a tablet into her palm. She didn't approve of nurses taking sleeping-draughts but this was her night off, and she couldn't lie there hour after hour tormented by love and anguish and fear. 'I wonder why Paul isn't back? Or has he run into the glass, too?'

That was her last conscious thought before she slept.

★   ★   ★

Suddenly the night exploded in tumult. Helen came out of her dreamless sleep to hear a bell pealing as though the Archangel Gabriel were ringing in the Judgment Day. Instinct pulled her out of bed and into a dressing-gown before her deadened senses recovered their normal acuteness. On and on the bell sounded. Even Blanche had never staged a show like this before.

As she reached the door of the sick-room she heard movements from the floor above, and Mrs. Hoggett's voice calling. But she paid no attention. Last time she saw Blanche's room it had been dark under night's shutter; now a light blazed. The scene that met her eye was like something perceived in a nightmare, a thousand miles from reality. In the bed Blanche lay with blood pouring from a wound in her breast; beside her stood her husband, one finger on the electric bell and an automatic pistol in his right hand. The front of his suit was heavily stained with blood, which seemed to be everywhere, on the unconscious woman, the sheets, the wall. Helen let the door swing behind her and came forward. Her eyes were enormous with fear, her whisper shrill with it.

'Paul, what have you done?'

ANTHONY GILBERT

Paul turned, his eyes focusing with difficulty. But when he spoke his voice was composed and hard.

'It was an accident. She overreached herself; she never intended it to be like this.'

Suddenly he seemed to become aware of the weapon in his hand, looked at it unbelievably, then threw it down on the dreadful bed.

'She's shot, Blanche is shot.' Helen's voice began to rise.

'Keep your head,' said Paul, grimly. 'You're the nurse, remember.' There was nothing lover-like about his voice now; those minutes on the hill might never have occurred. 'This isn't going to look pretty, you know.'

'But how—did she—?'

'Yes. She shot herself all right, but she didn't mean it. Nothing was further from her thoughts than removing the one obstacle between us. Take care. The old harridan's outside.'

The door was pushed violently open and Mrs. Hoggett appeared. 'What happened? I heard—' Then she saw the bed and let out a scream. This had the effect of bringing Helen to her normal composure.

'Be quiet. Don't behave like that in a sick-room.' She thrust Paul aside.

'She's dead,' exclaimed Mrs. Hoggett,

58

paying no attention to the girl. 'And you . . . Why, you must be mad. You couldn't hope to get away with this.'

Paul said as if to himself, 'I'd forgotten we even had the thing in the house. If I'd remembered I'd have unloaded it. But she remembered.'

'If you're trying to say she did it herself don't think anyone will believe you,' said Mrs. Hoggett. An instant later she added illogically, 'And if she had it would be you drove her to it.'

Paul paid no attention. 'How badly is she hurt, Nurse?'

Helen lifted a face as pale as milk. 'There's just a thread of pulse. It might stop at any minute I should think. All the same—get a doctor—quickly. Mrs. Hoggett, he'll want hot water and—are there some linen towels or anything that would do for bandages? Oh hurry, Paul.' (In her haste she forgot caution.) 'Get him now; anyone who'll come.'

'I'll get him, Nurse,' offered Mrs. Hoggett, promptly. 'Mr. French is all shocked—and no wonder.'

Her bitter malicious voice seemed to bring Paul back to life. 'I'll try Kemp first,' he said, pushing out of the room. They heard his feet going down the stairs.

'He could have rung from here,' said Mrs.

Hoggett suspiciously.

'How about the hot water?' demanded Helen. 'Don't touch *anything*, Mrs. Hoggett.'

'I should think not.' The woman shuddered. 'I can't bear the sight of blood. I never could.' She hurried out of the room. Helen leaned above the dying woman; there was no light in those narrow dark eyes, the blood welled slowly now from the gaping hole just above her heart.

The bullet must just have missed it, Helen found herself reflecting. It was not blood only but life welling away with each passing moment.

Paul came back. 'Kemp's coming. I warned him . . .'

'What did you say?'

'That she was fooling around with the gun and it went off.'

'But did Blanche know anything about guns?'

'Oh yes. I taught her. When we were first married we used to go to a week-end cottage she had in the middle of a wood, the loneliest place. Once a tramp tried to break in when she was alone. I got the gun next day. We haven't spoken of it for years. Helen, what chance has she?'

'It's a miracle she's not dead already. Paul, what made you come in?'

'I saw her light go on. I thought she was going to ring. Did Mrs. Hoggett say anything about seeing us?'

'She said she hadn't been out to-night.' They found they were talking in anguished whispers.

'This'll be jam for her,' muttered Paul. 'Helen, my darling . . .'

She interrupted mercilessly. 'Wasn't that a car? Tell him to come up at once.' Presently the whole horror of the situation would burst upon her; for the moment she was the nurse *par excellence*. If she could have saved Blanche's life she would have rejoiced.

They heard the car stop and Mrs. Hoggett opening the door; she said something inaudible, then Kemp's voice came clearly up the stairway, 'My good woman, keep that for the authorities. I'm only the doctor.'

He pelted in, thrusting Paul aside; Helen rose to make place for him by the bed. Whatever degree of shock he experienced he displayed none. After a minute he remarked, 'Does anyone know what happened?'

'Yes,' said Paul, flatly. 'I was here. She . . .'

'She never did that herself,' broke in Mrs. Hoggett from the doorway.

'It was an accident,' Paul insisted.

'Has anyone sent for the police? No? They should be called. I don't think there's much chance of Mrs. French recovering consciousness, but if she should be able to make a statement, if only to confirm what you've just said'—he nodded towards Paul—'they should be here to take it.'

He stood up and went across the room to wash his hands. 'Get the police,' he told Paul impatiently. 'There's no time to lose. I'll speak to them.' He took the receiver from Paul's hand. When he had hung up again he said in a perfectly expressionless voice, 'As I've just told Hebe here, I'm only the doctor, but this has come as a shock to the household—obviously—and if you take my advice none of you will make any statements except in answer to questions. It's for the police to find out the facts and the coroner— I'm afraid we must face the fact it's bound to come to that—to give the verdict. It would be a pity for anyone to say anything rash now. It's always so difficult to explain afterwards that you meant something else.' He dried his hands. 'Nurse.'

Helen came over to him. Mrs. Hoggett waited in the doorway. Paul moved automatically across to the windows and, drawing aside a curtain, looked out at the quiet street; the doctor's little green car looked like some sort of beetle . . . The doctor and the nurse seemed isolated, like people under a bell of glass. He couldn't hear what was being said. They were like people on a stage—all the world's a stage—he put up his hand to rub his face and saw the blood on it. With a muttered exclamation he plunged across the room, pushing past Mrs. Hoggett; they heard him go down the passage, a board creaked, his door slammed.

'What's he up to?' Mrs. Hoggett exclaimed.

'Gone to change his clothes, I should think,' said the doctor.

'Gone to do away with himself, I shouldn't wonder.'

'Oh, I doubt if he has a pair of pistols, and he's left that one on the bed. No, stay where you are' (to Mrs. Hoggett). 'In a free country a man has a right to change his clothes if he wants to. And in his circumstances anyone would want to.'

'He's a murderer,' said Mrs. Hoggett, flatly. 'He wanted her out of the way.'

'You'll be able to tell the police all about it,' said Kemp. 'They won't be long.' And a minute or two later their car could be heard.

'I'll let them in,' said Mrs. Hoggett, but at that moment the door of Paul's room opened and he shot past them.

'Wants to get the first word, I suppose,' said the housekeeper, 'all the same . . .'

'Tell that woman to wait outside, Nurse,'

ordered Kemp going to the bed. 'I can't have the sick-room disturbed.'

Mrs. Hoggett retreated, saying furiously, 'You ask him what they were rowing about before he went off this evening. He's a sly one all right but he won't be able to get out of this.'

Kemp looked at the girl beside him. For the first time Helen realised she was still in her dressing-gown.

'Naturally I don't know what story Mr. French will have to tell,' he remarked, 'but it's never much of a picnic when a wife dies in circumstances like these. Everyone concerned is clearly suffering from shock; sometimes it pays to make no statement without consulting a lawyer.'

Helen, still chalky but under control, said with the ghost of a smile, 'Mr. French *is* a lawyer.'

And then Paul came back, accompanied by a police sergeant.

They made a macabre group, with the blood-stained automatic lying where Paul had dropped it on the ghastly bed. The doctor was the first to speak.

'There's nothing more I can do. It's a question of time now. It wouldn't be safe to try and move her, and it wouldn't make any difference anyway. It's a miracle she should have lived as long as she has. I might add that it's never safe to attach too much importance to what people in her condition say.'

But they needn't have troubled, because about two hours later Blanche French died without recovering consciousness.

CHAPTER FIVE

BY NEXT MORNING the story was all over Bryan Mouncey. Blanche French had been alternatively stabbed, shot, poisoned, smothered and pushed out of a window. The cause was suicide, murder, accident while of unsound mind; the responsible agent was the husband, the nurse, the housekeeper, a burglar or the inmate of a lunatic asylum forty miles away who was known to have escaped during the previous week. Kemp, having warned the members of the household to keep their mouths shut until the inquest, and the police having talked vaguely about the law of slander, even Mrs. Hoggett held her peace. The reporters, smelling a possible *cause célèbre*, thronged the house, but she drove them all away, saying, 'I wasn't there, why not ask someone who was? And if you really want to know, the inquest's on Friday.'

There was even a paragraph in one of the chattier London dailies, that was noticed by Arthur Crook, the legal beagle of Earls Court, who observed cheerfully to Bill Parsons, his invaluable ally, 'Here's another husband in the *consommé*. Why they do it, go on getting married, I mean, beats me. Must be tired of life.'

'Suicide?' asked Bill.

'Or murder.'

'Husband responsible?' asked Bill.

'Could be,' said the optimistic Mr. Crook.

'On the premises at the time?' asked Bill.

'Doesn't say,' said Mr. Crook. 'But it doesn't matter. Just being her husband's enough to put him in the dog-house. He might have been playing bridge with his buddies five miles away but that won't stop half the place declaring he did it by remote control, and from what I've seen of husbands,' he added, slapping the paper down, 'it wouldn't surprise me if he had. Nothing,' added this man of law, grandly, 'really surprises me any more.' But he admitted later that even he was staggered by the story Paul French offered the court.

★   ★   ★

He said that, contrary to his usual custom, he had been away from his home on the Wednesday night.

'Since my wife's accident I have always tried to make no engagements for that evening as it is the day the nurse is off duty and my wife doesn't like being left alone. However, I had to keep this snap appointment'—he explained the circumstances, giving Roberts's name and address—'I tried to make Mrs. French understand that I had no choice. I got back shortly before eleven o'clock and, seeing a light under my wife's door, I went in to see if there was anything she wanted. The nurse,' he repeated, 'is off duty on Wednesdays.' In a reply to a question from the coroner he said that he was sleeping in a small room at the end of a passage. The authorities had thoughtfully provided a diagram of the lay-out of the first floor, for the coroner to consult, if so minded.

'I should perhaps explain,' Paul went on, showing his first mark of hesitation, 'that my wife had been rather put out by my decision to meet Mr. Roberts. If she had had notice she might have persuaded Nurse to change her night. Still, she seemed quite normal when I went in and I thought she had got over her annoyance. She said she wanted nothing and I remained chatting for a minute or two standing at the foot of her bed. As I turned to go, I said good night and I had almost reached the door when she said, in a most peculiar tone, "Not good night, Paul, good-bye." I swung round and saw that she had the automatic in her hand. It must have been concealed under the bedclothes during the minute or two we had been talking.'

'It was such a damn' silly story,' said Crook later, 'then it 'ud be difficult not to believe it.'

'When I saw the automatic in my wife's hand naturally I was horrified. I said, "What on earth are you doing with that thing? Put it down. For all you know, it's loaded."'

'Did you recognise it, Mr. French?' the coroner inquired.

'It's my property,' said Paul. 'I bought it several years ago—under licence—when we had a small very wild cottage, that is, the situation was very wild, and we had a fright once when a man escaped from an asylum near by. I taught my wife how to use it, though in point of fact Wednesday was the first time it has ever been put to serious use. Indeed I had forgotten its existence until I saw it in my wife's hand.'

'Where was it normally kept?'

'In my dressing-room, that is, the room where I have been sleeping since my wife's accident.'

'Under lock and key, no doubt?'

Paul looked guilty. 'In point of fact, no. The cupboard where it was did have a key once, I suppose, but nobody has seen it for years. The pistol was at the back of a shelf, which presumably explains why I seldom, if ever, remembered its existence. After all,' he added more warmly, stung perhaps by an expression of disbelief in the face of the coroner, 'one doesn't think of an automatic as a normal part of household furniture.'

'Precisely,' agreed the coroner, in glassy tones. 'Please continue, Mr. French.'

'My wife laughed, a very odd sound. "Oh, it is loaded," she said. "I've made sure of that." My first thought was that she'd had a brainstorm or something and that she meant to attack me. I thought the best way was to treat it as unemotionally as possible. I turned round and walked towards the bed, saying, "Give me that. You don't want an accident to happen." It was then I noticed that the safety catch was off.'

'Do you mean the court to understand that you had stored the weapon loaded?' The coroner sounded horrified.

'I should say that was most improbable, though after such a lapse of time I can't swear on oath . . . But there was ammunition in the cupboard and, as I explained just now, I had myself taught my wife how to use the weapon. When I had got quite close but not near enough to risk snatching the gun, my wife went on, in a perfectly cool voice, "Just stay there. I've something to say." "You don't have to say it with a pistol," I told her. We were both speaking very quietly. I suppose I realised she was temporarily deranged. At any minute I thought her finger might slip on the trigger. I still couldn't believe she intended to shoot me, though at that range she could scarcely miss. Then she said, "Don't be frightened. This isn't for you." And she turned the pistol so that the barrel pointed towards herself. I began to be angry. I abandoned the idea that she was mad. I thought it was a piece of unpardonable melodrama. "That's enough of this play-acting," I said. "Put that thing down at once. You must be out of your mind." She laughed. "That's what they'll say at the inquest, won't they? Such a polite fiction." I felt desperate. I wondered if I could possibly get at the bell beside her bed and attract somebody's attention. The bell rang into Nurse's room and though she wasn't officially on duty I knew she would come at once. The only thing was, of course, that my wife would realise I had rung the bell and that might spur her to precipitate action. I tried to bluff. "Take care," I said, "there's someone outside."'

'Did she believe you?'

'No. She said, "Then why don't you shout?"'

'I turned as if I were going to open the door and for a moment her gaze followed me. That seemed my one chance and I sprang, hoping to knock the gun out of her hand. Before I could touch her there was an immense explosion. I think she had forgotten she had the catch up and her finger on the trigger. I'm convinced, I shall always be convinced, she hadn't the smallest intention of taking her own life.'

'Then why do you suppose she had the gun at all?'

'I told you, she was putting on an act.' He looked round the unsympathetic court. 'Oh, I realise how this must sound to normal people, but my wife had the idea that money of itself was a kind of magic. If you had money you could buy anything. She had already said to me that I needn't bother with the convenience of clients, I could afford to snap my fingers at them. It was that that had precipitated a—a storm before I left. I think she hadn't really believed I would go. Now she was warning me what might happen if I disregarded her wishes another time.'

'Oh yes, Mr. French.' The coroner was playing it dumb. The jury didn't even pretend to believe it. 'Now, I think you said the weapon was normally kept in your dressing-room.'

'Yes.'

'Which, from this plan, is at the end of a corridor.'

'Yes.'

'So that your contention is that Mrs. French fetched the gun during your absence.'

'There was no one else on the premises

except the housekeeper, and I'm quite sure she wouldn't have laid a finger on it. She's already said that if she'd known it was in the house . . .'

'We shall be hearing Mrs. Hoggett's testimony later on. I understand your wife had recently broken her leg.'

'Yes. But that was several weeks ago. She was making excellent progress.'

'Good enough for her to have left her bed, gone down a passage, reached the weapon from the shelf, and returned, all without being heard?'

'She could get about quite well on sticks, in her room at all events. She had begun to talk of convalescence, though the doctor didn't think she was quite up to that yet.'

'On sticks, you said? Yet you contend that she could have reached a shelf . .'

'It wasn't difficult. The gun was kept in a shoe-box. I suppose if it had been something more striking I should have recalled its existence more easily, though even so,' he added in uncontrollable desperation, 'it would never have occurred to me it constituted a danger.'

'I see.' But how much he saw was not altogether clear. 'Please go on, Mr. French.'

'I was dazed by what had happened. I know I rang her bell, because my finger was still on the bell-push when Nurse Wayland came in. But I wasn't aware of the fact myself until she said, "You'll wake the whole neighbourhood," or words to that effect. Then I telephoned the doctor, he—but of course you can get his story from himself.' He stopped abruptly, like a machine that has run down.

There was an impressive pause. Then the coroner said, 'You do realise, Mr. French, that this is a most extraordinary story. The court probably feels as puzzled as I do over certain points. You say you don't believe your wife had any intention of firing the weapon. Then what was the idea in producing it?'

'She wanted to frighten me, and,' continued Paul grimly, 'she certainly succeeded. "This is what I might be driven to if you go out again and leave me alone." She would know, of course, that any violent action on her part would spell ruin for me.'

'A lady has to feel very strongly indeed to consider taking her own life—'

'I've told you, she never intended to. Why, she was the last person to commit suicide. Why should she?'

'That is one of the considerations before the court. How long had you been married, Mr. French?'

'Ten years.'

'Would you say it was a normally happy marriage?'

'I'd say it was a typical one. We weren't given to rows or recriminations; our tastes didn't always lie in the same direction, and, being a rich woman, my wife laboured under the delusion that her will should be law. We had had disagreements before . . .'

'But she had never gone to such extreme measures?'

'No. And when I left the house that night it never went through my mind—she was put out, but, well, every husband knows there are disagreements in marriage from time to time. Even now it's difficult for me to accept the truth. It seems like a nightmare.'

'And you still tell the jury that the reason for this—disagreement—was your insistence on keeping your appointment with Mr. Roberts? It seems to me and I feel it may appear to them in a similar light—that it was altogether too frivolous a reason for this very tragic dénouement. I know ladies sometimes lose a sense of proportion, but—suicide is . . .'

'Not suicide,' protested Paul, but his voice seemed weary now.

'It puts the jury in a remarkably difficult situation,' the coroner continued in even more severe tones. 'If there were any contributory factor which you have so far failed to mention, it might assist them.'

Paul turned to look at the people referred
to. The Woodentops, Crook would have said
in his bald fashion. Certainly their faces told
him nothing. Only—if there was no actual
condemnation there, there was no compassion
either.

'I'm afraid I'm only concerned with my own
situation,' he told the coroner. 'But I do urge
the jury to put the notion of suicide out of their
minds. She was very temperamental on
occasions, but she would no more dream of
taking her own life than I would myself. If that
had been her intent, why wait till my return?
She had enough sleeping-tablets to put an end
to things before I came back, and if she wanted
to incriminate me she only had to leave a letter
and, in my experience as a lawyer, letters from
suicides are better evidence than anything
else. No, I was meant to crawl, to say "On my
honour, I'll never leave you alone again."'

The coroner was shaking his head. 'But
Mrs. French was not alone in the house?'

'Certainly not. The housekeeper was always
in on a Wednesday, and she certainly would
have stayed in when she knew I was out. In
fact, she assured me she didn't leave the house
that night . . .'

'Mrs. Hoggett will be giving her own
evidence later,' said the coroner, for the

second time. 'What is so difficult for the court to understand is why Mrs. French should be brought to what you yourself admit to be the verge of madness simply because you had to keep a business appointment. I take it there was no doubt in her mind as to the genuineness of this?'

'I telephoned Mr. Roberts from her room; she could actually hear his voice on the line. No, the fact is, as I've tried to make clear, she was outraged at the notion that her money couldn't buy her her own way.' He looked uneasily to left and right. 'That isn't so singular as it may appear to a layman. I have had wealthy clients who have suffered from the same illusion. Why bother to keep an appointment that is inconvenient to me when financially it's of small account whether you please this client or not?'

Meaning, as the foreman of the jury instantly comprehended, that, having bought her husband, she didn't see why he shouldn't perform every trick demanded of him.

'Did she try and exact a promise from you?' the coroner persisted.

Paul put up his hand and touched his forehead; it was damp with perspiration, and he drew a handkerchief from his sleeve and held it for an instant to his face.

'No. No, I don't think she actually did that.

In a sense, there wasn't time. My one concern was to get the gun away from her. I've wondered ever since what would have happened if I'd turned and walked out of the room. I think now that if I had done that she might still be alive. But it was too big a chance to take. Suppose I had heard the explosion after I had closed the door behind me? I should have been censured by everyone, could even have been named as accessory before the crime. It was an intolerable situation,' he burst forth in a wilder voice, 'and only a man who has found himself faced with it can begin to understand my problem. If I had lunged for the gun it might have gone off without either of us intending it. My one hope was to distract her attention—and it failed.'

The coroner let him go. 'We may want to ask you some more supplementary questions when we have heard the rest of the evidence,' he said, and there was no sympathy in his voice. 'Call Nurse Wayland.'

Helen took the oath, not looking at Paul. Both knew that the worst danger was to come, when Mrs. Hoggett gave her evidence.

She could add very little to what Paul had already told the court. There had been nothing unusual in the dead woman's attitude earlier in the day. No, she had never appeared a suicidal type, had, indeed, spoken of going away for convalescence as soon as the doctor would agree.

'How long had you been on the case, Miss Wayland?'

'About seven weeks, almost eight.'

'Did Mrs. French ever in your hearing speak of self-destruction?'

'No, never. I'm convinced she never thought of it. She had no reason . . .'

'Will you tell us in your own words what happened that night?'

'I came in about a quarter to eleven. Mr. French had not yet come back. Mrs. Hoggett told me he had had to keep an unexpected appointment. She said that Mrs. French was asleep and had not rung since dinner-time. I went up to my patient's room, but the light was out and though I opened the door a crack there was no sound. I went along to bed, and, as I had rather a headache, I took a sleeping-tablet and I must have been asleep before Mr. French returned. At all events I didn't hear him come upstairs.'

The coroner glanced at his notes. According to his evidence he returned about 11.15. Something else seemed to strike him for he jotted down a word or two, then went on, 'And after that, Miss Wayland?'

'I was awakened by a roar and the pealing of a bell. I didn't appreciate at first the nature of the sound. I hurried along to Mrs. French's room, where the light was on and where I found Mr. French standing beside the bed that seemed drenched in blood. He said, "It was an accident, she never meant it."'

'Did you know of the existence of the weapon?'

'No. Neither Mr. or Mrs. French had ever spoken of it.'

'Where was the pistol? Did you notice? In Mrs. French's hand or . . .?'

Helen paused an instant. 'I think Mr. French was holding it. He seemed perfectly dazed. After a minute, during which the housekeeper appeared, I realised Mrs. French was not dead though it was obvious she was dying fast. Mr. French called the doctor and he said the police should be summoned. Mrs. French died about two hours afterwards.'

'Did Mr. French make any statement to you later?'

She shook her head. He kept saying, "It was an accident. She never meant it."'

The coroner pulled her up abruptly. 'This is very important, Miss Wayland. You are sure those were his actual words.'

'Perfectly sure.'

'*It was an accident. She never meant it.* He didn't amplify that?'

Helen thought. 'I believe he said, "She's

overreached herself'' or something of that kind.'

'Did he explain what he meant by that?'

'There was no time,' Helen protested. 'Mrs. Hoggett came in, then we rang the doctor, and as soon as he arrived we telephoned to the police.'

'I see. Now, Miss Wayland, in your opinion could Mrs. French have left her bed and fetched the gun from the dressing-room?'

'Oh yes. She was walking about her room on sticks and I know one day she got as far as the bathroom, which involved opening two doors and coming a short way down the passage. If she could do as much as that she could get as far as the dressing-room.'

The coroner put a number of further questions but the answers threw no more light on the situation. Asked what her impression had been of the relations between the dead woman and her husband, Helen replied that she had never heard them in any violent argument. Mrs. French was inclined to be possessive, she admitted, liked everyone to know that it was due to her that Mr. French had got his start in life. 'I was only there while Mrs. French was ill,' she added defensively, 'but she never said anything to me to make me think she was unhappy or dissatisfied in her private life.'

'Would you expect her to?' asked the coroner, dryly.

'Nurses get a good many confidences,' was Helen's simple reply. 'They're treated rather like bank managers, they have an official rather than a personal standing.'

'You had no criticism to offer of your treatment while you were in the household?'

'None,' said Helen. 'I was the nurse, it was a routine job, all invalids have their difficult moments, but Mrs. French had made a very quick recovery, in fact, Mrs. Esdaile was considering replacing me as I was wanted for another case.'

'Did Mrs. French know that?'

'Only if Mrs. Esdaile told her. It wasn't for me to make the first move.'

'So, in your opinion, there was nothing in her husband's behaviour to account for Mrs. French taking the violent action she did?'

'I wasn't in her confidence,' Helen insisted. 'I can only repeat I never heard any scenes between them. Mr. French was out a great deal. Mrs. French had very few visitors. I believe Mr. French when he says, as he told the police and the doctor from the outset, that she had no intention of taking her own life.'

CHAPTER SIX

IT WAS Mrs. Hoggett who set the court by the ears and started Paul's heart beating so painfully it was a wonder to him everyone present couldn't hear it. She said she had been nearly three years in the household and you couldn't say it was a happy one.

'What do you mean by that, Mrs. Hoggett?'

'Nothing definite,' Mrs. Hoggett mumbled, 'but you can always tell.'

'Woman's famous intuition,' said the coroner smiling grimly. 'I'm afraid that can't be allowed as evidence. Can you tell us anything definite that might lead the jury to understand Mrs. French's astounding action on Wednesday night?'

'Well,' said Mrs. Hoggett, pertly, 'we don't know what happened, do we? We've only got Mr. French's word for it. If Madam was here she might tell a very different story.'

'Have you any ground for saying that? According to what the court has heard already, it seems an average household, allowing for the natural repercussions that may occur where the lady holds the purse-strings.'

'I don't know about that,' said Mrs.

Hoggett coolly. 'I can only tell you there was the father and mother of a row that night when Mr. French told her he had to go out. For one thing, she didn't believe him.'

'Did Mrs. French tell you that? or did you hear her say it to Mr. French?'

'Some things don't have to be put into words.'

The coroner sighed. 'I find it so difficult to persuade witnesses that assumption is not proof. May we take it, Mrs. Hoggett, that Mrs. French did not actually say to her husband that she disbelieved his story?'

'She made him ring up this Mr. Roberts from the extension in her room.'

'And after that?'

'Well, after that she had to believe him, unless it was a put-up job.'

'More assumptions,' sighed the coroner. 'For your information, it has been established that Mr. Roberts did make the appointment with Mr. French for Wednesday evening and Mr. French kept it.'

'I didn't say anything different, only that Madam was rare put-out, accused him of neglecting her. She said he didn't have to fetch and carry like any pettifogging little attorney and he said a man didn't want to be Mr. Blanche Mullins all his life.'

The jury stiffened at that. But the coroner

cooled them down by saying, 'A very natural aspiration, Mrs. Hoggett, and one with which most husbands would agree. By the way, were you actually present when the words were said?'

'I'd gone up to know if they were ready for me to serve dinner and I couldn't help but hear. They were going at it hammer and tongs and never even heard me knock, so I went away again. If you ask me, she was jealous of the nurse. She did say "If Nurse was at home it might be a different story."'

'Did she ever say anything to you to support such a theory?'

'I've told you, she didn't speak to me. Only to give orders. She was like that. Just because someone else made her money for her . . .'

'This is highly improper. All we want here are facts. You say she was jealous of Nurse Wayland. In your information, had she any reason to be? I'm not asking for your opinion, I simply want facts.'

'I never saw them canoodling, if that's what you mean,' said Mrs. Hoggett sulkily. 'I've told you what she said.'

'Would you say that Mrs. French was a jealous woman?'

'Jealous? The whole place knew it. Mr. French couldn't have a new secretary but she'd find some excuse to go down to the office and look her over. And once when he took a client out to dinner, you should have heard how she created. Young lady was engaged to someone else, what's more . . .'

In her rage she failed to recognise that now she was testifying on Paul's behalf.

'So that, even if your statement is correct and she was jealous of Miss Wayland, it really proves nothing.' He turned to the jury. 'The young lady in question has an excellent reputation locally; it would be a thousand pities if any wrong impressions were to get about. Of course,' he turned back to Mrs. Hoggett, 'it would be a different story if you had any evidence of any improper behaviour.'

Mrs. Hoggett stared round her in a baffled sort of way. Here was her opportunity to speak of the meeting on the hill, but she had tied her own hands. So, 'I'm only telling you what I heard Madam say,' she assured him in sulky tones.

'What you *overheard*,' the coroner corrected. 'Afterwards, when you took up Mrs. French's dinner, did she say anything to you?'

Mrs. Hoggett sniffed. 'Not her. Thought herself too good to talk to me. Just that she didn't feel like eating, and she wasted practically all that good food. She did ask me to give her her sleeping-tablets before I left, and I put them by the bed.'

'Did she actually take a tablet? or possibly more than one?'

'I couldn't say. But she wouldn't have asked for them if she hadn't wanted them, would she?'

'You are here to answer questions,' the coroner told her crisply. 'It's for me to put them, and I cannot regard her request as being any proof that she did, in fact, take a tablet.'

It was easy to see what was implied. If the dead woman had taken a tablet how was it she was awake when her husband returned? Which would give the lie to his story.

Mrs. Hoggett then admitted that she didn't know how many tablets were in the bottle or how often Mrs. French took them. She had had them some weeks before when she found sleep difficult to woo. She added, however, that just before Nurse came in she, the witness, had gone upstairs and seen no light under Mrs. French's door. 'So she was asleep then,' she wound up, triumphantly.

'How long was that before Mr. French returned?'

'He came in about a quarter past eleven, I'd say. I waited up a bit after Nurse came in, just redding everything up for the morning. I like to find a clean kitchen when I come down.'

'The condition of your kitchen has nothing

to do with the case. So you went up about eleven o'clock?'

'Yes. And all the lights were out then. In these old houses the doors never fit properly, you can see the light under them, and there wasn't any under Nurse's door or Mrs. French's.'

'If you had gone up how can you be sure what time Mr. French came in?'

'I always make myself a cup of tea after I'm in my room. I was just drinking it when I heard the front door close, so I knew he was back.'

'You didn't see Mr. French to speak to?'

'No,' returned Mrs. Hoggett coldly. 'I was in my dressing-gown by that time.'

'Did you hear him come up?'

The woman hesitated. 'Well, not exactly, but I heard the board creak, and it's the only one, so I knew he'd gone along the passage.'

'Which board was this?' The coroner was frowning; with the best will in the world, you couldn't call Mrs. Hoggett an unprejudiced witness; his sympathies began to veer round towards Paul. A woman like this would ruin him if she could and the fact that she had produced no evidence worth the name seemed to indicate that no adverse evidence existed. And however rum the story might appear, you couldn't bring a man in guilty of murder without some sort of motive. It was true the deceased was a rich woman and her husband benefited considerably by her death, but it was equally true that he was in no way pressed for money—the police had made that abundantly clear.

'There's a board outside Mr. French's door, he calls it his burglar alarm. If you tread on it it can be heard even downstairs, gives a long squeaking sound. I heard it that night as I was carrying my crocks along to wash in my bathroom. That's how I knew he'd gone to bed.'

'You hadn't actually heard him come upstairs?'

'The stairs are carpeted too thick for that, and of course being late at night he'd want to be specially careful not to wake Mrs. French.'

'Why do you say that?'

Mrs. Hoggett looked astonished. 'Well, we all went round as if we had rags round our feet when Mrs. French was resting. It's no wonder we never had mice. They wouldn't dare so much as cross a floor.'

In those few words she had painted a picture of an overbearing woman alarming even her husband and her housekeeper into excessive quietude.

'The next thing I heard was a door closing, so of course I thought that was Mr. French going to bed.'

'But now you think you may have been mistaken?'

'Now I think it may have been the door of Mrs. French's room. Leastways it was shut when I came along.'

'But Nurse Wayland was there by that time.'

'Yes, she was, too. I suppose she might have shut it.'

'Is there anything particular to distinguish the sound of Mr. French's door closing from that of any other door in the house?'

Mrs. Hoggett shrugged. 'They all sound the same to me. It was only hearing that board creak made me feel sure . . .'

'But one moment.' The coroner had been examining the plan the authorities had provided. 'In order to make that board creak Mr. French must have been close to the door of his own room.'

'That's what I keep saying. That's why I thought it must be his door that closed.'

'But if he was there, then he had already passed the door of Mrs. French's room. I take it there is no second staircase?'

Mrs. Hoggett's expression said that one staircase was enough.

'So, unless you are mistaken, Mr. French had intended to go straight to his room—and then he changed his mind?'

What was it Paul had said? 'I saw a light under my wife's door and went in.'

The construction the jury were putting on the facts was clear to at least two-thirds of those present. Of course Mrs. Hoggett had heard the board creak, because Paul had needed to fetch the weapon from his dressing-room before retracing his steps to his wife's bedroom.

The coroner asked, 'You heard just the one creak?'

'Yes, sir. Of course, if you remembered, you could step over the board . . .'

'I have told you before, Mrs. Hoggett, you are only required to answer my questions, not to put forward any theories of your own. Or even hint at them,' he added sharply. 'How long elapsed between the sound of the creaking board and the closing of the door?'

'Well, not long, because I took it he'd gone straight into his room.'

'What was the next sound you heard?'

'I heard the shot and the bell, you could hardly tell which came first. The shot seemed to go on sounding like an echo—or of course that could have been shock, like the war when the falling masonry seemed to go on and on after a bomb had dropped. But the bell went on and on as if the push had stuck somewhere and it couldn't stop.'

'One more question, Mrs. Hoggett. Was it usual in your experience for Mr. French to go into his wife's room on his way to bed?'

'You mean of a Wednesday? Well, it had never happened before that he wasn't at home on Nurse's night out. He'd say good night, of course. Ordinary nights?' She paused. 'He'd go in, I dare say.'

'You dare say. But you're not certain.'

'I'm not one to pry,' said Mrs. Hoggett coldly. 'I'm glad enough at the end of the day to be able to put my feet up and drink my tea in peace. I'm engaged as housekeeper, I don't have anything to do with the sickroom. But I'll say this, I never heard Mrs. French moving around in the evening the way she must have done if Mr. French's story is true.'

'You've just told the court you didn't hear Mr. French come upstairs because the carpets are so thick. Doesn't that apply to the landings?'

'There's no carpet over the place where the board creaks.'

'You told the court just now that it would be easy to step over the board if you remembered. If you didn't wish it known that you were going into the dressing-room... Besides, where did you spend the evening?'

'After I'd done the washing-up and put

everything ready I had a bit of a read in the kitchen. There's no servants' hall there.'

'And if you were in the kitchen—did you have the door shut?'

'I never could abide draughts.'

'Can you be sure you would hear a board even if it did creak? You were reading, remember, no doubt you were engrossed.'

Mrs. Hoggett looked sullen. Then the coroner put the 64,000 dollar question. 'For the purposes of the record, we may take it that you did not leave the house that evening?'

Mrs. Hoggett was hoist on her own petard. She had not only assured Helen that she had been indoors, but later had repeated her statement to the police officer in charge. 'I didn't go out,' she said sullenly.

It was her last question and she came down from the stand with a face like thunder.

'Recall Mr. French,' the coroner ordered, and once again Paul took the stand.

'You have heard the evidence given by the last witness. Can you offer any explanation? Your own statement was that you went into your wife's room because the light was on.'

'That's true,' he acknowledged, 'but Mrs. Hoggett's statement is also true. When I went upstairs there was no light under my wife's door and, not wishing to disturb her, I went along to my own room. That would account for the creak Mrs. Hoggett says she heard. I made no particular effort to avoid treading on that board. If my wife was asleep it certainly wouldn't wake her. I was about to open the door of my room when I happened to glance over my shoulder and saw that a light had now sprung up. Whether I had roused my wife or not I don't know, but it was Nurse's night off, and if my wife did want anything I could supply it. She sometimes fancied a cup of tea or—it had turned very wet and unpleasant— she might have needed another blanket—at all events, I went back. I wasn't sorry for the opportunity. I told you we had parted on somewhat acrimonious terms . . .'

'And your wife was waiting for you, gun in hand?'

'No. She said, "I'm glad you've come in. I heard you come upstairs" or something like that. The rest of the interview went as I've described.'

It was like the game of here we go round the mulberry-bush. Paul French had an answer for everything and it all depended how much the jury decided to believe.

★ ★ ★

After the jury had filed out there was a sound in the court of breath being relaxed.

Neighbours turned to exchange glances. Talk about an ancient and fishlike smell, those glances said. A rich jealous woman—they all knew her reputation—had pressed a trigger and presented her husband with his liberty and a fortune in one tempestuous second. Only, thought the more logical of them, it wasn't quite like that. Could she have known that he was slipping away from her and taken this drastic and melodramatic way of killing the two of them with one stone?—one bullet actually, of course.

They recalled Dr. Kemp's evidence. After he had declared the cause of death, he had been asked whether he regarded his late patient as a well-balanced woman, or conversely as someone who might have taken her own life? He had stated emphatically that he had never noticed any suicidal tendency, her health was normally excellent, she had plenty of this world's goods, had her own interests, had been speaking to him not twenty-four hours earlier of going away for convalescence. She had even said she hoped her husband might be able to get away with her for a few days at least. 'On the other hand,' he added, 'she was very temperamental and liable to blow up a trifle, like a bladder, into something quite formidable.'

★   ★   ★

In the little room where the jury were immured the foreman, who had held this office at other inquests, was urging for an open verdict.

'I don't agree,' snapped a big solid jurywoman. 'Why should he be allowed to get away with murder?'

'We don't know that it was murder, and, even if we were convinced, it could never be made to stick in a court of law. Just think of the facts. He says the light went on and that was his cue. Do you think she was going to see an armed man come into the room and not yell blue murder? Why, she had the bell push under her hand, and by all accounts the nurse was pretty quick on the draw. Oh no, that cock would never fight.'

'We only have French's evidence that the light was on,' insisted another juryman. 'He could have fetched the gun and gone back to her room.'

'To shoot her in the dark? You aren't suggesting that, I suppose? Then, when he did switch on the light, why didn't she give the alarm?'

'She might have been asleep,' pointed out one of the hanging jurors.

'In that case why did he make such a boss

shot? There was always the chance she might recover consciousness and make a statement?'

'The same applies to the suggestion that she shot herself.'

'Ah, but French's defence is that she never intended to shoot anyone, the thing went off and blew a hole in her shoulder and upper part of the arm.'

'If he was guilty why on earth didn't he say she tried to shoot him and he tried to get the gun away and it was self-defence? Nobody could have faulted that.'

'Couldn't they?' The foreman's voice was sharp with sarcasm. 'When there were no signs of a struggle—there weren't, you know—no scratches, no torn nightgown. No, there are three alternatives. She did it herself, hoping to get him charged with murder. And if it was suicide that must have been in her mind or, as he says himself, she'd have taken a simpler way out, the sleeping-pills, for instance.'

Someone interrupted. 'If she'd taken a sleeping-pill she needn't even have awaked when he went in. He simply had to put on the light and shoot her.'

'And ask people to believe she shot herself curled up cosily under the bedclothes? She'd been lying against the pillows when the shot was fired, that much has been established . . .

97

And if she had shot herself under the clothes the wound wouldn't have been where it was. No, that's out. The second possibility is that French took the gun in with him and walked up to the bed and shot her. But in that case why didn't she scream? Mrs. Pigg or whatever her name is was on the *qui vive* and she didn't hear a sound. She didn't say in her evidence she'd even heard voices.'

'She thought he'd gone to bed. . . .'

'And she was probably running the tap to wash her tea-cup, etc . . .'

'The third possibility,' the patient foreman continued, 'is that French's story is the true one. I cast my vote for three, not because it's necessarily true but because it's just possible it may be, and a man has to have the benefit of the doubt.'

'The fact is,' put in a juror who had previously not spoken, 'we don't know how much didn't come out. There may have been some other reason for the scene that night. That housekeeper said Mrs. French didn't really believe her husband was meeting this business contact, not until he rang up. Then who did she think he was meeting?' He wagged his goat-like head. *'Cherchez la femme,'* he said. 'And I don't mean the nurse.'

'It hasn't occurred to you that the police haven't unearthed any secret liaison?' the foreman snapped. 'They've been going round trailing their net for the past thirty-six hours. If anyone knew of any funny business where French was concerned, they'd have found it out. And all of us who knew anything of them know what Mrs. French was like.'

'They say there's no smoke without fire,' insisted Juryman No. 6. 'Are we sure that Nurse is all she's cracked up to be?'

'Really,' protested the foreman, 'we are only asked to come to a decision on the facts put before us, not speculate as to something that might have happened about which there are no facts at all. Personally I don't see how we can ever be certain of the truth. He could have done it, of course he could, though it still beats me why she didn't raise a hullabaloo, unless he tapped her on the shoulder and asked her to sit up and then pulled the trigger before she knew where she was . . .'

'It could have happened like that,' muttered the disapproving woman juror.

'You heard what the coroner said; we can only go on evidence. There may not be much of it, and there's no support for any of the statements that have been made so far as I can see, but a man in French's position doesn't murder a rich wife without some fairly obvious motive. There's the nurse, but there's no evidence there and the girl's got to earn her living. Besides, some of us know about her. She's not the type to get into this sort of mess. If there's another woman, where is she? If he's in financial difficulties, why does no one know anything about them? And if he was going to put his wife out of the way, why choose an evening when admittedly they'd had words?'

'Because the next day might have been too late,' said the crusty juror. But that was just another opinion. Blanche didn't help them a bit, she hadn't even mouthed anything to the repulsive Mrs. Hoggett about writing a letter or putting through a telephone call to her lawyer. The lawyer aforesaid, Mr. Blissett, had told the authorities he hadn't heard from his client in more than a year.

At last the jury was won round. 'We call it suicide while of unsound mind?' suggested the goat-like one.

The foreman's face thinned with contempt. 'No. We bring in a verdict of death from shooting with insufficient evidence to show how it came about. That virtually accuses Paul French of responsibility without giving him an opportunity to defend himself in open court. That's known as British justice which is proverbially the best in the world. Sometimes I wonder if we shouldn't do better to adopt a more lowly standard. Better for the victim, that is.'

He opened the door of the juryroom and indicated that they were ready to return to the court.

DEATH TAKES A WIFE

He opened the door of the jury-room and indicated that they were ready to return to the court.

CHAPTER SEVEN

WARNED by the authorities that the crowds who had attended the inquest were hanging about in the hope of seeing him, and perfectly aware that the verdict was by no means approved by all those present, Paul kicked his heels in the small room that had been reserved for witnesses until a welcome burst of rain cleared the streets. Even so he found a few pertinacious reporters hanging round his gate. Head down against the rain, and the cameras all pointed mercilessly at him, he thrust his way through them, saying between his teeth, 'No comment.' Then he gained the refuge of his house and slammed and locked the front door. Instantly he was aware of a sense of emptiness amounting almost to dereliction. A cold air hung in the hall and about the staircase as though life had deserted the place. Defiantly he pressed a bell but no Mrs. Hoggett answered his summons, and when he went along to the kitchen he saw that this also was deserted. The fire had burnt out, the grate was cold and clean, the table empty, the very plates on the dresser had an air of disuse. In the room she had occupied the glass lay face downwards on the dressing-table, the bed was covered, the blankets folded neatly. Not a doubt about it—Mrs. Hoggett had fled from what she clearly considered to be a sinking ship. The sense of cold and emptiness growing within him, Paul made a survey of the house. Helen had left it the previous day, returning to the Nurses' Home, and he had not seen her until she appeared to give evidence. Her pallor and distress must have touched any but the stoniest heart, but he wondered cynically how much good it had done him. Since their love could not be publicly acknowledged, the sightseers as a whole probably attributed that exhausted look to fear—of being found alone with him perhaps. He came down the stairs and picked up his hat. He couldn't stay here with the ghost of Blanche haunting the stairways; by dark he'd be hearing the reverberation of the shot that had ended her life. He would go out, get himself a good meal somewhere. But in the hall he stopped. It was no good; wherever he went he would be recognised.

'And why not?' he asked defiantly. 'I've been cleared of her death.'

But it wasn't true and he knew it. Someone far less knowledgeable than a lawyer could have told him he had merely been found not guilty, and that verdict, he shrewdly suspected, was due to lack of concrete evidence rather than any firm belief in the jury's mind that he was in no way responsible for Blanche's violent end.

He sat for a long time in his study, not even troubling to turn on the electric fire, then, when the cold invaded his bones, he went to the kitchen where there were tins in the cupboard and got himself some kind of a scratch meal. He put on the wireless but that only seemed to intensify his solitude. He thought of people he might ring up, but uncertainty as to their attitude towards his dilemma kept his hands off the telephone receiver. The next day would be Saturday when the office would be closed, but there was nothing to prevent his going there. They had been remarkably busy recently, and there would be business awaiting his attention. Norris never came in on a Saturday and Paul had seldom done so. Blanche had taken a poor view of a husband who couldn't even devote his week-end to her entertainment.

The long evening wore away interminably. It seemed impossible when the clock chimed in the hall that it should only be nine o'clock. If there had been a dog, a cat even, a bird in a cage. He began to understand the significance of loneliness and the drugs men took to allay it. Old women took to writing poison pen letters or, on a minor scale, backbiting ones to their neighbours. Men cuddled a bottle. He found the whisky but that didn't prove what he wanted. At last he went into Blanche's room where the sleeping-tablets were in a medicine chest and took sufficient to induce sleep. To-morrow, thank God, there would be work.

The morning brought a spate of letters. Some were unsigned, most had identical contents. They congratulated him cordially, cynically, obscenely, on not being asked to stand trial on a charge of murder. The last letter was from Norris. He said that he had been wanting to discuss the future of the firm for some time past. As Paul doubtless appreciated, he, the writer, was anxious to retire and enjoy his remaining years—he was now past sixty—at leisure. A man called Fielden had made an excellent offer for the practice. 'In the circumstances you will probably feel, with me, that you would be happier in some other locality,' wrote Mr. Norris, his handwriting as smooth as his habitual voice. 'The Dene is bound to have unfortunate memories for you, and you are still a comparatively young man. I gather that Fielden does not want to buy a partnership, but to run the business himself; he has a son to inherit in due course.' He named a price that was certainly not ungenerous. 'No doubt you will let me know your views,' the letter wound up. 'You will probably be taking a short holiday in any case after your ordeal . . .'

There was another page but Paul barely skimmed it. The meaning was only too clear. Nobody, or practically nobody, would want to confide his affairs to a man who might have murdered his wife.

'Dead men tell no tales,' said the proverb, but dead women may win the rubber. Still, he had already contemplated leaving Bryan Mouncey. Everything now depended on Helen. If she sided with all the others—but she couldn't, she couldn't.

'I've got to be fair to her,' he thought, 'give her her chance.'

He wondered if he dared ring her up. But probably that old witch at the Nursing Home had told them not to put any calls from him through to her, and, besides, his very calling of her might start the gossip afresh.

He made himself coffee, drank it black, got his hat and went out. If this chap, Fielden, was going to take over, there was no time to be lost clearing up outstanding cases. And in his work he lost himself for several hours, shrinking instinctively from the moment when he must close the office and return to the derelict house.

★   ★   ★

At the Nurses' Home Mrs. Esdaile was talking to Helen.

'You've had a piece of luck,' she told the girl grimly. 'I had a *cri de cœur* this morning for a reliable nurse to take an old gentleman to Bandol where he's resolved to die. He could die perfectly well in Bournemouth, of course, where he is at the moment, but he doesn't trust the Government to let him out of the country once he's dead.'

'What on earth could they do?'

'Open the coffin and search for contraband. Oh, it's been done, smuggling goods abroad in a coffin, I mean. I don't choose to believe you know any more about this French affair than you've revealed in the court. You're a first-class nurse and it would be too bad for a thing like this to break you. Ordinary people may like reading about murders, but when it comes to employing nurses who were involved, however innocently . . .'

Helen stopped her. Her eyes were blazing.

'You've no right to call it murder. A jury found him innocent . . .'

'Don't be a fool,' said Mrs. Esdaile scornfully. 'They didn't find him guilty and that, I should say, is more than he deserved. If he has any sense he'll clear out, too. In fact, I dare say he won't have much choice. Norris isn't going to like this any more than I do. Now, listen to me. To-morrow—no, Monday—start getting travellers' cheques and so forth—you've got a passport? Good. I'll telegraph Mr. Bellairs's doctor that you're ready to leave at once. His lawyer in London is making all the travel arrangements and he'll see about the currency. You'd better go to his office and collect the tickets and any other documents. And take that look off your face,' she added in a grim voice. 'You're getting a wonderful break and don't forget it. With any luck you won't be back in this country for several weeks—and by that time Mr. French, if he has a grain of sense, will have shaken the dust of the place off his feet and people will have begun thinking about something else. The less you see of him before you go the better. Bryan Mouncey's no different from any other place—they can all add two and two—I don't say they won't make it five, but the point is they'll all agree on the same total.'

'If I walk out now,' said Helen, 'he'll think I'm like everyone else and believe he did it.'

'Of course he did it,' said Mrs. Esdaile again. 'You're not going to tell me that Blanche French would set her husband free and leave him a rich widower, in order that he can enjoy himself with someone else? If she'd meant to kill herself she'd have taken him first. I hope, Nurse, you're going to be sensible about this. I don't deny that Paul French has some excellent qualities, and I've always heard he's a most successful lawyer, but he's a murderer, whatever the jury may have said. Don't forget that and don't get carried away by any romantic claptrap about history not repeating itself. Once a man's reached the point where his own interests are more important than the life of another person he's over the borders of sanity, if he can't be certified under the McNaughton Rules.'

By Sunday night Paul was in little doubt as to his standing in Bryan Mouncey. At six o'clock he was sitting by a smoky fire with *The Observer* in his hands, not seeing a word that was printed therein. Ever since the inquest he seemed to have lived in a state of suspension. Sunday was often one of the most social days of the week, and he had told himself he couldn't suddenly become a recluse because of what had happened.

He had scarcely spoken to a soul all day, had thought first of going to the golf club, but, with his bag on his shoulder, had suddenly changed his mind; had started out for the Cat and Chickens, seen someone he knew on the other side of the road, opened his mouth to call a greeting and realised that either by chance or of intent the other fellow hadn't seen him. Quickly he had turned back. At last he got out his car and drove over to Mellingford; there was a country club there where he had sometimes taken Blanche at a week-end, but when he walked in and asked for a table a slim young man with smooth black hair said he was afraid all the tables were reserved.

'We're always full up on Sundays,' he said, carelessly.

Paul knew it was necessary to ring up in advance, but to-day he saw a deliberate attempt to label him a pariah.

'I'll have to make do with a snack at the bar then,' he said doggedly, but the young man said they didn't do snacks on Sunday—Catering Wages Act and all that. He might have stopped for a drink, but he didn't. He came straight back and put the car away, then found some biscuits and cheese—that slut Hoggett hadn't even left him with a fresh loaf of bread—and sat drinking whiskies and soda and looking at nothing. Commonsense assured him that Parratt really hadn't seen him; he knew from experience the necessity for telephoning in advance for a table, it was unreasonable to expect the place to do snacks on a Sunday, but, though he had faced a coroner's jury with composure, now a soft knocking at the door sent his heart into his mouth.

It would be that slut, Hoggett, he decided, come to collect her back pay. He thought grimly it would give him immense pleasure to point out that, as she'd left without giving notice, she wasn't entitled to a bean; then he knew he was going to let her have it; there was gossip enough as it was, and it would seem that he was trying to pay her out for doing her best to get him swung.

Throwing down the paper he pulled open the door—and Helen came slipping over the threshold. His delight and amazement at the sight of her drove all sense out of his mind. But when he would have put his arms round her she drew back, and at once the dark colour came flooding into his cheeks.

'Do you have to come to the back door?' he asked roughly. 'You've been using the front entrance for the last two months.'

She sent him a look of such love and grief that he felt stupefied with shame.

'It doesn't matter,' he cried quickly, remorsefully, 'you could come down the chimney for me. Sit down—I'll give you a drink—oh Helen, Helen! How pleased Blanche would be to see me now.'

'I had to come,' said Helen, taking the glass and putting it down untasted, 'though Mrs. Esdaile would be furious if she knew.'

'What are your movements to do with Mrs. Esdaile?' he asked, angrily. 'This is your free time, isn't it?'

'She can't stand her nurses being mixed up in anything'—she hesitated—'shady.'

'And no doubt she's convinced I shot my wife. Perhaps she could tell you why. For money? If she could see my bank book. . . .'

Helen laid her hand over his. 'Darling, don't. Ever since the inquest I've been wanting to come, and she must have known I would, because she's kept me at her beck and call all these forty-eight hours. But—I swore I'd come before I went away—if it had to be midnight.'

'*You're* going away?'

She explained about the old gentleman who had made up his obstinate mind to die in Bandol. 'I didn't want to go at first, but now, since the letters have started arriving . . .'

'You've had them too?'

'Not many. But—and you, Paul?' as the meaning of his last words sank in. 'What are you going to do?'

'Follow your example.' He told her about Fielden. 'Not that I shall mind leaving Bryan Mouncey. It would have been impossible to stay anyhow once I'd split with Blanche, and, believe me or not, that's what I intended to do, even if you never spoke to me again. There's a limit to what a man can bear. I haven't any particular plans at present—eventually I might settle in London, people won't go on remembering this for ever, and the suicide, because that's virtually what it was even though she didn't mean it to end this way, of a tyrannical woman is pretty small beer outside Bryan Mouncey. Helen—there's one thing I must ask you, I haven't had a chance before. You don't think I was responsible for what happened?'

'But, of course, we're both responsible,' said Helen, as though surprised by the question. 'We can't shirk that. Whatever happened on Wednesday night, we took Blanche's life.'

'Now you're talking hysterically,' he began, but she shook her head. 'There'll be no peace for us unless we acknowledge the truth. Blanche's life was you. She may have had an odd way of showing her affection, but you were her whole existence. And she'd been forced to recognise that we were in love, and even if you had decided to stay and I'd gone to Philadelphia in the morning, her world was shattered. It could never have been more than a bare keeping up of appearances, like one of those bombed churches in London that look all right till you're close to and then you see they're nothing but an empty shell. To all intents and purposes, she was dead before the shot was fired.'

'I don't agree with you,' said Paul, bluntly, 'but I can see I should be wasting my breath arguing with you; and we've so little time. Helen, listen to me for a minute. I want to talk to you about the future—our future. Oh, I realise you can't be asked to make up your mind now. I wouldn't let you, even if you were ready. But—you're going away. When you come back . . .'

'I shall never come back to Bryan Mouncey. I can nurse anywhere . . .'

'I feel the same. In fact,' he added recklessly, 'after this I should be more use to my clients than ever, I shall be able to put myself in their places. To come back to ourselves, I suppose if I were noble I'd say put the whole of the past out of your mind, turn over a new leaf, start again. I don't see that that's possible, not if you feel a tithe of what I do. But—think well, take time, take a year. Yes, a year. Remember that if you decide in my favour you won't ever be absolutely sure the past won't crop up. Someone may walk through the door who knew us here, or someone who read the papers. If we have children you'd have to face the fact that one day someone might tell them their father was a possible murderer. They may recognise you—

"Wasn't that the girl who gave evidence in that fishy case?"—no, Helen, don't try and stop me, this must be said, and said now while I'm still honest enough, brave enough, to face the truth. Loving me could wreck your life, it hasn't done much for you to date. So—think well. Don't be afraid I shall change, nothing will ever change me. At the end of a year I'll find some way of getting in touch . . .'

'How?' asked Helen, and he knew from her voice that she could no more go from him than he from her.

'I'll think. I know. I'll put an advertisement in the *Record*. Do you remember how we used to vie with one another to find the most extraordinary advertisement of the week?' He even laughed at the recollection, then stopped. 'You can laugh all right when it's you and that girl alone together,' Blanche had said.

'I remember,' said Helen. 'If ever I wanted to get in touch with anyone that's what I'd do, you said, and Mrs. Hoggett came in, looking as if she thought we were both mad.'

'In a year then—start looking in the *Record*. I'll put it in three times, something you'll recognise. If there's no reply I shall know you've changed, or circumstances have changed. Or, of course, if I should see the news of your engagement or marriage—'

'Ah Paul, don't.' For the first time her

admirable control seemed about to collapse. 'That's cruel. And I mustn't stop. Mrs. Esdaile has eyes that can see through walls . . .'

'She's warned you against me, I can see that. Ever since it happened I've wondered if you still believed in me. If you hadn't come I'd never have been sure.'

*　　　*　　　*

Helen walked slowly back to the Nurses' Home. Her mind was in a turmoil. 'When I see him I shall know,' she had thought. 'It won't be necessary for him to say a word. I shall know.' And at the back of her mind had been the fear that he might turn to her for the strength he could no longer sustain, make some admission of guilt, say, perhaps, that Blanche had threatened him and he had killed her in self-defence. But, at least, she thought, I shall be certain; it was the uncertainty that was beyond bearing. And now all she knew was that, innocent or guilty, her love was unchanged, at any moment when he sent for her she would come.

The next day Helen went to London; she came back to Bryan Mouncey only for an hour or two and she and Paul did not meet again. But Wednesday brought Mrs. Hoggett to The

Dene, as bold as brass, asking for her back wages, implying that she was owed a bonus . . .

'For trying to get me hanged?' exclaimed Paul.

'I had to tell the truth, didn't I? No, I meant all the extra work when Madam was ill. Having nurses in the house is always difficult . . .'

'Not in this case,' said Paul quietly, so quietly, that she took alarm and sheered off the subject. She asked for a reference, she was going to Brighton, to a Mrs. Luke, killing two birds with one stone, though she didn't say as much to Paul. She knew how to wait, did Mrs. Hoggett. Her time would come.

Paul wrote her out a cheque. 'If you're not satisfied,' he said, 'write to my wife's solicitors. Only I don't advise you to drop a hint that you cooked your evidence in any way, or withheld some confidence that might have affected the issue. And that,' he wound up grimly, 'is worth more than six-and-eightpence.' He blotted the cheque and passed it across the table.

'It's a nice house you've got here,' remarked Mrs. Hoggett conversationally, pushing her heavy body to its feet. 'Ought to fetch a good price, specially just now. Clever of you to put it on the market while it's still in the news.

ANTHONY GILBERT

Well—p'raps we'll meet again, p'raps not.
You did know Miss Wayland had gone to
France with an old gentleman, didn't you?
P'raps she'll be luckier than me. Old
gentlemen are sometimes grateful.'

She caught his eye and suddenly she paled.
'What surprises me isn't the murders that are
committed but those that aren't,' Crook used
to say. If ever she'd seen murder in any face
she saw it now. Snatching up her formidable
black gamp, she stumped out of the room.

CHAPTER EIGHT

OLD MR. BELLAIRS was a card. Helen had supposed that by leaving the country she would leave the French affair behind her, but not a bit of it. The old gentleman had seen the newspaper report and they were scarcely settled in Bandol before he asked her, 'Now, m'dear, tell me the truth. Did that fellow really shoot his wife? Must have been mad to think he could get away with it. There must have been simpler ways of getting rid of her.'

'He hadn't thought of getting rid of her as you call it,' Helen began.

'Rum thing is he persuaded a jury to bring in an open verdict. Used to know a chap in London, lawyer called Crook. Be bloody, bold and resolute was his motto. He'd have liked your Mr. French. No harm making a note of the name,' he went on airily. 'Never know when it may come in useful.'

He was the liveliest dying man Helen had ever met. A few weeks the doctor had said piously, always supposing he survives the journey. But Mr. Bellairs carried on for five months; when he reluctantly died Helen learned that he had left her £100. 'Give yourself a nice holiday,' he said. But an invalid, who had had her eye on the girl for some weeks, jumped in before the sods were turned on the old gentleman's grave, and offered her her return fare and expenses in return for light nursing and companionship. She was herself going home and an obtrusive daughter-in-law was proposing to come and collect her, but Mrs. Anson intended to return the long way, via Paris. 'If I say I've got a nurse,' she implored . . ., so Helen found herself packing her things and taking almost a month to get home. When they parted Mrs. Anson gave her quite a nice old-fashioned gold bracelet, shaped like a snake with ruby eyes. 'I never liked it,' she said happily, 'but I hear they're coming in again.'

The daughter-in-law, looking like a pot of vinegar with a grey pudding basin in place of a cork, met them at the airport and scolded Helen for allowing her patient to fly. Then she whisked her into a rattletrap of a car that nearly shook all the old lady's bones together and they disappeared with a whiff of petrol and in a cloud of mud, because, as usual, it was raining in England.

Helen had already written to Mrs. Esdaile saying that she proposed to look for a nursing job in London, and Mrs. Esdaile wrote back that she supposed she knew her own business best. The Dene, she added, had been taken by a delightful family, four children, two wolf-whistling budgerigars and a goat. That, so far as Helen was concerned, was her last link with Bryan Mouncey.

She was lucky enough to find a penthouse apartment, up 86 stairs, and all the work she could tackle. She made friends, entertained a little, bought a picture to hang on her bare walls and was surprised one evening by a ring at her bell. Her thoughts flew to Paul, but how could he know she was there? and anyway the year was not yet up.

It wasn't Paul but Miles Gordon who stood outside. 'Heard from Ma Esdaile you'd flitted from Bryan Mouncey,' he said, 'and I can't blame you. I'm in London myself now. How about coming out to dinner?'

At dinner he said, 'You know French did a flit? Silly of him really. The gossip died down in no time. Wonder where he went. I suppose you didn't hear?'

She shook her head. 'I did hear he might come to London. He doesn't write.'

'Married again perhaps,' suggested Miles glibly. 'Women never seem to mind how many chances they take and even if he did do for Number One that's all the more reason he wouldn't try again. Not engaged yourself or anything?'

Again Helen shook her head; she had no

voice with which to reply. The moment Miles said, 'Might have married again,' she knew it was all up with her, if she had had proof that Paul had shot Blanche, and he still wanted to marry her, she would say Yes.

As the year drew to its close she found herself waiting for the first possible day when Paul's insertion might appear. The anniversary of Blanche's death came and passed, then the day of the inquest, then the funeral. But on the anniversary of their last meeting she found a couple of lines in the *Record* Personal Column.

HELEN, and a reference. Canticles 2. 10.

She knew it was his. She took out the bible she had been given years ago as a confirmation present and looked up the text. It said:

Rise up my love, my fair one, rise and come
away
The winter is past, the rain is over and gone.

After a number of spoiled efforts she wrote her answer, just her name and address on a piece of paper, and put it in an envelope. And set herself to wait a little longer, just a little longer.

He must have gone to the headquarters of

the *Record* and called for the reply in person
for next night, before she thought he could
come, he was there waiting for her outside her
own front door. After the first moments of
giddiness and disbelief had passed, she saw
with surprise that he looked practically
unchanged, except that there was now an air of
confidence about him that previously he had
lacked. His hair hadn't turned grey, he wasn't
abnormally thin. On the contrary, he was
more assured than she ever remembered him.

She said as much. 'Why not?' he inquired.
'Except where you're concerned. All these
past weeks as the day drew nearer I began to be
afraid of opening my paper. In case I saw your
face, your name. A year's a long time, and if
you hadn't wanted me none of it would have
seemed worth while, the work, the
chances . . .'

He told her about himself. He had bought a
practice in London. One of the partners went
with it, he said. A queer little chap called
Phillips. More like a gnome than a man and
apparently utterly incurious. 'I might have
dropped out of the skies for all the interest he
took in the past.'

'Did you tell him anything?' she asked.

'About Blanche? Just that I'd had to leave
the countryside where I'd been practising
because my wife died in rather mysterious

circumstances. That it could have been suicide, though that didn't seem very probable, that the jury had returned an open verdict . . .

'He just waved his hand and said, "Very unpleasant for you, my dear fellow. Really, when you think what life has in store for us I sometimes wonder we dare get born at all." Mind you, he's bone-lazy, would shuffle all the clients off on to me if he could, but he's got some quality—part integrity, part sheer charm. How he's stayed a bachelor . . .' He paused abruptly. 'Come to think of it, I don't know that he is. He doesn't talk about his private affairs. I know he lives alone in a flat in Lancaster Gate. For all I know he has a second raffish establishment in whatever is the modern counterpart of Maida Vale.'

Hours later she made an omelette for them both and produced half a bottle of claret. 'Not right, I know,' she apologised, 'but it's all I have.'

He had done something she hadn't thought possible. Blanche had been in her grave for twelve months, yet to Helen the tombstone had seemed no more than a curtain behind which the dead woman was shrouded. At any moment the curtain might fall and there she'd be with her black hair and narrow peering eyes. Now she was in the grave for good, almost as though she'd never been anywhere else. Paul had firmly slammed the door on the past, slammed it for her as well as for himself. So she believed, and that belief gave her a happiness she had never hitherto known.

By the time they parted she had agreed to marry him very quietly at a registrar's as soon as the necessary time had elapsed. He had an eye on a small house in Kensington that was nearly ready for occupation.

'You believe in laying your plans in advance,' she said, and for an instant a flicker for which she couldn't altogether account crossed his face. 'You don't seem to have had much doubt what my answer would be.'

'I didn't let myself think you might have changed.' Suddenly his voice was grave and his hands held her so harshly she could have cried out. 'It would have made nonsense of everything I've been working for. I told you once—you're my life; for that, to preserve it, I'd let everything else go.'

They would have to wait until Helen had given notice to the Association for whom she was working. Officially this should be a month but Helen thought, with unfounded optimism, that she might easily get away sooner. When Paul left her it was past midnight. A cloudy day had blown itself out, the sky was dark and clear with stars abounding. Walking back, since all public transport had come to a standstill and in any case he was so full of energy he wanted the freedom of movement, Paul felt as though the past was dead at last. ('These lovers,' Crook would have grumbled. 'No more sense than a pin. The past dead indeed? As if he were a butterfly emerging from a chrysalis or a snake shedding its skin. He'll find out that he can't shuffle off his past till he shuffles off this mortal coil.')

But to-night no such fears beset Paul, walking past the Victoria and Albert Museum, where the light of the street lamps fell on the autumn leaves turning them into golden parasols. Blanche was in her grave, the old story was dead; he doubted whether they even spoke of her at Bryan Mouncey any more. As for Mrs. Hoggett, he never so much as gave her a thought.

★　　★　　★

Their plans went less smoothly than they had anticipated. There was no trouble about giving notice at the registrar's. Paul knew one pang of foreboding when he gave their names and profession, but the juxtaposition of French and Wayland struck no answering chord in the large smooth grey-headed man who noted down the details. Bride's name and address, condition (spinster); his own standing—widower, lawyer, it went as easily as butter from a hot knife. Then he went round to the house-agent to start proceedings there. Until the place was ready they could live in furnished premises—better that than a hotel. He told Phillips he was going to be married.

'Dear me!' said Phillips. 'How dashing of you. I hope the lady doesn't contemplate a long honeymoon. I really don't know how I could manage here without you.'

*   *   *

It was the Nursing Association who upset things by refusing to release Helen until she had worked out her month's notice. They were short-handed and she was booked for a new case. When she started work Helen had agreed to a month's notice on either side, and though she pleaded her cause she didn't move the matron an iota.

'You've never been married before? I thought not. You're like mice, you girls, all longing to rush into the trap, expecting the best cheese. It doesn't occur to you that life isn't an unlimited supply of cheese, or that one day you may look out between the bars and wonder why you were in such a hurry.'

'It's only a month,' Helen consoled Paul, but he was instantly apprehensive. He would have scoffed at the notion that he was superstitious, but now that he and Helen had met again he regarded every day separating them as a potential enemy. 'It's bad luck,' he insisted. 'Something might happen. You might get knocked down or nurse some contagious old witch . . .'

'Does it ever strike you that nurses practically never catch infectious diseases?' Helen asked, trying to rally him.

But his dark mood persisted. 'I shan't feel you're safely mine till I've heard you say *I will*,' he told her. And he repeated, 'Till that day anything might happen.'

What did happen was Mrs. Hoggett.

*   *   *

She waited until the eleventh hour, until the night before the wedding. Patience was her strong suit. After Blanche's funeral and the break-up of the household at Bryan Mouncey she had been convinced that Paul and the nurse would meet again. Paul had disappeared, but she supposed Mrs. Esdaile would have Helen's address. Mrs. Esdaile simply returned the letter with 'Address

Unknown' written on it. Mrs. Hoggett hung about trying to pick up hints. Eventually she had heard that Helen was nursing in London.

'And he's gone to London, too. Now, how'd they get together?'

She remembered that silly conversation— 'If ever I wanted to get in touch with a loved one I should put an advertisement in the *Record*,' Paul had said. It was a bow drawn at a venture, might come to nothing. Of course the separation might be permanent; she went to Somerset House to check up on their marriage records, but they knew nothing there about either party.

Then she saw the advertisment in the Personal Column in the *Record*. It hadn't occurred to Paul that his cryptic message would have any meaning for anyone else; he had forgotten, if he ever knew, the length of Mrs. Hoggett's memory and the strength of her malice. She recalled that half-laughing conversation she had overheard months before and when she saw the appeal to HELEN she told herself, 'It could be him, and, if so, what's the odds he'll go up and collect the answer himself?' If he didn't, she thought, she'd try and get it over the counter. She didn't know what regulations prevailed. Perhaps if she simply said she'd come for any letters for Box No. V. 158 they'd give her the envelope. Worth a chance anyway. She hung about outside the city office the following morning and, sure enough, presently she'd espied Paul coming along. When he came out, slipping an envelope into his pocket, she was convinced she was on the right track. He had turned away and jumped into a stationary bus, going on the top deck; she went inside, and, when he alighted she followed on the farther pavement. She saw the office and noted the name. First blood to her, she thought. A little more sleuthing and she discovered his home address, a furnished flat in a nice district. He'd have to put up the banns at the local registrar's, she thought, unless he meant to get married by special licence, and the books of registrars are open to the public eye. So, piling one brick on another, she learned the approximate time of the wedding and waited her opportunity to pounce.

*   *   *

On his wedding eve, Paul worked late at his office clearing up outstanding affairs and remembering that it would be three weeks before he saw the place again. The house he had bought was almost ready for occupation, he had engaged a housekeeper to take over as soon as he returned. He had sold all Blanche's furniture and Helen had never possessed any. 'We shall furnish from scratch,' he told her, and that seemed to him a good augury for their new life together.

It was seven o'clock and he was preparing to leave when the knock fell on the door. He thought vaguely it must be the cleaners, women to whom hitherto he had never given a thought. Going to the door and saying, as he opened it, 'I'm on the point of leaving, the place is all yours,' he fell back, silenced and horrified.

Mrs. Hoggett's squat figure and toad-like face barred the way.

'I thought you'd rather I came out of office hours,' she said, as cool as you please. 'I noticed the light in the window so I knew you couldn't have gone. And, of course, after to-morrow it would have been too late.'

Insensibly he had retreated and she had followed him into the room. Now she settled herself in the client's chair and laid a pair of black fabric gloves on the edge of the desk. Her hands were so large with short broad fingers that the gloves seemed almost square.

'What do you want with me?' demanded Paul, harshly.

'I've come for advice. Well, nothing so strange about that, is there? You are a lawyer, and a very successful one from all accounts.'

'London,' he told her, controlling himself with an effort, 'is lousy with lawyers. Why come to me?'

'It's generally best to go to someone you know. It's about my husband, Mr. French.'

'Your husband? But I thought you were a widow.'

'I'm sure I never said. Madam asked me if I had any ties and I said no. It's been hard on me really, no man to support me and no widow's pension either.'

'You've got your legal remedy. You can apply for maintenance.'

'To tell you the truth, I wasn't sorry to see Hoggett go. Created something shocking he did and broke up the furniture when the drink was in him, which was most of the time.'

Paul believed he saw light. 'You mean, he wants to come back to you now you're in a steady job?'

'Well, that's over, the job, I mean. Mrs. Luke is giving up her house and going to live with her daughter in America. A very nice lady,' she added warmly. 'Appreciative, too. That's what gave me the idea really, that and me not being so young as I was and having had a lifetime of taking orders, it struck me it 'ud be nice to give them for a change.'

Phillips used to say that women clients must frequently have been cats in an earlier incarnation. Cats are said to take the long way round and some of these women could outdo any grimalkin yet born.

'If you could explain a little,' said Paul politely. 'He's not pestering you—are you afraid of what he may do in the future? You can always ask for protection if he threatens you . . .'

'You haven't got it right, Mr. French. Nothing would please Sam more than to know I was in my grave. Why, he's already gone round telling everyone he's a widower. Not that I've seen him for ten years,' she added.

Paul was hopelessly at sea. 'If you haven't seen him, what on earth is the trouble? You don't want to marry again?' he added, sharply.

'After what I've seen of marriage?' Now her full brown eyes rested squarely upon him. 'No, but I'd like to understand my rights. Here's Sam keeping this other woman and her brats in the lap of luxury, I dare say, though when he was my husband it was all I could do to get him to pay the rent. You don't marry to go out charring and so I used to tell him.'

'It's not a crime to take up with someone who isn't your wife. The law isn't a court of morals,' Paul pointed out.

'As I should know,' agreed Mrs. Hoggett, smartly. 'But there is a law to stop you marrying a new wife when the first one's living.'

'So that's what's happened?' Paul began to see daylight at last. 'You'd have to show that he knew you were still alive . . .'

'Well, I am, aren't I? He could have found out if he'd wanted to. Doing nicely now, his own shop and all. Fulham way,' she added. 'Mind you, she may have had a bit, I wouldn't know.'

'Mrs. Hoggett, I'm very busy, as you can see.' Paul's fingers itched to catch her by her bunchy scruff and propel her into the passage. 'What precisely is it you think I can do for you?'

'As I was saying,' returned Mrs. Hoggett, who clearly was in no hurry, 'I've had my share of taking orders. Now it's time I was in charge. I've seen just the little place I'd like, newspapers and tobacco (and sweets, of course,) price reasonable but cash down. The chap who's got it is suffering from asthma, going to live with his brother-in-law. I've seen the books, they show a tidy profit, living quarters behind, fridge, and all. Of course, I'll need furniture, Hoggett broke up our home like I told you. Well, can the law make him put up something on my account?'

'It depends on his circumstances. And yours. Did you leave him or . . .?'

'Walked out on me at the beginning of the

war. Might as well be killed by a bomb as any other way, he said. A nasty sharp tongue he had from the start. Married his tart in 1948. What I was wondering was—I'm no dog in the manger, I don't want to take him from her if that's her fancy, there's no accounting for tastes—could you write, as my lawyer, and say it'd be best for him to meet my demands, best for himself and his baseborn family?' The continued malice of her tone made him draw back as if she had been one of the mythical dragons that spat flame at the passerby.

'Have you never heard of blackmail?' he demanded, anger and disgust for the moment crowding out his fear. 'If you want money and think you have a claim, you should go and see him and put your cards on the table. I can't possibly advise you of your chances, without knowing his side as well as yours. But it sounds to me remarkably as though you were holding a pistol to his head.'

He could scarcely have chosen a more unfortunate metaphor and before the words had died on the air he recognised it; he felt the colour receding from his cheeks. It was too much to hope that his visitor would let so tempting an opening pass, and of course she didn't.

'Well, of course, that's always a silly thing to do. Risky, I mean. You could never be sure you'd get away with it. All the same, I've made up my mind to have my little place. I've got a bit of capital, Mrs. Luke was a very generous lady, and I can't help feeling that when the case is put to him, Sam 'ull see sense, too. There was something else I really came about. I suppose Mrs. French didn't mention me in her will?'

'If she had you'd have heard officially long ago. But, of course, she didn't. Why should she?'

'To show appreciation like. I could have got better jobs, and I'm sure she never showed me much favour. Still, of course, she didn't expect to die when she did.'

'If she'd lived another ten years I don't suppose she'd have put you in her will,' prophesied Paul rashly. 'You hadn't been with her three years, and you had your wages.'

'There's some things no money 'ull repay. What I was thinking was perhaps you'd feel like giving me a bit of a hand. It's the chance of a lifetime, it won't come again, and even with what I've been able to put by and what I can hope for from Sam, I'll still need quite a substantial sum. £1,200 this chap's asking, I might beat him down a bit for cash. But I need £600 and I need it now. So how about it, Mr. French?'

'If the business is as sound as you say you

should be able to raise a mortgage. Any respectable building society . . .'

'Ah, but that 'ud mean starting in debt, and Sam taught me what that's like. I've no fancy to have people coming to my door and asking to be paid and finding there's no money in the kitty. That's the sort of thing gets you a bad name.'

'If I were to lend you the money you'd still be in debt,' Paul pointed out.

'It 'ud be different, though. I mean, you wouldn't press for repayment if times were hard, would you?'

'Why should you be so sure of that?'

'It wouldn't look well, not if you was to bring the case to court. Mind you, no one said outright you killed Mrs. French, but . . .'

Paul rose to his feet. 'That'll do, Mrs. Hoggett. I told you, blackmail's a dangerous game to play and, as you've just said, no charge was ever brought against me.'

Mrs. Hoggett had remained seated. 'Well, no, but they could reopen the case, couldn't they, if fresh evidence came to light?'

'How can there be fresh evidence at this stage?' he asked contemptuously, but his heart was going like a piston rod.

'Well, you should know, Mr. French. What do you suppose the verdict might have been if they'd known about the bell?'

'The bell? But they did know. What are you talking about? Nurse told them, you told them, why, even I told them.'

'Ah, but I didn't mean that bell,' croaked Mrs. Hoggett softly. 'I mean the first one, the one she rang when she saw you come in with the gun in your hand.'

The silence was complete; for a moment to Paul everything seemed to have gone out of focus. When his surroundings began to settle again he said for the second time, 'What on earth are you talking about?'

'You know what I'm talking about. If the court had known there were two bells . . .'

'There weren't,' said Paul, flatly.

'Oh yes, there were. I heard them. A bell, just a short peal and then the shot, and then the second bell everybody knows about.'

'It's taken you how long—about a year—to think this up,' Paul accused her. 'If it was true or if you even believed it was true—why didn't you stand up in court and say so?'

'You could have said it was you ringing, couldn't you? There wouldn't have been any proof. But you and me know . . .'

'It didn't ring,' said Paul, steadfastly. But his heart misgave him. Suppose she went round spreading this yarn? What had she said at the inquest? The bell and the shot came together, it was difficult to tell which came first. And now she'd had time to think and was convinced it was the bell. Of course, she couldn't prove it but she could put the idea into a number of minds that had plenty of room for ideas. The police wouldn't like it, but she need only say, 'Well, I couldn't be quite certain at the time and I didn't want to give false evidence, but my impression now is'... Only, of course, reflected Paul, desperately, she knew he couldn't let it get that far. It would undermine the whole of his new life, both with Phillips and with Helen. She'd got him in a cleft stick and they both knew it. But he fought her doggedly.

'I warned you a few minutes ago that blackmail was dangerous. I'm warning you again.'

'Don't get me wrong,' Mrs. Hoggett implored. 'I didn't like her any more than you did. If you want my opinion, some women simply ask to be murdered. Only—you can't go round putting them down like a lot of dogs, any more than you can get tired of one woman and go out and marry another and not expect to pay for it.'

'You're barking up the wrong tree,' Paul assured her. 'Go out and tell your story if you think anyone will listen to you. But you may find it awkward explaining why you've kept your mouth shut so long. The police . . .'

'I wasn't thinking of the police,' said Mrs. Hoggett, composedly. 'Miss Wayland doesn't know about the bell, does she? Well, of course not. She was asleep.'

'She wouldn't believe you.' Paul's tone was curt with scorn.

'Well, she might say she didn't, and of course it might be true. But it's funny how thoughts grow, like seeds. And if there should be any more talk about it—you'd be surprised what the papers think is news. Mrs. French has been dead for a year, and you might say forgotten, but if it was known that the widower, who inherited her fortune, was marrying the nurse in the case—well, it 'ud be worth a little paragraph and, perhaps, a picture. Happy couple leaving registrar's. Better luck this time, Paul French. The *Morning Sun* 'ud eat it,' she added simply.

Paul opened his mouth to protest, then closed it again. It was perfectly true. It would be jam for the *Morning Sun*, and though the talk would die down again . . . .

As though she read his mind Mrs. Hoggett went on, 'They'd ask for an interview, I dare say. Well, naturally you and Mrs. French— the new Mrs. French, that is—wouldn't say a word, but you know what these newspaper boys are. Never say die, that's their motto. They'd look around for someone who might

140

be able to give them a word, and they're ever so persuasive, they might get me to say just a bit more than I meant. It wouldn't be very nice for the young lady. You do like to start your marriage with a clean sheet.'

She had him hip and thigh and she knew it. For Helen he would dare fire and water. And he realised that this harpy was perfectly capable of putting her threat into action.

'You're a brave woman,' he said at last, 'though it doesn't always do to strain your luck.'

'That's just what I'm saying, Mr. French.'

'Between two fires—myself and Mr. Hoggett—you might get quite badly burned.'

'Are you threatening me now, Mr. French? But, of course, I know it's only your way of joking. I'm sure no one would be surprised if it should get out that you wanted to help me a little after the time I had with Mrs. French.'

'Stop talking about my wife,' said Paul roughly, covering his eyes with his hand. Mrs. Hoggett sat as mute as a fish. Though in fact she was the angler who had the wretched fish squirming on her hook and they both knew it.

'I'll tell you what I'll do,' said Paul at last. 'Take it or leave it. I'll lend you £500 against your I.O.U. Then no one can accuse you of blackmail or myself of yielding to it. I shall lodge the I.O.U. in the bank. That way everything will appear open and above board. If you refuse—but why should you? You may in some obscure fashion want to be revenged on me, though I can't imagine why, but such a feeling is seldom worth £500.'

'That's not quite so generous as I'd hoped,' she said, her hands picking at the clasp of her big black bag.

'It's the only offer I'm going to make. Make up your mind.'

She took it, of course. He wrote out the cheque and gave it to her.

'Let's have one thing clear,' he said in a warning tone. 'This isn't the first of a series of payments. It's a loan and I shall expect it to be honoured.'

'I dare say you won't be too hard on me,' observed Mrs. Hoggett, rising at last and pulling on her shapeless fat gloves. 'I'll look in again in a year, say. The first year's always the hardest. You could regard it as an investment, couldn't you? Yes, that's what I'll do. I'll let you know at the end of the year how I'm getting on.'

The telephone rang and he took off the receiver. Mrs. Hoggett, watching him like a lynx, saw his face change. 'That'll be the girl on the line,' she thought accurately. 'Well, he's over the moon all right.' She ambled across to the door and softly let herself out.

'Bet he doesn't tell her anything about me,' she reflected.

And she was right.

*   *   *

The next morning Paul French married Helen Wayland in a flurry of fine rain. Two other couples impatiently waited their turn. Each had brought a small party, and a brace of Fords stood against the pavement. They speculated a little as to the ownership of the Bentley. It was over so quickly neither could quite believe they were married. Paul remembered the tedious overdressed ceremony eleven years ago, then suppressed the thought. Blanche was in her grave and let her stay there till Judgment Day. As for Mrs. Hoggett, he was married now, Helen was his, let her do her worst, she could never separate them.

CHAPTER NINE

SAM HOGGETT in 1958 had a flourishing little ironmongery business, near Walham Green Station, a wife whom he frankly considered far too good for him—('What you see in me, Cathie, is more than I can guess?' 'Go on,' said Cathie, 'take a look in the glass now and again, why don't you?')—and three young children. At ever longer intervals he remembered a black-haired exuberant chap bearing the same name who married a woman called Ruby Bertha Forrest, why he couldn't now remember, but his relationship to that shadowy figure was so remote he scarcely connected the two. In middle life he had become a rather solid, tall figure of a man, sober of mien, an indefatigable worker, not teetotal but as good as, so far as the local, The White Goat, was concerned. It stood tantalisingly almost opposite Hoggett's, but all the bar saw of Sam was the time it takes to drink a pint four nights a week. Fridays he always worked late doing the accounts, he might drop in afterwards, he might not, it was all according. Saturday and Sunday belonged to his family, and when you'd seen Cathie and the kids you wouldn't be surprised. Unlike most of his neighbours, he didn't close the shop during the lunch-hour, saying it was then that plenty of chance customers became regulars. Nosing down the street for somewhere to buy a packet of soap flakes or a new saucepan, they saw him and came in. He employed a fellow called Bernie, 'my young man,' he used to say, though Bernie was married with two kids of his own. Bernie went to his dinner 12.45 and was back at 1.30, when Sam dashed home to Cathie. If Bernie got less than the statutory hour Sam only took thirty minutes.

One day round about one a woman entered his shop; he saw at a glance she wasn't one of his regulars, but no reason why she shouldn't be. 'Packet of panscourers,' she said.

'Any special sort?' He dived under the counter to show her what he stocked. When he was facing her he saw it was Ruby. He was a big man and florid but every vestige of colour left his cheeks.

'Why, Sam,' said Ruby calmly. 'This is a surprise. Finding you working, I mean. Must have got you in the way of it in the war.'

He found his voice. 'You're dead,' he accused her. 'Far as I am concerned, I mean.'

'Not me. Suit your book, I dare say, if I was. Husbands are supposed to support their wives, not like you, walking out on me the way

145

you did. Or p'raps you're just an employee. But no, of course not. That's your name over the front. That's what drew me.'

Sam put his big hands flat on the counter. 'They swore you was dead,' he insisted. 'I asked everyone.'

'If they did that on the Book it was perjury. Who's everyone, when they're at home?'

'Police, W.V.S., your boss—I even saw some of your mates when I came up. They all swore you was under the pavement with the rest of the night shift.'

'Bet you went out and bought yourself a new tie when you heard that,' said Ruby, derisively. 'A nice bright one. I'm surprised at you, Sam, believing all you hear.'

'I was down at Bristol at the time, doing essential work,' said Sam, doggedly. 'Then I saw this report and I wrote. My wife was working on one of your shifts, I said, giving your name and details. I couldn't be sure which, because I know these factories change, like nurses in a hospital. They looked up their records and said you were on the night-shift that Tuesday and there weren't any survivors. Didn't even dig the bodies out, they was buried so deep.'

'That's right.' Ruby nodded. 'Direct hit. I heard it. Lucky me, not to be down there, I thought. No mistaking what had happened. I thought those bricks were going on falling for ever. Like a waterfall, it was, only it was masonry, not water.'

'Why weren't you on duty?'

'P'raps I guessed there was going to be a raid. Psychic, see? But no, it wasn't that, of course. Matter of fact, I did sign on, that's why everyone was so sure I was there, I suppose. But I wasn't feeling so good, I had arthritis in the knee, ever so stiff, and all that standing—place was as cold as a tomb, too—I dunno who got all the coal in the war, not much of it came our way. Well, when we stopped for a break about twelve I sneaked off home. No sense winning the war if I was going to be dead, I thought. Bomb fell about an hour later. A lot of fire, too. I stood at my window and looked out. You could see there weren't going to be any survivors there.'

'No one who was going to remember Bertha Hoggett had sloped off at half-time?'

She looked at him oddly. 'No one's called me Bertha since you slung your hook,' she said. 'Ruby wasn't good enough for you, was it? Well, next day the place was swarming with relatives. Not that there was anything they could do. Everyone was under tons of rubbish. Finally I heard they closed the place—like that air raid shelter that's got 1,500 bodies in it, and no one being sure to this day who they are.'

'But why didn't they know next morning you hadn't been there?' Sam insisted.

'Because I didn't choose to tell them, that's why. I'd had enough of being ordered about by young madams at the Labour, young enough to be my daughters. Do you know what one of them had the sauce to say to me, when I said the pay wasn't up to much? "We must all be prepared to make sacrifices in a war," she said. "Think of the men in the forces." I could have slapped her silly face. In all that bother and rush nobody was going to notice me, so I packed my things and went north. I didn't report to the Labour there, got a job in a canteen. Not much money but you did get the chance of something over and above your rations. And, seeing I was dead, I couldn't be called up any more. And I hadn't got any loving relatives to fuss about me. Just you.'

'I came up on my day off,' said Sam. 'I saw the authorities and the W.V.S. I asked where you'd been lodging and I went round. You didn't take much with you,' he added.

'Well, it would have looked queer if I'd been bombed with every blessed thing I possessed. No, I just went into the Town Hall next morning and said I'd been bombed out, and they gave me a ration book and some clothing coupons—lots of chaps were doing it that never lost as much as a pane of glass—mind you, I'd had those in my bag the way we all did, and my identity card, but no harm getting what you can. So you were at Bristol all that time, were you? Doing well, I dare say.'

'Well enough.'

'And now more than a dozen years later, you find you're an old married man again. Looks to me you're a reformed character, Sam. Shows the war wasn't all waste.'

'I don't know what you've turned up for like a bad penny,' said Sam, 'but I tell you straight if you try and spoil Cathie's life, I'll do you.'

'Who's Cathie? The girl-friend?'

'Cathie's my wife.'

'She can't be. I'm your wife.'

'I married Cathie all open and above board, in church, too. We had the banns called and everything. If you were going to step in and stop things, you've missed your market. It's all in the service. Speak now or for ever hold your peace.'

'How could I speak when I wasn't there and didn't even know? Mind you, I don't want to break up your life, only being your wife does give me some rights.'

'Not any more. We were all washed up before the war and you know it.'

'It wouldn't be the first time the war had

brought a couple together again. Any family?'

'Three kids.'

'That's nice. I quite see you wouldn't want them to know they were—well—'

'Don't forget what I told you. I meant it, every word.'

'I really believe you would, Sam. Though how that would help your Cathie—No, let's be sensible. As I see it, you're doing nicely.'

'I need to, the family I've got.'

'Your own house, I dare say. Car most like. TV.'

'No TV. Cath and me don't hold with it, not for the kids. All right for old people, I suppose. And no car—yet.'

'Get it on the H.P.,' suggested Ruby.

'We don't go in for that. What we can't afford to pay for, we go without.'

'You've changed all right. Your Cathie must be a miracle-worker. Not that I don't agree with you. But it does leave me a bit out in the cold. If you're fair, Sam, you'll see I haven't had much of a turn, making my own way almost from the start.'

'Why not?' asked Sam, unsympathetically. 'Nothing else to do. Idle women only get into mischief.'

'I'm not sure the law couldn't make you pay me something. You wouldn't want it all to come out—because bigamy's bigamy, even if you did do it in good faith. Kids are cruel, too! You wouldn't like to see your kids pointed at. And if anything was to happen to you, I don't think your Cathie 'ud get the widow's pension, any more than I have. Doesn't really make sense, does it, Sam? I'm not a wife nor a widow, nor yet a corpse.'

'What did you come for?' asked Sam. 'Cash?'

'No need for us to be unfriendly,' said Ruby, treating him to her steady baleful stare. 'I've got to look after myself the same as you. Now, there's a little business I could walk into if I could put up the money. I'm not asking you to buy for me, I'm not that unreasonable, I'm the saving kind and sometimes the ladies I've been with have made me presents or remembered me in their will, but there's more expenses than just buying the goodwill. The fact is, I need £300 cash.'

She had settled on the sum of £300 as being the highest she was likely to twist out of her reluctant husband. Asking for too much was daft; and you could always come for a second helping. That moment when he'd hesitated about the car, a blind man could see he was hoping to get one soon, and since he didn't believe in H.P. that meant there was a little nest-egg somewhere.

'I believe you think £300 grows on trees,'

Sam accused her. 'Look out.'

Another customer had come in. 'Afternoon, Mr. Hoggett,' she said cheerfully.

Ruby looked round as if considering. 'You serve this lady while I make up my mind,' she offered. She walked round the shop taking things off the shelves, examining them and putting them back a bit crooked. No sense in it really, but Sam owed her something. It wasn't so much his getting on in the world as daring to be happy with this Cathie-creature and speaking with that note of pride of his three kids. Cats do it better, thought Ruby, banging down a glass butter-dish so fiercely that it cracked.

'Must have been damaged,' she said swiftly. 'You ought to send it back.'

The customer had gone out, with an odd humorous glance over her shoulder.

'That costs two-and-threepence,' said Sam.

'Put it on the income-tax. You get something for expenses, don't you? Well, Sam, do I get my £300? You could always raise a mortgage on a snug little business like this, you know.'

'I can't discuss it now,' said Sam, desperately. 'Someone else could come in any minute.'

'I could always drop round,' she said matily. 'I'd like to see your Cathie.'

'If you do that you'll never see a penny. Give me an address . . .' But she shook her head.

'I didn't escape being buried under the factory to fall in the gutter and crack my skull open,' she said. 'Haven't you got an office or something behind the shop?' She nodded towards a closed door in the background.'

'I don't have visitors after hours.'

'I'm not visitors, I'm your wife.'

'All right. But I'm not making any promises, and if you try hanging round my house you won't get as much as a used postage stamp. How do you know this business is worth the money?'

'I've got a gentleman putting up nearly half,' she told him coolly. 'Housekeeper to his wife, his late wife, that is. *And* a lawyer looking after my interest.'

It was the word lawyer that decided him. 'Come round Friday night,' he said. 'I work late Fridays after the shop's closed. We'll see then. . . .'

But, like Paul, he knew he hadn't any choice.

★   ★   ★

'Well, you look like a wet week-end and no mistake,' said Cathie affectionately, when he came in that night. 'Sit down and have a cuppa

153

and I'll put a spoonful of whisky in it. You work too hard and that's a fact.' She was a cheerful comely young woman looking less than her thirty-five years. She had a baby on her arm and two older children came running out. 'Get your Dad's slippers, Maureen, there's a dear. Bobby, see if the kettle's boiling.'

'You got our car yet, Dad?' Bobby asked.

'Who said anything about a car?' Hoggett demanded.

'Why, you took us to see that Morris Mr. Hake's got. Smashing job. Ted Burton's father's got a Consul, but I don't go so much for these Fords myself.'

'You won't go for anything but your bicycle for a long while yet, my lad,' Sam told him. 'And don't forget to oil it.'

Bobby was nine years old and naturally yearning to outdo Ted's father's standards.

'Wish I had a bicycle,' mourned seven-year-old Maureen.

'I told you, you wait till Santa Claus comes round,' Cathie consoled her. 'You've got that trike Bobby had . . . Put out the cups, love.'

'You didn't have to bite their heads off, Sam,' she reproached her husband later. 'They're good kids, but only kids. They all talk the same way.'

'Keeping up with the Joneses,' said Sam. 'I

know about Ted Burton. Never pays his rent till it's a fortnight overdue, shouldn't be surprised if he owed on the car as well. And they've just got one of these new tellys, twenty-one-inch screen or some such nonsense. It's no wonder Mrs. B. has to go out to work.'

'Oh well, she doesn't mind. Wasn't brought up to housework, she tells me.'

'She doesn't have to tell you,' said Sam. 'Brought up among the pigs from the look of that house.'

She leaned against his arm and kissed him lovingly. 'Oh Sam, you old Londoner. Pigs are ever so particular these days.'

''Pologise to the pigs. Fact is, Cathie, I've had a bit of a blow. A bad debt in a quarter I couldn't have looked for. Swallow up our car this year, I'm afraid.'

'Oh Sam—after all your saving.'

'Could be worse,' Sam pointed out. 'If I couldn't meet my obligations . . .'

'But it isn't your debt,' she protested.

'Well, you might say I was responsible for the goods.' He moved uncomfortably. He'd never lied to Cathie before. He hadn't believed it when she'd promised to marry him. He'd not said much about Ruby, but that he'd been married and she'd died in the war. Why, she didn't even know her predecessor's first name. Bertha, Sam said in one of his rare references. So no wonder when the trouble broke Cathie never connected the two. He couldn't tell her the truth now, but it made him feel mean. Life's unaccountable, hits below the belt in a way you'd think shocking in a human being. It wasn't the conflict of right and wrong that flummoxed a man—anyone not a moron could distinguish between the two—but the conflict of right with right. The next morning Cathie told the two elder children that Dad had had some bad luck—been bilked—'You be a bit nicer than usual,' she told them. The children were indignant. 'Why doesn't Dad get this man sent to prison? He's cheated him, hasn't he?' 'That wouldn't get us our car, and if he's in prison he won't be able to work and pay us back.' Cathie knew all the answers. You have to when you've got three kids.

They soon got over it, of course. Children do. Cathie hadn't cared particularly about the car one way or the other. It was Sam who wanted it—for her. He'd have given her the moon and the stars if she'd fancied them, or died in the attempt.

★　　★　　★

When Ruby went round the following

Friday Sam had the money there, all in notes.

'Take it away and count it somewhere else,' he'd told her with suppressed violence. 'You'll find it all right. And don't think this is like the annual flower show and when you've made a muck of your shop you can come back to me. Cathie and me and the kids are going to have to live on the smell of an oil rag for the next twelve months thanks to you.'

CHAPTER TEN

WHEN SHE was quite a young girl Helen had agreed with her friends that you simply couldn't be a second wife.

'Your husband would always be comparing you with the first,' they told each other.

And when that first wife had died in mysterious circumstances the situation was still more unfavourable. Yet, within a few weeks of her marriage, she found she didn't think of Blanche at all. Of course, it was a fortunate thing that none of the furniture reminded her of her predecessor. She and Paul furnished with modern pieces, all light and easy to clean. It was Helen's first chance of looking after a house, and she never found the time hang heavy on her hands. Paul had got a housekeeper, a Miss Margetts, the very antithesis of Mrs. Hoggett. She gave the impression that her employers were simply an essential bit of her life's furnishings, but she had her own existence. The qualities that made Paul a successful lawyer—'He really gives you the impression he minds what happens to you,' one client had been heard to remark—made him popular out of working hours. And now with Helen as his wife his popularity increased. They were so much in love, so full of warmth and the pleasure of life, that quite soon people were saying, 'We must get the Frenchs. They always make things go.' Helen was introduced to Phillips, who held her hand for a minute, looking into those grey-blue eyes with their long sparkling lashes and said in a regretful tone, 'Almost thou persuadest me— to follow your husband's example, I mean. Still,' and here his gnomish smile flashed out, 'nearly isn't quite, is it? And I can't feel nature cut me out for matrimony.'

It was easy to see how Paul revelled in this popularity and success. Sometimes Helen was a little scared—for him, never for herself. She couldn't believe that one day someone wouldn't ferret out the truth. 'Paul French? Isn't he the chap whose rich wife got herself shot and the matter was never cleared up?' It was bound to come, she thought, and when it did, how much would it matter to Paul? The answer was it would matter terribly. Blanche had done him an immense disservice throughout those years of servitude. Now his natural gaiety of mind and independence of spirit shone out like lamps. But when these doubts visited her, which was seldom, she would recall Mrs. Esdaile's parting words on her disappearance from Bryan Mouncey.

'Never look back. That's the secret. The

place for people to spend their lives brooding over the past is the graveyard. There'll be all the time there is then.'

As the first happy year drew to its close Paul began to be haunted by Mrs. Hoggett's promise.

'I'll be back at the year's end to let you know how I'm making out.' In vain he told himself she had only said it to torment him. But he couldn't altogether crush his fears.

The anniversary came and passed without a word from her. He and Helen celebrated it *à deux*. The only fly in their ointment was their continued childlessness. 'There's time enough,' he reassured his wife. 'I don't mind having you to myself for a time. In fact, there are days when I have a secret dread that I should make a jealous parent.'

'Not you,' said Helen. 'Still, as you say, there's lots of time.'

Of course, she would remember when she was alone, he hadn't given Blanche a child . . . But you couldn't imagine Blanche as a mother. No, it would be all right. Just a matter of patience. She and Paul had any number of friends who hadn't started a family for three or four years after their wedding. And when you had so much it was ignoble to wish for more. 'By this time next year,' she told herself cheerfully, 'I may be wistfully thinking how free we were a year ago.'

So she brought herself back to contentment.

*   *   *

When it did happen it was like history repeating itself. Like picking up a book and finding to your surprise that you know what's coming when you turn the page, and then looking up and realising that the marker has slipped and you've gone back a couple of chapters.

Paul had suddenly got a commission to go north at literally no notice. One of their most difficult clients was dying and he was dying in the northern home of a married son. He sent for his solicitor in a great hurry.

'Will trouble,' said John Phillips, resignedly. 'Who said that the love of money is the root of all evil? Sometimes I think these chaps who live from hand to mouth are the lucky ones. There's nearly always trouble when a rich man passes out. I know of one case where the family made out a list of their father's possessions and pushed it in front of him on his deathbed, asking him if it was true he'd given this to A. and that to B. It wouldn't surprise me,' he added, with his familiar impish grin, 'to learn that he's left everything

ANTHONY GILBERT

to that so-called housekeeper of his. One thing, she's brought him a lot more comfort than any of his own children. So take an outsize bottle of oil up with you, my dear fellow, to calm the troubled waters and Heaven be your friend.'

Once again, therefore, at a crisis in his life, Paul was working late. Helen hadn't yet been told of the change of plan, but he had no fears as of yore that there would be a scene when she realised their week-end plans would have to be cancelled. Blanche would have been furious. Helen said, 'When you marry a man of parts you must be prepared to take a second place while he's working on his first million.'

And to-night, as before, just as he was prepared to call it a day, he heard the footsteps, the hand on the door, saw the door opening and looked up to see the same frog-faced malicious woman on the threshold.

She scarcely seemed so much as to have changed her clothes since her last visit.

'I expect you've been wondering why you haven't heard from me,' she said, coming in and closing the door behind her, 'but the fact is I've been having a bit of trouble.'

'I'm sorry to hear that,' said Paul, sincerely.

'It's only temporary,' Mrs. Hoggett assured him.

She sat down and he waited for her to put

162

her gloves on the table as she had done before. When she had so placed them she went on:

'I'm sorry if this isn't a very convenient time for me to call, but then I dare say no time would be particularly convenient. Still, I don't mean to keep you long. For one thing, I've got to get back to the shop. I've left a boy in charge, the one that does the paper deliveries, and you know what boys are. Can't give the correct change for half a crown and never in my favour, of course.'

She needled him with her impudent conspiratorial stare. 'Doing nicely, aren't you?' she murmured. 'Well, I wish I could say as much.'

'I wondered at the time if you weren't biting off more than you could chew,' Paul reminded her. 'It seems to me there are two things everybody thinks they can do—write a book and run a shop.'

'Oh, it won't last,' Mrs. Hoggett assured him quickly. 'I was never one to give up heart and I'm not afraid of hard work neither. And it is hard work, I have to be in the shop by six to catch the early trade, papers, and chaps coming in for Woodbines and such, and I don't close till eight of an evening. That's often the time you get the best trade, folk going to the pictures and wanting some chocolates for the girl-friends, kiddies turned adrift to amuse themselves and always clamouring for an icecream or a Mars bar. I'm quite well situated, mark you . . .'

Paul interrupted grimly, 'Do I take it that you're not here to repay the loan I made you?'

She fixed him with her dull brown gaze. 'I don't think you ever expected to see that again, Mr. French. In a way, I could say it was just the reverse. The truth is, I'm being pressed just at the moment. Naturally, it's only a temporary state of affairs, and a year isn't long to get established . . .'

'I understood it was a going concern when you took it over,' retorted Paul, hardily. But his heart was beating painfully. This is it, this is it, he was thinking.

'Ah, that's just the point,' Mrs. Hoggett told him. 'That man, Robinson, behaved something shocking to me. You could call it downright dishonesty. He showed me his books, a long list of regulars, good turnover, a little gold-mine he called it, and only giving up because of his heart. Bad, see. And so it was, though not the way he meant. What he didn't tell me was that he was going into partnership with a fellow in the next street in just the same line—his son-in-law it is. And, of course, he's taken a whole lot of his regulars with him, leaving me only the casual trade and what I can build up. Mind you, the chances are there.

Once I can get on an even keel, so to speak, I'll be all right. It's just the first year or two when people are getting to know you and appreciate the service you're prepared to give.'

'And during that time,' suggested Paul, politely, 'you need to be subsidised?'

'Just a little temporary help,' she amended. 'It wasn't only the customers he welched on, he never said a word about the fridge needing a new thermostat. It had to run at 9 to freeze up at all, though of course, when he showed me over, it was set at 3. There was a bit of delay getting that put in and there was a time when I couldn't take deliveries of ice-cream at all, and of course that didn't do me any good. And there was dry-rot in the roof—oh, it's no wonder he didn't mind getting out. You had the builders at your house last year, I noticed, so you'll have some idea what that costs. And prices going up every month.'

'Your solicitor should have looked after all that for you,' Paul told her in harsh tones.

'That's what I told him. I dare say if I'd shown good sense I'd have come to you. You're a lawyer, aren't you, Mr. French, and you'd have had a personal interest, so to speak. Well, there it is. There's debts owing that have to be paid—no, I wasn't meaning that £500. I don't think you were expecting to hear about that when you saw me to-night.

But, if I can't settle with the wholesalers, I might as well have poured my savings down the drain, and I know I can make a go of the place if I can get a fair crack of the whip. Only—if customers see your shelves bare, it makes a bad impression, and rumour flies faster than—than a Javelin plane.'

Paul said slowly, 'I don't know the extent of your indebtedness, of course, but if you're in this jam at the end of a year, doesn't it occur to you you might do better to cut your losses?'

'No,' said the woman, coolly, 'it doesn't, and I don't care about putting my hand to the plough and then looking back. It's a great neighbourhood for new faces, a lot of the houses let apartments and there's flats and lodgers and the new people will most likely come to me. I've only got to get really established and I'm on to a good thing for life. I've had enough of waiting on other people...'

'What do you consider you're doing now?'

'Ah, but that's different. There's an end product, so to speak, and that's for me, not for whoever's paying me my bits of wages. I'm sure you must have made investments in the past that didn't pay off right away.'

'I warned you,' said Paul, 'I couldn't come to your assistance again. And if you were thinking of tackling Mrs. French, I should tell you she has no private means.'

'I don't think you'd like it to come to that,' observed Mrs. Hoggett, easily. 'Mind you, I'm not giving up heart, only I had to put more into the place to start with than I reckoned on. I didn't want to press you too hard, but if I'd had more sense I'd have made it £1,000 instead of £500. Still, we could call it the same in two instalments, couldn't we!'

Paul played desperately for time. 'Do you realise I don't even know the whereabouts of this shop?' he temporised. 'For all I know, you could be taking me for a ride.'

She stiffened at once. 'If you're suggesting it doesn't exist . . .' she opened her big stuffy bag and produced a trade card.

'I'm not on the phone. I've no time to bother with a lot of silly calls when there's customers waiting. But come along any time I'm open and you'll find me there. No need to stand on ceremony. Just walk straight in and if there should be anyone there I can tell them you're the legal gentleman that looks after my interests, can't I?' She laughed, without humour. 'Don't forget to come, though, or I might get tired of waiting. Or the creditors might. Then I'd have to look elsewhere.'

'Your husband?' he suggested.

Her face darkened. 'It wouldn't do me much good pulling him into court. Mind you,

I don't say he didn't recognise his responsibilities, but then he's only in a small way, not a gentleman like you.'

He felt shaken with a storm of anger; it was as though she had put her hands on her fat hips and was jeering at him.

'If you had my wife in mind,' he said, 'I can assure you, one, that she wouldn't believe a word you say, and, two, that you would wreck any possible hope you cherish of getting further help. And now I must ask you to leave me, I've got to catch a night train north.'

Moving leisurely, she got up and walked to the door, stood waiting for him to open it; hearing her feet clump down the stairs—she didn't trust the lift and the attendant went off at six o'clock—took him back to the days of his servitude at The Dene. In a film, he thought, she'd fall down and break her neck, or trip under a bus on the way back. But that was fiction. In real life the tragedies assailed the young, those with a future to lose, while the senile, the vicious, the insane went on and on . . .

The telephone bell roused him. Again (as on that occasion a year ago) it was Helen. 'Darling, what has happened? You were coming back early. Remember?'

'I had an unexpected client,' he said, confusedly. 'She's only just gone.'

'You're too good-natured. You let them impose.' He felt himself begin to shake with anger. This was how Blanche had started. Were all wives the same?

'Darling, are you all right?' Helen pleaded. Oh, the love, the tenderness of that voice. Blanche would have been impatient, resentful. They didn't seem to belong to the same world. And yet he had to restrain himself not to shout back, 'Leave me alone to manage my own affairs.' The strength of his own feelings alarmed him. It was Mrs. Hoggett, of course; he couldn't really feel like that towards Helen. With an effort he ironed the exasperation out of his voice.

'Since you are on the telephone, darling, I've got a bit of tiresome news. I have to go north to-night in connection with some old bustard's will. I'll tell you when I come back. Be an angel and pack a bag for me for a couple of nights or so.'

'What time's your train?'

At the cheerful good sense of the question he felt his composure returning. Blanche wouldn't have believed him at first, and if and when she did she'd have demanded a thousand details that he couldn't supply. His voice sounded cheerful enough as he said, 'I'm just going to ring up and find out. Phillips sprang this on me. A hell of a joke, he thought. You know the way his gnome's face wrinkles up at the prospect of passing the buck to someone else? I'll get on to the station right away and then I'll come back. There'll probably be a train about midnight. With luck I might even get a sleeper.'

* * *

His luck didn't hold quite that far, but he was told it was improbable the train would be full and, since the client would be paying expenses, he resolved to travel in as much comfort as possible. He dotted down the times of the two alternative trains on the first bit of paper that came to hand and by chance it was Mrs. Hoggett's professional card. He slipped this into his pocket, found his hat, switched off the light and took a taxi home.

* * *

The Twemlows, four sons and two daughters, all married and all equipped with their partners, were waiting for him like greyhounds in the slips. As Phillips had suspected, the wicked old man had left everything to Miss Tite. All six disappointed heirs-expectant shouted their intention to contest the will despite the doctor's assurance that, if everyone was as sane as the late Twemlow, the Ministry of Health could close down its mental hospitals in the morning. Miss Tite, the calmest person there, folded her enormous hands, on one of which a disproportionate diamond ring glittered, and spoke of the impiety of going against the wishes of the dead. The youngest Twemlow son said he'd pitch the old witch downstairs before he'd let her collar the estate and a son-in-law suggested a compromise. All of them behaved as though Paul were responsible for their situation, and he was accommodated in what used to be called bachelor's quarters, which meant a slip-room on the north side of the house, about a quarter of a mile from the bathroom. The two nights lengthened to four, but on Thursday Paul wrote firmly to Helen that he'd be home on Saturday midday, catching an unearthly train that left at 7 a.m., and suggested they should celebrate their anniversary by going to a theatre, if Helen would get the seats. And afterwards they would dine extravagantly to take the taste of Twemlows out of his mouth.

Helen, who had missed him even more than she had expected—it was their first separation since their marriage—bubbled over with delight when she got his letter, and ran to the telephone to book seats for London's most popular show. She was lucky to get two excellent returned stalls. Having written a cheque in payment she found she was out of stamps. Paul, that methodical man, always kept a supply in his dressing-room, so she went to help herself. Under the book of stamps was a card and her glance fell idly upon it. Then she stiffened, stared, first incredulous, then dismayed—and after that alarmed. Old sins have long shadows, proclaimed the proverb. There was the shadow falling over their sunlit path.

MRS. R. HOGGETT (late E. R. ROBINSON) (the card ran) 14 Dorking Road, Camden Grove.
Newspapers, tobacco, confectionery.
Daily morning delivery.
Open till 8 p.m.

Forgetting about the envelope in her hand, Helen picked up the card. What on earth was it doing in Paul's desk and how long had it been there? Chancing to turn it over she saw some hurriedly scribbled train times on the back and, putting two and two together, realised that Mrs. Hoggett must have been Monday's late visitor.

'But why not tell me?' she said aloud and Miss Margetts popped her head round the door to say, 'Did you speak to me, Mrs. French?'

'No,' cried Helen, confused. 'I suppose I was talking to myself. Oh dear, one of the first signs of old age.'

Miss Margetts, who had neither time nor taste for nonsense, shut the door and went away.

Helen went on staring at the card. Her thoughts went like this.

'He saw her Monday night, but he didn't tell me. So—he didn't want me to know. Why not? Because she means trouble. What sort of trouble could she stir up two years later?' The answer, of course, was—something to do with Blanche's death.

'And something he and she know and I don't,' Helen continued to herself. 'And he doesn't mean to confide in me or he'd have told me at once. Only—what on earth could it be?'

She knew that Mrs. Hoggett had had no thought of entering commerce immediately after Blanche's death, since she had at once applied for and obtained a post in Brighton, since when Helen had heard nothing of her. How long had she had the shop? How long had Paul known about it? And (at last, she came to the 64,000 dollar question)—Who had paid for it? As Crook would have said, 'Give me three guesses and you can have two back on a dish with parsley round the edge.'

The only reasonable assumption was that Paul had, at the very least, assisted in financing the enterprise.

The effect of this discovery on Helen was horrifying. The doubts that had threatened to submerge her at the time of Blanche's death, and that she had thought stilled for ever, now came surging back with redoubled force. She had never believed Blanche would kill herself and leave Paul free. And yet, if Blanche had had the gun, how was it she was the one who died? But Paul explained that, she told herself. He tried to stop her . . . Doubts, like sand in a gale, and answers to refute those doubts, went whirling through her mind. After a long time it occurred to her that Paul's unexpected absence till the following day afforded her a heaven-sent opportunity to do some investigating herself.

On Fridays Miss Margetts went out after lunch and seldom returned till about 11 o'clock. As a rule Paul and Helen went out, too, since the housekeeper was a despot in her own kingdom and secretly resented her employers so much as boiling an egg. On this Friday Helen had decided to go to the Cavendish Cinema where a new Spanish film was being shown, and dine by herself (since

Paul's uncertain return had prevented her from making concrete plans) at the Blue Dolphin, but her discovery of the card altered this arrangement.

'I'll go to the earlier house,' she now decided, 'then have a sandwich and take the bus to Camden Grove. Not much sense getting there before eight, because she'll be busy in the shop. And I'll find out the nature of her hold over Paul if I have to stay there all night.'

It never occurred to her Paul might prefer her to keep out of the whole affair. It would have occurred to Blanche, but she would still have intervened out of jealousy and rage. Helen's motive was love of her husband. It seems unjust that such widely different motives can have precisely the same result.

The day dragged endlessly. The clock loitered, every tiresome acquaintance she possessed seemed to ring up. But at last it was time to go. She clung to her decision to attend an earlier house at the Cavendish, so that she could describe the film if she were asked. It was not until she was inside the cinema that she wondered why she had taken the trouble since, of course, she meant to tell Paul as soon as he came back that she knew about Mrs. Hoggett. It then came to her as an icy shock that perhaps she wasn't going to tell him, after all. She was so bemused by the whole situation and its suddenness that she felt she could hardly think straight.

Nothing went quite according to plan. The picture proved to be a very long one, so there was no time for a meal at the Blue Dolphin or even a sandwich at a snack bar. The journey to Camden Grove was very slow and as she alighted from the omnibus she saw that the clock stood at three minutes to eight. She had been unable to find Dorking Road on Paul's map of London, and the first two people she asked proved to be foreigners who were unable to help her. Eight o'clock had struck when she came upon a tobacconist in the High Road closing his premises for the night. When she asked for a direction he looked at her in surprise.

'You're sure you mean Dorking Road?' he said doubtfully.

'Quite sure,' said Helen.

He shrugged, supposing her to be one of the new kind of Health Visitors making a call after working hours. He walked a few steps with her, pointing out the way, then forgot her existence until something occurred later to pull him up with a jolt. He wished then he'd paid more attention to her appearance, but how on earth was a fellow to know?

CHAPTER ELEVEN

HELEN'S first thought on reaching Dorking Road was that Mrs. Hoggett was not very advantageously placed, since the street appeared to end in a cul-de-sac and the few shops dwindled into a row of thin pinched houses of dingy brown brick, with Victorian windows mostly veiled by lace curtains, every floor let to a different family and no doubt lodgers galore. In the High Street a good many people had been moving about, and although in the main the shops were closed, there were Espresso bars open, and cafés and sweet-shops still showing bright lights. Long queues stood outside the cinemas, and cars and motor-cycles filled the evening with sound. But here it was as if a sheet of glass had fallen, everything seemed muted and colourless.

She found Mrs. Hoggett actually standing at the door of her shop, looking furiously up and down the street. She was so much incensed she did not even recognise her visitor, but turned sharply, crying, 'Did you see a young fellow go past? A young thief, I should say. Well, did you?'

'I didn't notice anyone,' said Helen, somewhat taken aback by this unceremonious reception.

'Asked me for a glass of water—felt faint,' continued the infuriated voice. 'Must be going out of my sense to be taken in like that—I go into the inner room to get it for him and when I come back the till's open and cigarettes gone... And no insurance. Well, did you want something? You've left it pretty late. I shut at eight o'clock, and that's a longer day by half than most.'

Helen said, 'Mrs. Hoggett,' and at that the woman turned and saw her for the first time. 'Why, it's *you*, Miss Wayland.'

'Mrs. French,' corrected Helen, wondering if the mistake were deliberate.

'Yes, of course. Well, I didn't expect to see you coming along, but it's all one to me.'

Ungraciously she moved aside and Helen entered a not very prepossessing or methodical room, with sweets in jars and stands on one side, tobacco of various kinds on shelves, and the cheaper weekly periodicals and children's magazines on a small counter against the farther wall. Drabness, a drabness that equalled the proprietor's appearance, seemed the key note of the place.

'Right through,' ordered Mrs. Hoggett in the same ungracious voice and, rather dazed, Helen moved towards a door standing ajar. Mrs. Hoggett stayed to lock the shop door and draw down the blind. Helen found herself in a sitting-room that seemed all of a piece with the rest of her surroundings. Whatever Mrs. Hoggett believed in, it clearly was not comfort. A bare ink-marked table, two sparsely stuffed arm-chairs, a few ornaments, a flat dresser that served as a sideboard, an old-fashioned wireless set she had brought from Bryan Mouncey, completed the furniture.

'Sit down and make yourself at home,' called Mrs. Hoggett; a note of sarcastic triumph now tinged her flat voice. She came in, drawing a spectacle case from her large black bag, and increasing her likeness to a toad by setting a pair of horn-rimmed glasses on her lumpy nose. 'I suppose he's told you to get a receipt,' she said. 'Well, I'm ready.' She shifted the glasses impatiently.

'Those are new, aren't they?' asked Helen, trying to make sense of what had just been said.

'Got 'em yesterday. Of course I waited too long. Once upon a time they'd have been free. Now I have to pay through the nose for them, and they call that a free Health Service.'

She dropped into one of the chairs and sat there, looking like a bad-tempered Buddha, the sort you buy in junk shops and before which nincompoops burn joss sticks on lonely winter evenings. 'Well, Mrs. French, how does married life suit you?'

'I'm very happy,' said Helen in a low voice. 'Mrs. Hoggett, I've only just heard you had this shop.'

'I'll say,' said Mrs. Hoggett, as grim as a winter dawn. 'Still, you don't have to waste time offering me congratulations. All you have to do is hand over the money . . .'

'Money?'

'The money your husband was going to pay me, of course,' said Mrs. Hoggett impatiently. 'Just like a man to leave the dirty work to his wife, isn't it? Well, let's have it and I'll sign the receipt, and then I'll get along with my accounts. I do them at the end of the week—Saturday being a busy day here . . .'

'Mrs. Hoggett, my husband doesn't even know I'm here to-night. I only heard about this shop by chance, so I thought I'd come along . . .'

'It's a long way from South Square to Camden Grove just to buy cigarettes,' snapped Mrs. Hoggett. 'Really, Nurse, I'm surprised at you. I should have thought with your experience you'd have thought up something better than that. Why did you really come?'

'All right,' said Helen. 'I came to ask you a question. What hold do you imagine you have over my husband?'

'So he didn't tell you? I didn't think he would. Did he even tell you he helped me to open the business?'

'No. But he's always generous . . .'

'He can afford to be. I saw the figures of the first Mrs. French's will. As for generous, he owes me his life, and that's worth more than £500.'

'That's nonsense. You did your best to get him convicted with your story about the creaking board.'

'He got out of that very well,' allowed Mrs. Hoggett, grudgingly. 'But the bell's another matter.'

'The bell?'

'Yes. The one Mrs. French rang when she saw him coming at her with the gun. Oh yes, of course he shot her. I never had any doubts and I sometimes wonder if you did. Still, a rich widower . . .'

Helen felt suddenly faint. She wrenched at the scarf she was wearing, took it off and laid it on the arm of her chair. It was one that they had bought in Paris on her honeymoon, a deep rose-pink colour with an original ceramic design. 'That's one scarf you won't find all the shopgirls in London wearing when you return,' the salesgirl had said.

'I think you owe me an explanation,' Helen forced herself to say. A small fierce fire burned in the grate, and with a mutter she rose and took a straight-backed chair farther off. 'I'm sorry, it's so hot. What bell, Mrs. Hoggett?'

'The bell that sounded just before the shot.'

'There wasn't one. I should have heard it . . .'

'Not you. It took the shot to bring you out of bed. But it sounded all right. I waited for you to answer it, and then I heard the shot and . . .'

'You're making a very dangerous accusation,' said Helen, but her voice shook.

'If the jury had known about that bell they wouldn't have hesitated about their verdict. Well, think of it for yourself. Your husband had had a regular scene with his wife, all about you . . .'

'Who says that?'

'I heard her myself, and if you could have seen his face when I came in—lucky for Mrs. French I did, or he might have strangled her there and then. Not that it was much help as it happened.'

'Do you mean to say,' said Helen, 'that that's all you've got on him? Well, go out and tell the world and see how much attention they pay.' She heard her voice grow shrill, and quieted it with an effort. 'To say nothing of the fact that the police would be down on you like a cartload of bricks, wanting to know why you'd suppressed that piece of evidence. Of course, you hadn't thought it up in time.'

'Mr. French clearly doesn't agree with you,' returned Mrs. Hoggett, her dull brown eyes fixed unwinkingly on her visitor. 'He paid over the £500 as meek as milk, and he'll pay the next instalment, too. Even if he doesn't happen to mention it to you.'

'All right,' said Helen, preparing to depart. 'Try it and see. But don't forget about the police.'

Mrs. Hoggett picked up the poker and rattled the coals in the grate. 'If you're going back,' she said, 'just tell your husband that if he can't spare the instalment I shall be having the bailiffs in before the end of the month. There was bad debts I didn't know about, but I'll be in the clear soon, with a bit of help. But if Mr. French won't see it my way, I shall tell the bailiffs he went surety for me, they should apply to him. They don't want a bankrupt business on their hands, he'd find them on his doorstep all right. He holds my I.O.U. for the first £500, you know, or did he forget to tell you that, too?'

'Paul will only have to say that he never undertook any responsibility for your debts and they'll go away.'

'They may, but what about the Press? They're always out for a story, and it won't take them long to tie up the ends. Here's a man whose wife died in very strange circumstances, who came into all her money and subsequently married the nurse who was in the house at the time, and on his wedding eve he planks down £500 to the housekeeper.'

'A very generous gesture,' repeated Helen. But hope was dying in her heart.

'They might wonder why he waited so long. And then if they came talking to me, as of course they would, I might get panicked, not being used to newspapermen, see. Suppose I was to let out, quite innocent-like, about seeing the pair of you that night on Parsons Hill, the husband and the nurse, remember? But losing my head and not liking to let out I'd left Madam alone, and afterwards it being too late? You saw me yourself. You said as much with the police there. And back he comes and within the hour she's dead and he's free? Do you think people aren't going to put two and two together? Not just a few yokels as you'd call them, but fine educated people like you and Mrs. French know nowadays.'

'Suppose they do?' asked Helen. 'That's about all they *can* do.'

'Is it? Don't you ever read criminal cases, Mrs. French? I do. Not detective stories, I wouldn't waste my time with them. You know you're only trying to pick a lock, when all the while the key's in the author's pocket. But there was Crippen. He must have thought he was safe, with his wife under the cellar flags and the neighbours accepting his story that she'd run off with a lover and died in the Riviera. And then someone got suspicious, just as someone might get suspicious here, just an ordinary citizen, and that person went to the police. And, even if you don't read such books, you must know what happened to Crippen.'

'The two cases aren't on all fours! Crippen had murdered his wife.'

Mrs. Hoggett's silence said more than any words could have done. After a moment she went on in the same assured tones, 'Now you see why I thought he'd sent you with the money to-night.'

Helen half rose. 'There's no sense my staying. My husband doesn't know I came. But—don't think you've won the rubber. People like you forfeit your right to a place in the community . . .'

'Are you threatening murder, too?'

'No, no. Of course not. All the same, I'm not going to let you get away with it. I'm not going to have Paul turned into a nervous wreck, and I won't have the father of any child of mine dragged through the courts. Oh, I'll find some way, never fear. You shall know what it's like to hesitate before you open a letter, to feel your heart pounding at the ring of a bell . . .'

Mrs. Hoggett's faced paled as dramatically as it had coloured. 'Why do you say that?'

'Because I'll make it true. If we're to live in the shadow you'll live there with us, you'll know fear—and doubt—Is this the day the enemy will strike?'

'You're getting hysterical,' shrilled Mrs. Hoggett. 'But if you think you can alarm me, you're wrong. Me afraid of a door-bell indeed?'

At that instant the sultry air was shattered by the imperative continuous pealing of the shop bell.

The eyes of the two women met. Mrs. Hoggett sat as firm as a rock in her straight-backed chair. Neither spoke. The bell pealed on.

At last Helen said, 'Don't let me stop you answering it.'

'It'll be some lazy chap thinks I'll open up this hour of night,' snapped Mrs. Hoggett, contemptuously. 'Let him ring, that's what I say.'

'Mightn't it be the police?' suggested Helen. 'Didn't you say there'd been a—a burglary?'

Mrs. Hoggett sniffed. 'Not much use

complaining to the police in these parts. Get a stone through my window in the morning like as not. Justice—well, Mrs. French, you know as well as me there's no such thing.'

But it seemed clear the ringer had no intention of departing; the incident became a battle of nerves. At last the woman jumped up. 'I'll sort him,' she said, trampling through the shop and noisily withdrawing the bolt. She had not quite closed the door so that Helen, although she saw nothing, could hear Mrs. Hoggett's voice exclaim, 'What do you think you're doing?' And then in a different voice 'You!' Steps sounded as someone came in. Mrs. Hoggett's voice rose again. 'You can't go through there,' she shrieked. 'I've got company.'

The visitor must have paid no heed or said something to the effect that he was going where he darned well pleased, because an instant later she cried out in a yet louder tone, 'I told you, you can't go that way.'

At that Helen panicked. Whoever the stranger was, she mustn't be found here. It did not occur to her that, since the newcomer would not know her identity, he would not connect her with that earlier tragedy. All she understood was she had to go.

Pushing back the chair, she darted across the room and through a door in the opposite wall. This brought her into a narrow passage, covered in brown linoleum in a worn key pattern. At the farther end another drab door led into a little yard, with a dustbin set so close to the entry that she almost dislodged the lid. Emerging at last, she found herself in a kind of alley. Light poured from a public house—The Mitre—on the corner. It seemed to be doing a good business; the swing doors were in perpetual motion. Not that way, she thought desperately. Too much light—too many people. There was a narrow opening at the farther end of the alley and she half-ran towards it. Within three minutes she was lost in an inextricable maze of small streets. She moved confidently enough at first, scanning the distance for the sight of the familiar red bus that would warn her she was near a high road, but none passed. One or two people stood outside houses, talking together, and she went by them with her head down. Radios blared and the television masts on the roofs made her think of a picture of a harbour that hung in her room at home.

These houses were like those in Dorking Road, shabby and paintless. She turned a corner, passed a fish and chips shop still doing a roaring trade, a little ale-house called The Running Horse, almost cannoned against a couple inextricably intertwined, muttered an apology and swerved abruptly across the road. Round another corner, along another road, by a public house called The Green Pastures, past a block of modern flats—that gave her hope— surely they would be near the high road—by a bomb-site not yet rehabilitated, hearing whispers in the dark, cries, scuffles, groans of satisfaction and delight—it was like a nightmare, the bad dream you have that you are walking down a black road that goes on for ever and that you know will end in a glass-crowned wall.

Suddenly it was over, the ordeal and the irrational fear. At the corner of the road she saw a flash of red, lights sprang up, she began to run. A minute later she was passing a huge bright cinema, another minute and she was on a bus. Less than half an hour after that, surprisingly, she was fitting her key into the lock of the front door.

The house was perfectly quiet and gratefully empty. She snapped on lights, and the shadows went away. In this familiar setting security must surely abide. Yet common sense warned her that retreating armies don't vanquish an enemy. She turned quickly and from the sideboard she took a whisky-bottle. She seldom drank spirits but the damp night seemed to have chilled her. Feeling warmed and encouraged she carried the empty glass into the kitchen, rinsed it under the tap and returned it to its place.

Then she went upstairs and automatically began putting her things away, the hat in its box, the gloves in their drawer, the scarf . . . She stopped, looking round, perplexed. She couldn't see the scarf, yet she knew perfectly well she had been wearing it that evening. She must have dropped it in the dining-room when she poured out the whisky. Wearily she went down to get it. She didn't want Miss Margetts to find it lying by the sideboard. But it wasn't there, after all, nor in the kitchen, nor on the stairs.

It must have fallen off the bed, she decided, but it wasn't there either. So, then, she had dropped it out of doors—in the cinema, or the cafe . . .

Inexorable memory flashed before her eyes a picture of herself folding the scarf and laying it on the arm of the chair in Mrs. Hoggett's back room, and then crossing the room away from the fire. Her heart resumed a calmer movement, her pulse quietened. Nothing to panic about, nothing at all. She looked at her watch. Too late to go back to-night. The shop might be shut and if not there was the visitor—so—wait for the morning. In the morning she'd telephone—no, there hadn't been a telephone in the room. Well then, she would go over immediately after breakfast and collect it. She could be back long before Paul returned . . . that brought her up short again. If she intended to tell Paul about her excursion, where was the hurry to retrieve the scarf? She refused to face that problem now, undressed and slipped between the sheets.

The whisky that should have made her somnolent seemed to have aroused her imagination. She lay wide awake staring into the darkness, tormented by recollections of Blanche, Blanche of whom she seldom thought these days, who had lain in her grave for two years gone. Once, when a board creaked, she started up with a sudden hideous vision of the door opening softly, the light clicking on, or, worse still, no light coming on, only feet in the darkness approaching the bed. 'Is that what happened the night Blanche died? Did she experience this sudden appalled premonition of danger? Did she snatch out her hand and switch on the light and find Death coming towards the bedside?' Imagination was running riot now, it was like a high wind in a garden, reducing all the order and seemliness to confusion. 'I'm mad,' thought Helen, 'I'm mad. It all comes of getting lost, losing my head, finding I had left my scarf with someone I had never meant to see again— that and the hour of the night.' After dark the witches and warlocks come into their own, the dead rise from their graves and vampires are abroad. She put out her hand sharply and turned on the bedside lamp and the ghost of Blanche laughed—'I did that, I did that.' But it hadn't saved her, she'd died without a word, a kiss, a prayer. A dreadful death really more dreadful in a way, seen in retrospect. Helen reached for the bottle of sleeping tablets that she'd scarcely opened since her marriage, she shook two into her palm, swallowed them with water and switched off the light. Long before Miss Margetts returned at eleven o'clock she was deep in sleep.

CHAPTER TWELVE

THIS TIME no screaming shot awakened her, but a knock on the door that brought her bolt upright in bed. Automatically she turned to where Paul should have been, then remembered that he wouldn't be back till midday. Last night's alarm now seemed absurd. Of course she would tell her husband she had seen Mrs. Hoggett; that would cancel out her advantage, though not, Helen feared, Paul's conceivable liability. Because the woman was perfectly capable of putting her threat into action and referring the bailiffs to rich popular Paul French.

The knock sounded a second time, the door opened and Paul came in, a tray in his hands.

'*Bonjour, madame.*'

She stared. 'Paul. But you're up in the north.'

'Then my ghost makes a very efficient substitute.' He came across and put down the tray, there was a smell of excellent coffee.

'Miss Margetts following with the savoury or whatever it is,' he said. Then he put his hand in his pocket and pulled something out. It was her rose silk scarf.

'Here's a thing and a very pretty thing,

who's the owner of this pretty thing?' he chanted.

Relief turned her sheet-white. So she hadn't left it at Mrs. Hoggett's last night, after all.

'Where on earth did you find that?'

'It had floated down into the area. Lucky I saw it really. You must have untied it standing on the step, or else forgotten to tie it in the first place.'

'Thank goodness, Paul. I was afraid I'd lost it. I feel quite superstitious about that scarf.'

'Had you missed it?' her husband inquired.

'Yes. When I put my things away last night. I knew I was wearing it when I went out . . .'

'Where did you go?'

Now was the time to tell him the truth, but for some inexplicable reason she retained silence. Miss Margetts would be up any minute—it could wait—

'I went to the cinema to see that Spanish picture.'

'Good?'

She nodded. 'Lovely to see all that beautiful hard sunlight.'

The door opened and in came the housekeeper, carrying a covered plate and toast in a small silver rack.

'Will you have another cup of coffee, Mr. French?' she suggested.

Paul said he might as well so she went off for

a second cup.

'Why are you here?' asked Helen, puzzled. 'I mean—I didn't expect you till midday.'

'The business suddenly folded up after lunch and I caught the slow train that arrived at midnight. Actually I hoped to get one that got in four hours earlier, but I just missed that through sheer bad luck. A good thing I did come, or I might have been a corpse by this time. Those Twemlows must have been birds of prey in a previous incarnation. Honestly, darling, I've seen more alluring things in the aviary at the zoo.'

She said wonderingly, 'I didn't hear you. As a matter of fact, I had a bit of a headache, I took a sleeping pill.'

'You seemed dead to the world when I looked in, so I slept in the dressing-room.' He poured her out some coffee, then turned to take the second cup from Miss Margetts's capable hand. She had brought the paper up and this she laid on the bed.

'Late again,' she said, 'and Grey hasn't got any leeks. I told him, if you can't send us leeks when we want them we shall have to transfer our custom.'

'You're nearly fifty years out of date,' Paul told her, picking up the paper.

'I'll run down to the market after breakfast. They may have leeks there. There's another of these horrid murders,' she added casually from the doorway. 'It's getting so it's not safe for women to be living alone nowadays. This makes the third—one in Cardiff and that old woman in Manchester and the police without a clue.' She sniffed. 'If they had any sense they'd keep a dog or have a chain put on the door. Women weren't made to live alone, most of them haven't the gumption.'

'Teddy-boys?' murmured Paul, taking the cup from Helen's hand.

'I'd give 'em Teddy-boys,' said Miss Margetts.

Helen poured out the coffee and buttered some toast. 'Have you had anything to eat?' she asked Paul. 'Have some of this?'

There was no reply and she looked up to see his face rigid and absorbed.

'Paul!'

He lowered his paper. 'Well, of all the coincidences. Helen, you remember Mrs. Hoggett?'

'Well, of course. Oh, no! *She* isn't the one.'

He nodded. 'Looks like it. He began to read:

Police last night, attracted by a light burning at a very late hour, entered a tobacconist's shop in Camden Grove and found the body of the proprietor Mrs. Ruby Hoggett, aged 59, on the premises behind the shop. Head injuries, believed to have been caused by an iron poker found near the body, are thought to be the cause of death. Police are pursuing investigations. Foul play is suspected.

Paul let out a short laugh, that was so surprising she stared at him unspeaking.

'Foul play is suspected,' Paul repeated derisively. 'As if people hit themselves over the head with iron bars. Well, she can't say I didn't warn her.'

'What do you mean, you warned her? When? Of what?'

Paul put out a hand and laid it over hers. 'Keep calm, darling. Of course, it's a shock. When you read about murder you never expect it to be about someone you once knew. And yet every murdered person must have some relations and friends.'

'Is that all the paper says?'

'Yes.' Paul looked surprised. 'Well, they only found the body last night and the paper probably goes to press in the small hours.' He glanced at the watch on his wrist. 'We've missed the news, though they don't generally feature murders on the B.B.C. at this stage unless they've got some clue as to the criminal.'

'Have they?'

'It doesn't say. I've read you all there is. Darling, don't look so distracted. It's dreadful, of course, but . . .'

'What did you mean when you said you warned her?'

'Oh, she came to me just before we were married, when she was opening this shop. She wanted money, of course.'

'And you gave it her?'

'Yes. She timed it very neatly. I didn't want the Press all round us on our wedding day.'

'No. What did you mean when you said you warned her?'

He asked a question in reply, 'Did you know she had a husband living?'

'Mrs. Hoggett? I always imagined she was a widow. At least, I don't suppose I really thought about it.'

'Mr. Hoggett had the good sense to leave her some years ago and apparently he's set up very snugly with a substitute Mrs. Hoggett.'

'And she found out?'

'She only had to go to Somerset House, and, assuming he married in his own name, all the evidence would be there.'

'It's bigamy, isn't it?'

'I suppose he could say he thought she was dead. After seven years, if there's no evidence, you're allowed to take the chance.'

'And she was getting money out of him?'

'Trying to. I don't know how successful she was. I gathered he was a bit of a disappointment to her. Then she'd picked up £100 from her last employer. I wonder what skeleton she had in her cupboard.'

Helen waited but he said no more.

'She was expecting a second instalment, wasn't she?' she said at last.

'A second . . .?' Paul laid the paper down. 'What's all this, Helen?'

'You'll have to know,' said Helen. 'I went to see her last night.'

'You went . . .? How did you know where she was?'

She explained about the stamps and the card. 'I couldn't bear the thought that she was putting a stranglehold on you. I thought if she knew I knew that would be the end.'

'What did she tell you?' asked Paul, carefully.

'The story about the bell. It's nonsense, of course. Surprising really she couldn't think up something better.'

'Any stick does to beat a dog. Helen, you do realise your own position? What time did you go to see her last night?'

'I got there just after eight.'

He looked back at the paper. 'It doesn't give even a speculated time as to her death. She was alone?'

199

'And furious. Someone had just tricked her into leaving the shop for a minute, and then robbed the till. She was just closing, it was a minute or two after eight. Because she didn't recognise me for a moment, she said, "You've left it pretty late, haven't you? I'm shutting."'

He said abruptly, 'If I'd wanted you to know about her I could have told you, couldn't I?'

'I'm your wife, Paul. You must share the bad things with me as well as the good. Besides, I thought if she knew I was in your confidence, so to speak, that would spike her guns. She said you helped her.'

'As I've just told you, I lent her £500 against her I.O.U. which my bank holds.'

'That's what she said. Paul, will that come out now?'

He frowned. 'It depends. If they don't make an early arrest they'll start looking through her papers . . . Helen, what time did you leave?'

'I think about 8.30. I didn't look at my watch.'

'Did she say anything about expecting another visitor?'

Helen looked astonished. 'But he was there. I mean . . .'

'What? Helen, for goodness' sake, what are you talking about? Do you mean someone else knows you were there last night?'

'No. At least, I hope not. But someone came ringing at the bell and wouldn't go away. She thought at first it was someone wanting cigarettes and expecting her to open up—at least, that's what she said, but, of course, she was trying to bluff me.'

'Why do you say that?'

'Well, if you wanted cigarettes after eight o'clock, you wouldn't have to knock a shop up to get them. The place was ablaze with public houses—and there was probably a slot machine somewhere too. They seem to be everywhere nowadays.'

'You mean, whoever it was . . .'

'It was someone she knew. I heard her say "You!" as if she couldn't believe her eyes, and then, "You can't go in there, I've got a visitor." That was when I left.'

'Without catching a glimpse of whoever it was?'

'I just picked up my things and fled. It sounded like trouble, and I didn't want to involve either of us.'

'Think hard, Helen. Did she say anything else, anything that might help to identify him? Was it him, by the way?'

'I don't know,' Helen discovered astonished. 'I only heard *her* voice. I took for granted it was a man.'

Paul was silent for a long minute. Then he said, 'Be guided by me. Don't take this story to the police, not yet, anyway. If you could assist with any detail it would be different but you can't. You can't really tell them anything, except that she was alive at half-past eight and the medical evidence would probably tell them that. Did you touch anything? But of course you must have done. They'll sift the whole place for finger-prints.'

'I don't think I did. Wait a minute. I didn't take off my gloves till we got into the inner room. Then I put them with my scarf on the arm of the chair. I had a scare about the scarf,' she broke off, 'when I couldn't find it last night I thought I must have left it there. I was going back to ask this morning. I thought there'd be plenty of time before your train got in. Why, Paul.' For his face had changed, grew stiffer, even paler than before.

'If you left at half-past eight you must have been back by nine.'

'Well, not quite, because I lost my way. I didn't go back to the high road, I went up the lane—I came out by the private door at the back. He and she were in the front, you see.'

'But—couldn't you have got into the high road that way?' He sounded puzzled.

'I could, but there were some people coming towards The Mitre—that's a public-house on the corner—and I didn't want to be seen.'

'What difference would it have made? They weren't likely to know you.'

'No, of course not. All the same . . .'

He sat so still that she put a hand on his arm. 'What is it? Paul, you look frozen, like a dead man . . .'

'If you do have to tell the police this story later,' he said, and his voice now matched his appearance, 'don't add that last bit. Say you mistook the turning or something. I know the police. They'll hammer away at you to know why you were nervous at being seen.'

She caught his meaning and her own face paled. 'You mean, they might think—*I*—but there was this 8.30 visitor.'

'He's hardly likely to come forward. To all intents and purposes, you will be marked down as the last person who admits to seeing her alive. Means, motive and opportunity— that's the police force's unholy trinity. She was hit over the head with a poker—did you notice one in the room?'

'Yes. She used it to poke the fire. It got so hot I moved my seat.'

'Motive—plenty of that, from their standards. Opportunity—Helen, you wouldn't think this could happen twice to the same people. First me and Blanche and now you . . .'

'They won't believe there was an 8.30 visitor. Is that what you're trying to tell me?'

'Put yourself in their shoes. Suppose you had lost your head and taken up the poker—isn't this exactly the story you would tell?'

She sat, appalled. 'But—there'd be finger-prints on the poker? And I didn't handle it, so . . .'

'Finger-prints can be wiped off. Or, if the assailant wears gloves, there wouldn't be any in the first place. Helen, this is a hell of a mess. There's another point,' he added. 'They'll ask why you didn't go back for the scarf last night? It wasn't late, it wasn't wet, not till after ten . . . It turned into a pretty dirty night—'

'You're forgetting the visitor.' Her tone was very dry.

'Ah, yes. But . . . If only she'd said something that gave us a pointer.'

'She probably has other enemies . . .'

'No doubt. Her husband for one, but you can't go shooting arrows of suspicion at someone who may be perfectly innocent, and has probably suffered as much from her as we have. Oh, come in.' This to Miss Margetts who put her head round the door to know if she could collect the tray and what orders they were giving for lunch.

'We shall be out,' said Helen quickly.

'Lunch and dinner.'

'You told me dinner—I'm sure I hope you'll enjoy the theatre. Well then, I'll get the cupboards turned out. It's time.' She swooped on the tray and marched out.

'You don't suppose she was listening,' said Paul apprehensively.

'She's not Mrs. Hoggett.'

'No.' The silence came down again like a curtain. To Helen it was as stifling as if it had been made of concrete material. She saw that their positions now were reversed. Two years ago she had fought a temptation to believe he might be guilty of murder. Now he had to struggle against a fear that she might be charged with the same offence.

'I didn't do it,' she cried desperately.

'Darling, of course not. You don't have to convince me.' But hadn't he spoken rather quickly, and with almost too much conviction? 'You'd better dress now if we're going out to lunch. And take my advice, don't say anything yet. The police may make an arrest in the next twenty-four hours and then no one need ever know you were there at all.'

★   ★   ★

There was more news about the Camden Grove murder that afternoon. Walking back through the Park, saying, 'It's absurd to be afraid of going into our own house,' yet knowing they were so afraid, afraid of the incautious word, of the mysterious telephone call or the policeman on the step—because it's by the minutiae of crime that men are pulled in, the blood-stained match, the dropped cloak-room ticket—they caught sight of a paperseller's poster-board.

MYSTERY WOMAN in CAMDEN GROVE MURDER

they read.

Paul dropped his coppers through the slot of a wooden box by the stand and took up the newspaper. Together they read it, sitting side by side on a free Park seat, like any other couple, ghoulishly yet cheerfully interested in the latest crime.

It seemed that a woman called Beatrice Peacock had been going into The Mitre with two men friends when she noticed a woman come out of the back door of No. 14, look both ways and hurry off down the lane. She was certain of the number because she had observed to one of her companions, with the ghastly appositeness that sometimes attend the casual comment, 'Wonder if she's been doing Ma Hoggett,' an indication of the odour in which the neighbourhood held the dead woman. Mrs. Peacock gave some description of the woman, young, nice figure, fair hair, wearing a dark costume and a small light hat.

'It's a wonder she didn't add the scarf,' said Helen dryly. 'That would have made the identification complete.'

'I suppose there can't be more than two million women in London wearing light suits and small hats and having passable figures,' Paul agreed.

'But only one of them visiting Mrs. Hoggett last night.'

'There's no reason I can see why anyone should connect you with this—apparition. Did you speak to anyone in the district?'

'I asked one or two people the way, but they were all foreigners or dumb. Oh—' she stopped—'I asked a man who was closing his shop the way to Dorking Road. He might remember. He seemed a bit surprised that I was looking for it, now I come to think of it.'

'Did you say Dorking Road or Mrs. Hoggett?'

'Dorking Road. I'm quite sure of that. But he's pretty sure to remember.'

'What will he remember? That a young woman who might be this Mrs. Peacock's young woman asked the way. Don't attach too much significance to that. How about coming home?'

'I didn't speak to anyone after I left the house. The bus conductor was talking to someone at the top of the bus and just put out his hand for the fare. There were only a few people on board. I doubt if any of them would dare swear to me. All the same, Paul, I hate it. If the police ask me . . .'

'We've got to hope it doesn't come to that. They may pick up the 8.30 visitor at any minute. In the meantime, remember you're practically the leading lady in the local amateur dramatic society and put on an act.'

          ★   ★   ★

The Sunday papers went to town on the affair. *The Yardstick* devoted a vitriolic leader to the inadequacy, numerically and otherwise, of the police force.

'This is the third elderly woman to be murdered within the month,' it bawled to its readers. 'So far no arrests have been made; we are told the police are pursuing investigations, with as much success as tourists looking for the Loch Ness Monster.'

It featured photographs of all three women—'Mrs. Hoggett's must have been taken some while back,' said Paul, 'and she was no beauty then.' And then in enormous capitals. 'Next Time It May Be You.'

'Some chap enjoying himself knocking the Force,' remarked Sergeant Bennett sourly to his wife. He had been employed in the Manchester search, with not so much as a cocktail sausage to show for it. 'Seem to think we ought to be equipped with a sort of natural radar. Like to see them tackle it.'

He grumbled his way through breakfast and Mrs. Bennett, a patient woman, went to look for the soda mints. She hadn't much patience with murderers, a cross-grained lot that couldn't hold their tempers. Why, only think what most policemen's wives put up with, day in, day out, and how often did you hear of them breaking down, and no one to suggest justifiable homicide if they did.

CHAPTER THIRTEEN

IN CAMDEN GROVE it made something to talk about that wet Sunday morning. Neighbours told each other they weren't surprised, silly stuck-up old goat. Kept herself to herself and welcome, they said. Supposed to be a widow but nothing known for certain. No children, she'd told someone, no visitors neither. Hardly any letters. Took over from Tod Robinson about a year back. Should have been warned. Tod never let anything go that was worth hanging on to. New to the job, too, any fool could tell. One way and another, not a popular woman, not much of a loss really. Still, you've got a right to your life, even if you aren't exactly the parsley round Life's trencher. So let the police wade in and do their stuff.

The police lost no time. Thirty-six hours after the old woman's death they had learned that an unemployed labourer, called Alfred Savage, had displayed unusual affluence on Saturday night at The Running Horse. Here he had been seen to offer cigarettes all round, not Weights or Woodbines, but the kind that cost nearly 4s. for 20. Someone had chipped him.

'Been robbing a bank, Alfie?' 'Found a quid in the gutter,' said Alfie promptly. 'Well, a quid won't buy you much these days.' It bought four men a round of mild and bitter, and that meant the other three also stood a round apiece and then Alfie chipped in again and someone who had his wits about him observed to his ever-loving on his return that some chaps had luck and no mistake. A quid indeed! More like three or four, unless his eyes were deceiving him, and though you might find one quid in the gutter, (though no one he knew ever had), you didn't find quads. The wife, having a sharp tongue, told a neighbour who wanted to borrow a cupful of sugar it was a pity *her* husband didn't go scavenging in gutters like Alfie Savage, and by Sunday night the story had got round to the authorities. They asked Alfie if he'd like to answer one or two questions at the station. 'No compulsion, mind,' they said.

'Sense of humour you chaps got,' said Alfie. 'Shall I want me birth certificate? Ma has her lines, if that's what you were thinking.'

The officer said pleasantly that it wasn't a crime to have marriage lines, so long as you only had one set at a time, and suggested he'd suddenly come into a bit. Alfie told the story of the pound note. 'Some old geyser must have dropped it or maybe left it by a window and it blew out,' he offered.

'Don't you know you have to hand treasury notes in?' asked the station sergeant.

'How'd I be expected to know that? Never found one before. Anyway, you rozzers are a lot better paid than I am.'

'Never heard of stealing by finding?'

Alfie laughed. 'A diamond brooch p'raps or a wallet. But not a quid. How could anyone identify that?'

'You say you bought the cigarettes on your way to The Running Horse?'

'That's ri'.'

'Remember where you got 'em?'

'Well, a tobacconist, of course. I didn't find them in the gutter.'

'Remember which one?'

He shrugged. 'I don't go into 'em often enough to know.'

'Well, was it in the High Street?'

'I dessay.'

'Didn't get 'em from Mrs. Hoggett, I suppose?'

'Who's she?'

'Has—had—the shop in Dorking Road.'

'What?' His eyes hardened, his manner crisped. 'The old geyser who got herself bumped off? Here, you're not trying to pin that one on me.'

'Just asking,' said the sergeant, peaceably.

'What time did you buy the fags?'

'Never thought of looking at my watch,' sneered Alfie. 'Getting forgetful, aren't I?'

'That won't help you,' said the sergeant sharply. 'This is murder, remember.'

'So what? I didn't murder her. I got to The Running Horse round about eight, I think.'

'The Running Horse is in Maybury Lane on the corner. You go straight from your place?'

Alfie said again, 'Tha's ri'.' He wasn't the brightest boy in the class, but even he couldn't help seeing which way the arrow was pointing—convict's arrow, if he didn't look out.

'Then you wouldn't go by the High Street.'

'So I wouldn't,' Alfie agreed.

'And the only place you'd pass that sold fags would be Ma Hoggett.'

'Well, then, it could have been her. I told you, I don't remember.'

'Come on, let's have it,' said the sergeant, 'and forget about the quid you found in the gutter. You wanted some fags and you couldn't pay for them, so you got 'em the hard way. You're not going to try and tell me she gave 'em to you.'

'Gave 'em? If that old besom found a flea she'd walk a mile in the rain looking for a dog she could sell it to.'

'And you didn't pay for 'em, because you

hadn't got any money when you left the house, tried to borrow five bob from your dad, only he hadn't got any either ... So it looks like you helped yourself. Bit of a smash-and-grab, like.'

'Next thing you're going to tell me you found my fingerprints on the till,' said Alfie. Suddenly he looked frightened. 'O.K.,' he said, uneasily. 'Say I did help meself, that doesn't mean I killed her, does it? Never saw 'er after she went to fetch me that water. Come over faint, see?'

'Nice trick to play on an old woman, young chap like you,' said the sergeant disgustedly.

'I heard her bawling after I'd scarpered,' Alfie insisted. 'Corpses don't yell blue murder.'

'Funny thing,' said the sergeant. He sounded unsympathetic. 'No one else seems to have heard her. And we all know she's not the kind to turn the other cheek.'

'Look here,' said Alfie in desperation, 'didn't I read the blind was down and the door locked? Well ...'

'The blind was down,' the sergeant agreed, 'but the door wasn't locked.'

'So your chap only had to turn the handle and walk in. No jemmy, no acetelyne blow-lamp. No enterprise in the Force these days, is there?'

But none of that helped him. He was in the cart good and proper and he recognised the fact.

* * *

The midday papers carried the news. CAMDEN GROVE MURDER: MAN DETAINED.

Helen bought a paper and read all about it. The police might be reticent, but neighbours had given the reporters a treat. Here was something that idiotically, neither she nor Paul had considered—the taking of an innocent man. For she, and probably she alone, could prove it hadn't been his hand that struck Ruby Hoggett down. She had been alive and venomous as an adder half an hour after Alfie had gone on his lawless triumphant way.

'We ought to have foreseen this,' she told Paul when he came home that evening. 'Now we haven't any choice,' said Helen. 'We can't let an innocent man be accused.'

'Unless he was the one who came back at 8.30,' suggested Paul, but there was no conviction in his voice. 'She said "You!" you said.'

'Of course he wasn't.' Helen's voice was flat with denial. 'He'd keep out of her way, you

can be sure of that. As for the "You!" it
sounded as if she recognised someone she
hadn't expected to see, someone she didn't
want to see.'

'Blackmailers always have enemies,' Paul
agreed. 'I'll come with you, Helen. It's not
going to be very pleasant, I fear.'

It was even less pleasant than they had
anticipated. At first when they said they had a
statement to make about the Hoggett mystery
no one paid much attention. Too used to
crackpots drifting in with fallacious evidence,
Crook could have told them. But when Helen
said in crisper tones that she had proof that the
man they had arrested couldn't be guilty, the
authorities began to sit up and take notice. A
sergeant was fetched along to take their
statement, and when he heard it he said if
they'd wait he'd see if the inspector was
anywhere about. The inspector was, a little
dark dried-up chip of a man who didn't evince
any gratitude at this new piece of evidence,
but proceeded to treat Helen as though she
were branded as a criminal already.

'You do understand you should have given
us this evidence right away, Mrs. French?' he
said.

'I hadn't any evidence to give. I didn't and
don't know who attacked Mrs. Hoggett. It's
true I knew she was alive at 8.30, but until you

pulled in this Alfie Savage that didn't seem particularly important. I've no idea when she was killed.'

'Oh, I thought you were suggesting whoever it was came at 8.30 was responsible.'

'That would be tantamount to bringing an accusation against some person unknown. I didn't come here really to help you to solve the mystery of Mrs. Hoggett's death, but to persuade you you'd arrested the wrong person.'

'If you'd come to us at the start we should never have arrested young Savage at all. If you're apportioning responsibility—was there any particular reason why you should have kept quiet all this time?'

'We neither of us knew about the murder until Saturday,' Paul interposed. 'This is Monday night. I don't suppose it's done young Savage any harm to cool his heels for a few hours. After all, he did snatch the money and the cigarettes.'

'I asked Mrs. French a question,' said the inspector, forbiddingly.

'Of course there was a reason,' Helen replied. 'The press would drop on us like a vulture, will drop on us now. Mrs. Hoggett was my husband's housekeeper at the time of his first wife's death. At the inquest she gave evidence that might have been highly damaging. Oh Paul,' she made a movement of remonstrance, 'it's no good, all this is going to be aired now. My husband helped her to open this shop . . .'

'Is that so, sir?'

'Mrs. French has just said it.' Paul's voice was as hard as a Brazil nut.

'I see. You knew about this, Mrs. French?'

Helen was prepared for that one. 'My husband told me,' she replied promptly. 'It was a loan, perfectly open and above board. The I.O.U. is with my husband's bank. She was to come back and report progress in a year, and, of course, we hoped she would start repaying the loan. Unfortunately, either she wasn't such a good business woman as she had imagined or else she had astoundingly bad luck, anyway, she wasn't in a position to pay back any of the money, in fact, the boot was rather on the other foot.'

'You mean, she wanted another loan?'

'I don't think she actually said that, did she, Paul?'

Oh, how carefully they'd rehearsed this and how coolly they told their story. They weren't leaders in the local amateur dramatic society for nothing.

'She said she owed money. I asked her if she thought she was likely to make good if she had a little more time; she was absolutely sure of it.

So I said one of us would come along and see the place—as a matter of fact, we only had her word for it that it existed, and, though I didn't doubt that it was there, it seemed sensible to take a looksee before getting further involved.'

'Yes, Mr. French. When was this?'

'She came to see me at the beginning of last week. I had to go north unexpectedly . . .'

'So I thought I'd pay a surprise visit,' Helen chimed in. 'If people are expecting you they're rather inclined to set the stage, either make things look better or worse than they really are. So on Friday evening I went down . . .'

'Why the evening, Mrs. French?'

'There wouldn't have been much sense going during the day, she'd have been busy in the shop. I'd been to a cinema, the house was empty, I got into a bus and went to Camden Grove.'

'On the spur of the moment, would you say?'

'I thought of it earlier in the day.'

'And your husband knew you were going?'

'I don't see that that's of any significance,' remarked Paul in a puzzled tone. 'As a matter of fact, I didn't know. I imagine my wife thought I was more likely to be talked round than she was.'

'But you wouldn't have objected?'

Paul smiled. 'Are you a married man, Inspector?'

'I don't see what all this has got to do with it,' Helen broke in. 'Mr. French and I are married, we do things together. I went down to Camden Grove and found Mrs. Hoggett in a great tizzy because someone—I suppose Alfie Savage—had tricked her into leaving him alone in the shop and had then helped himself. She recognised me after a minute and asked me to come in.'

'You say that was just after eight.'

'Yes.'

'And this anonymous visitor called—when?'

'About 8.30.'

'So that you talked to Mrs. Hoggett for roughly half an hour. What did you talk about?'

'She asked about Mr. French, said the usual things, I hope you're very happy—you know—I asked about the shop. She said she'd had some bad luck, but she was sure she could pull it together. I was less sure. To begin with, I thought it was badly placed, in a cul-de-sac...'

'Did you tell her that, Mrs. French?'

'No,' said Helen, brought to an abrupt halt.

'Then that's not really important. Did Mrs. Hoggett ask outright for money?'

'Oh yes. She thought that was the reason for my visit. When she found I hadn't brought her any money she was—outraged.'

'What precisely do you mean by that?'

'What I say. She behaved like a prima donna whose time was worth £5 a minute. Why had I come if I hadn't brought the money. I said we wanted to see the place. Neither of us had ever been down there.'

'You mean, Mr. French, you lent the money blind?'

'Yes,' said Paul. The inspector waited, but Paul said nothing more.

'So, Mrs. French, when you had explained you hadn't brought any money, did Mrs. Hoggett resort to threats?'

'I object to that question,' said Paul, sharply. 'You're trying to put words into my wife's mouth. She has told you what Mrs. Hoggett said.'

'On the contrary,' said the inspector grimly, 'Mrs. French has merely told me what *she* said. Now Mrs. French, when Mrs. Hoggett realised that you had brought no money, what happened next?'

'I think that was quite early in the conversation. Then I said I'd come to see the place—that's when she put on her outraged look.'

'Did she explain why she should expect Mr.

French or you to help her further?'

'She seemed to think that as my husband had made her a loan in the first place he was in some way implicated, I mean, that if she went bankrupt he would be involved. If you call that a threat . . .'

'What would you call it?' asked the inspector.

'Sheer nonsense,' said Paul, sailing neatly in like an actor on a cue. 'Of course I wasn't involved. I had suggested to her that if she was in debt at the end of a year she mightn't be cut out for a commercial career. That's really what decided us to look at the place.'

'And it was about then that the bell rang,' Helen hurried on. 'It seemed rather melodramatic, because we'd just been saying something about jumping out of your skin every time you heard a bell—I suppose it could be bailiffs, I've never had them myself—and then this started pealing and pealing. At first she didn't want to open it, said it was only some impudent fellow expecting her to sell him cigarettes after hours. I suggested it might be the police . . .'

'Why the police?'

'Because of Alfie Savage.'

'I'm not aware she'd reported the larceny.'

'She was shrieking fit to beat the band, someone might have overheard and told a policeman. Anyway, we know now it wasn't the police. I can't help you much further, because for one thing, I don't know the names of any of her associates, and for another I never heard the visitor's voice. At least, I heard the sound of someone speaking, but the words were quite undistinguishable; I'm not even sure if it was a man or a woman. All I am sure is it was someone she recognised.'

'What makes you so sure of that?'

'The way she said "You!" Whoever it was was coming into the inner room where I was, so I left the place by the back door.'

'Why did you do that, Mrs. French? The visitor wasn't likely to recognise you.'

'I thought there might be trouble, and I didn't want to be involved and the whole story about Blanche French's death dragged up. You know yourself it's just the kind of thing the gutter Press would revel in.'

'Then I take it you're the woman Mrs. Peacock saw leaving by the gate?'

'I didn't see anyone else there and if the times fit . . .'

'And you went straight home?'

'Camden Grove is unknown country to me. I took a wrong turning and missed my way. I didn't get back till 9.30. I'm afraid I haven't any alibi for that—though why you should want one I can't imagine—because my husband was at that moment in the train coming south and the housekeeper, Miss Margetts, goes out on Friday nights and never gets back till after eleven. Is there anything else?' she added after a moment.

'There's one thing,' said the inspector slowly. 'You're a lawyer, Mr. French. I know ladies don't have much respect for the law, but you must have known it was her duty to give us all the assistance she could.'

'Then I suppose I'm like the Scots gardener who, told by the vicar that it was his duty to love his wife, said he wasn't special struck on duty. I agreed with my wife that she could tell you nothing you couldn't find out for yourself. If Alfie Savage wasn't responsible, then clearly Mrs. Hoggett had a visitor later in the evening. The doctor could give you approximate time of death.'

('Anyone can see you haven't had a lot to do with the police,' Crook was to remark later. 'They can outsmart any Alec living.' It would have been obvious to him, if it wasn't to the Frenchs, that they were totting up quite a big account, and the Income Tax Commissioners have nothing on the police when it comes to settling bills.)

'Did you notice the poker with which the murder was committed?' the inspector continued, unsmiling. He could do *his* laughing later and well he knew it.

'I saw Mrs. Hoggett poke the fire with it.'

'You didn't handle it yourself?'

'Of course not. Why should I?'

'It's an odd thing, when we came to examine it for fingerprints, there weren't any on it at all.'

'That doesn't strike me as very peculiar. If I'd just hit someone over the head with a blunt instrument, my first consideration would be to rub my prints off the handle.'

'Really, Mrs. French? Would it? Now that's very interesting.'

'Any child of seven years old would do the same,' put in Paul. 'The whodunnit writers have got us all educated as far as standard one.'

(That was another black mark against them.)

At last they were allowed to depart with the warning that if they were thinking of quitting town they should leave their address with the authorities first.

'For one minute,' Helen confessed as they went back to South Square, 'I thought they were going to arrest me out of hand.'

Paul smiled vaguely, glimpsed a taxi and hailed it. No sense telling her at this stage that that was how it would most probably end.

CHAPTER FOURTEEN

DURING the early days of Helen's married life Miles Gordon uprooted himself from Bryan Mouncey on the strength of a lecturing job in London. He was wanted to give evening classes, and he was still near enough the foot of the ladder to let nothing go by him. He wasn't one of your swells who will design a cathedral, consider a public library, but draw the line at anything less distinguished. 'I'd design a sheepfold if anyone would pay me for it,' he said. He liked his lecturing, he liked the excitement and the full swell of life in a big town. He found a couple of rooms, one of which served very well for a studio, and got on with the job. On the night he read about Helen's visit to the police station—you could be sure the enterprising Press weren't going to miss that—he walked into The Duck and Drake just off the Strand and found himself virtually cheek by jowl with a big drum-major of a man in a bright brown suit, with fox-coloured hair and eyebrows and a face like a slab of moulded chocolate.

'Well, if it isn't my favourite crime detector,' he said, cheerfully. Crook had friends of every kind, sex, age, colour and reputation. The Ancient Mariner would have approved of him, though Crook would have been hard put to it to say who the Ancient Mariner was. 'Glad to see you,' Miles went on unconcernedly, as though nothing could give Crook greater pleasure than this encounter, 'seen the evening paper? My hoodoo's hoodoo'd herself into a real spot at last.'

'Who's your hoodoo?'

Miles explained. 'Jolly for Paul French, I must say. All that story resurrected. Mind you, whoever put the Hoggett out of her misery has my sympathy. A horrid woman.'

'What's the odds Mrs. French takes Alfie Savage's place in the next thirty-six hours?' asked Crook.

'Why on earth . . .?'

'Line of least resistance. She was there, she can't prove anyone else was, deceased was a menace, well, of course she was, weapon lay to hand, she was a nurse, presumably knew all the vital spots, can't prove what time she came back—why, it's all served up on a plate. Mark you, they'll have to look for this mysterious visitor, but in a city of eight million souls it wouldn't surprise me if they didn't find him. Wonder if they've got anyone in mind to look after her interests?' he added yearningly. Life was dull just now, he'd have welcomed something to liven it up.

ANTHONY GILBERT

He didn't have to wait long.
The next day he was in his office at Bloomsbury Street when the door shot open and a young man tramped unceremoniously in.

'You Mr. Crook?' said the unannounced visitor. 'You don't seem to have a bell or anything.'

Crook gave him the once-over. Patron saint of the skiffle group, he decided.

'At your service,' he intimated politely, and from force of habit shoved the box of cigarettes in his direction.

Alfie took one and introduced himself.

'Never ought to have put me inside in the first place. That's one thing I wanted to ask you. Can I bring a case?'

'I shouldn't advise it. You did pinch the fags, didn't you?'

'That's not the same as hitting an old woman over the head.'

'True. You out on bail?'

'I dunno. They told me I could scarper, but I'd be wanted at the courts if and when notified. Heard about this Mrs. French?'

'Last night. Friend of hers was telling me. Friend of yours—Mrs. French, I mean?'

'What do you think? Came down to the station to say it couldn't have been me that knocked the old girl off because she was there

228

at half-past eight and she was crowing like a
cock then. Barmy, of course.'

'Who? Mrs. French or the old girl?'

'Mrs. French, of course. Fancy putting
yourself in the rozzers' hands. Shows she
doesn't know anything about them. String
you up as soon as look at you, just to get
another notch on their stick.'

'If you were going to ask me to represent
you in a libel action I'm not on,' said Crook,
politely.

'It's not me. It's Mrs. French. If she knows
so little about the police, she clearly doesn't
know enough to come in out of the rain.
Thought it might be up your street,' he added
casually.

'I didn't realise they'd taken Mrs. French
for the murder,' said Crook pleasantly.

'Well, if they haven't yet, you'll see they
will. Don't tell me they're going out of their
way to find some other chap, with this served
up on a plate?'

'Had a word with Mr. French?' Crook went
on.

Alfie waved a contemptuous hand. 'He
can't know much, if he is a lawyer, or he'd
never have let her do it.'

'Not a married man, I take it,' murmured
Crook. 'You I mean.'

'I should say not,' disclaimed Alfie

indignantly.

'If you were, you'd know you had about as much chance of stopping a runaway train as preventing a woman doing something she'd set her mind on. Come to that, she's done you a good turn. You should be grateful.'

'Why do you think I'm here?' demanded Alfie, more indignantly than before. 'What she wants is someone like you that can prove black's white. Mind you, I don't say she did it—I dunno—but that's what the rozzers are going to plump for. Line of least resistance, that's them.'

'Fancy us agreeing about something,' said Crook, cordially. 'How do you think the husband will take it?'

'Jump at the chance if he knows his onions.'

'You've got a nerve,' Crook congratulated him, 'though nothing to the nerve you're expecting me to have.'

Alfie turned towards the door. 'Just my idea,' he said. 'Up to you, of course.'

'Leave your address,' suggested Crook.

Once again suspicion clouded the brown eyes.

'Might want a bit of help yourself one of these days,' explained Crook. 'Honoured, I'm sure.'

Alfie spelt out his address. Crook unexpectedly shoved out an enormous paw.

'Does you credit,' he said. 'Glad to have met you. Just wondering how I could muscle my way in. Before you go—know anything about the dear departed?'

'Just that she's departed and it's news to me she was dear to anyone.'

'Widow?' murmured Crook.

'If I was married to that I'd make a bee-line for the cemetery,' was Alfie's retort.

'You and me talk the same language,' approved Crook. 'Well, be seeing you—maybe.'

'Who says there isn't good in everyone?' he murmured to Bill Parsons when Alfie had slouched off, whistling a raucous rock-and-roll tune. 'Fancy that boy taking the trouble . . . Yes, I know she may have saved his life—you can still get the rope for violence while committing theft, if it is only cigarettes and three quid from the till—but if some in high places were as prompt in paying their debts, a lot of us would be living more comfortably.'

The police were in no hurry. They had already had to release their first choice—mind you, they weren't to blame, anyone would have done the same thing in their place—but they didn't want to come a second cropper, and this Mrs. French wasn't likely to vanish into thin air. She hadn't given evidence at the inquest. The coroner had said he understood it would oblige the police if he deferred the proceedings, since action might be taken in another place, and Mrs. Hoggett was quietly buried with no mourners and only one enormous wreath sent by the *Daily Gossip*, who never missed a trick, and saw a whole galaxy of fireworks coming out of this case before it was signed off and tucked away.

It didn't occur to the authorities that Arthur Crook might be going to muscle in on the affair; and again, you couldn't blame them for that. He usually waited till they'd made the arrest, and they had to go through the motions of hunting for the anonymous visitor, even if in their heart of hearts they didn't believe in his existence.

Miles Gordon, who, like Browning's hero, never bowed his head but marched breast forward, into quagmires if need be, chose a time when he knew Paul would be at his office and came round to call on Helen. She was delighted to see him, asking how he was getting on.

'Fine,' he said. 'Which is more than you can say, all things considered.'

'That's absurd. I'm happily married . . .'

'Oh yes.' He lighted a cigarette and dropped a match on the carpet. 'Point is, how long are the police going to let you remain in that desirable estate?'

'They can't interfere between Paul and me.'

'No?'

'If you're thinking of Mrs. Hoggett, as I suppose you are, it hasn't made any difference to us.'

'I'm not a matchmaker,' Miles protested, 'and what Paul French thinks is nothing to me. It's what the police may think that I have in mind.'

'They're very unreasonable,' Helen allowed. 'They seem to think it's my fault I can't identify the murderer.'

'If that's all they've got against you, you're in luck.'

'I don't understand.'

'Are you sure they're not convinced you could do a good identification job, just by looking in the glass?'

It seemed incredible to him that she should turn so pale and seem so shaken. Surely she must realise that it was not only the police who held that opinion.

'You mean, you think I...? But that's absurd. Mind you, there have been times when it would have been a pleasure...'

'Let's stop all this fun and games for a moment,' suggested Miles, abruptly. 'My dear girl, just stop and ask yourself what proof there is that X exists at all—barring your word?'

'Mrs. Hoggett's dead body,' returned Helen, stubbornly.

'That isn't proof of anything except that someone whanged her over the head—by the way, it seems it wasn't the blow that killed her, she fell against the marble kerb round the fire, but I doubt if that will alter the jury's verdict.'

'Why did you come, Miles?' Helen inquired, and now she was pale as on the night she flashed open Blanche's door and saw her lying on her bed, nearly smothered in her own blood.

'Because I think you ought to have a chap watching out for you.'

'What on earth for? I mean, he can't represent me at the inquest, because the inquest has been deferred. And I haven't been accused by anyone, except you, of murdering Ruby Hoggett.'

'That's what you think. Wake up, Helen. I can't imagine what that husband of yours is thinking of, not taking some steps.'

The door opened and Paul came in. 'Hallo!' he said. 'Gordon, isn't it? Helen, you didn't tell me . . .'

'She didn't know. I came on my own initiative. Matter of fact, I'm trying to sell Arthur Crook to her.'

Paul looked staggered. 'Crook? Yes, of

course I know who you mean, but he's a last-ditcher.'

'Has it occurred to you that may be what you want or will be wanting shortly? It's not just my idea. It was Alfie Savage, and a chap like that has forgotten more about the police than any of us three know.' He told them about Alfie's visit. 'Look at it straight,' he urged them. 'The police have got to get someone and they won't be able to mark time much longer. The letters in the Press are getting a bit hypercritical. It only wants one more old woman murdered for the balloon to go up.'

'I can't see what another woman getting herself hit on the head has to do with Helen.'

'If you were the police you might. At least they've got a reasonable suspect in this case, someone who was admittedly on the premises more or less at the time Mrs. Hoggett was killed, and who—let's face it—preferred her dead to alive.'

'But if I was responsible,' broke in Helen, 'I wouldn't have told them about young Savage.'

'Oh, you might not be past doing an old woman who was threatening your future and still have qualms about letting a boy of twenty swing for it. Look. Take my advice and let Crook in on this. He's got interested—you can thank Alfie for that. And he has the supreme advantage of believing that X does exist.'

'Why should he believe it if no one else does?' asked Helen, stubbornly.

'Oh, perhaps because the police doubt it. Crook and the police never have seen eye to eye, and as he'd tell you himself, you can't teach an old dog new tricks. There's another thing. The fact that you aren't taking any steps, French, gives people a chance of saying, "Well, perhaps he thinks she did it too and like Brer Rabbit, he feels the safest thing is to lie low and say nuffin." Husbands not being forced to give evidence against their wives,' he added. So, albeit a bit reluctantly, Paul agreed.

★ ★ ★

And 'If you wanted to commit suicide why not throw yourself under a bus?' Crook inquired plaintively a few hours later of Miles Gordon. 'French has already faced one tacit accusation of murder to get this girl, then you come along and suggest . . .'

'I merely suggested to him you might be invited to take a hand. You know yourself . . .'

'Don't start telling me what I know,' said Crook. 'I don't know anything at the moment except Mrs. French's story. And that's the

236

way I like it. It's always best to start from
scratch.'

          ★   ★   ★

He went to work with a will. There were, he
said, three starters in the field. Helen.
Hoggett. Paul French himself. And he added
a fourth—X who may conceivably tie up with
one of the others. 'Now, we can eliminate
French because he was on a train coming
south at the time of the murder. No harm
checking up on his story, I suppose, but the
odds are he's out. Mrs. French was there and
we know it; we also know she had a good
motive for murder. Only—nurses are
generally pretty cool-headed people, they
have to be not to have murdered half their
patients. She must have known the stink
there'd be if the woman was found dead, with
foul play suspected. The story she tells all
hangs together, and she's told it two or three
times to two or three people. Trouble is, of
course, she never expected to have to tell it.
Then Hoggett. We know he exists, because
Mrs. H. told French so. First thing is to run
him to earth. Also she told him he's set up
house with another dame. Might be worth
checking the registers at Somerset House.
Now it's common sense that when one party to

a marriage meets with a fatal accident the suspicions of the force are automatically directed against the surviving partner; and good sense too. If a man or woman is so exasperating someone thinks it's worth the risk of putting them out for the count, the most obvious person, the one with the greatest motive and the greatest opportunity is the one they live with. Jamieson can start on that first thing in the morning. Then we'll start putting the screw on and finding if he also had a visit from the late R.H. and, if so, with what result.'

★   ★   ★

Now Crook was on the warpath. While Jamieson confirmed the record of the second marriage and, from the birth registration of the latest child, discovered Hoggett's private address, Crook went to see Tod Robinson and learned that payment for the business had been made in notes. Crook, by methods known only to himself, learned that a sum of £300 in fivers and single notes had been paid into the dead woman's account rather more than a year before.

'Let Mr. Sam Hoggett talk his way out of that one,' said Crook grimly.

*   *   *

Among the dead woman's papers the police had turned up a marriage certificate and a wedding picture dated 1928, showing a tallish young man with a flourishing moustache, a buttonhole and what Crook described as a wedding simper. Ruby couldn't have been a beauty at any stage of her existence, all you could say about the photograph was that she still looked like a toad, but a toad thirty years younger. Another man might have wondered what the young Hoggett had seen in her, but not Arthur Crook. He knew that sort of question ranks with the unsolved mysteries of the world. All the same, he reflected, it was a pity there was no National Health in those days. Chap might have bought himself a pair of spectacles and realised what he was getting.

Ruby's history was easier to come by. Blanche had got her from an agency run by a Mrs. Rose, where she had registered as a widow, husband killed in a raid, she had said. No kids. Aged 36, and every blooming hour of it, thought Crook unchivalrously. Worked in a factory that got bombed, went north for a bit of rest and stayed there for the rest of the war. In 1946 she got a job as housekeeper in a seaside town, and did this sort of work until Mrs. French engaged her in 1955. The references she had brought to Bryan Mouncey didn't help much. An airmail letter went to Canada where Mrs. Luke, late of Brighton, had joined her married daughter. An answer came back with commendable celerity. Mrs. Luke had found Mrs. Hoggett clean, honest and reliable, a reasonably good plain cook, punctual and sober—all the virtues, only it stuck out a mile that Mrs. Luke hadn't liked her much. She had given her a present of £100 before leaving for Canada, as she understood Mrs. Hoggett was opening up a little business and was short of furniture.

'One born every minute,' thought Crook, philosophically. Well, there it was. £100 from Mrs. Luke, £500 from Paul French: three hundred pounds odd in bank notes—and maybe Hoggett can answer for that. The remaining £200 had either been her savings or were money she'd coaxed out of some person or persons unknown.

240

CHAPTER FIFTEEN

A MAN called Jamieson went to call on Cathie Hoggett. He found a good-tempered girl with a face full of fun, carrying a baby like a parcel under her arm. As soon as she saw him she said she was sorry, they didn't buy at the door, and if it was H.P. her husband didn't allow it. Jamieson talked his way into the house, representing himself as collecting facts for a kind of housewives' poll.

'If you knew it, you're the first that doesn't pay anything on the Never-Never, so don't spoil my luck. I shan't keep you long.'

Popularity polls were the order of the day, anybody who subscribed to a newspaper knew that, so Cathie good-naturedly let him in and answered his questions. A picture emerged of a thoroughly contented household, though the husband was twenty-five years older than the wife.

'I'm his second,' she said. 'Bertha—that's the first Mrs. Hoggett—got killed in a bomb raid.' No, she couldn't say she'd recommend such a disparity in age to everyone but it suited her all right. There were three kids, a boy called Bobby and a girl called Maureen—and the baby. Yes, a big gap, but they didn't mind.

Babies were nice—didn't he think so? Jamieson said he was a bachelor. They were buying their house, had the whole place to themselves, Sam wasn't the sort that liked sharing—independent, you might say. That got Jamieson nicely started on Sam. He learned he had an ironmongery business, believed in hard work, was so punctual you could set your clock by him. Shop opened at 8.30, closed at 6, 1 on Saturdays. He was always back by the half-hour, and he spent his evenings at home. Not a drinking man and with children you couldn't often get to the pictures. No TV, not good for the kids, and anyway they were company for each other at the day's end. Good about the house he was, papering and painting, coming out with her of a Saturday afternoon and then, weather permitting, always ready to take the children out. Not one of those men that couldn't stand kids. Often they went to Barneys Wood, the big park-place about a mile distant. In the summer she'd pack their tea, and the kids liked to go swimming.

'In the lake?' asked Jamieson, when she paused, feeling he must say something to keep up appearances.

'No. That's too deep. Bathing's forbidden. But there's a pool there. Sam can't swim, didn't get taught that sort of thing when he

242

was at school, but I like a dip as well as anyone. Sam takes us to the seaside in the summer, all except last year, and that was only because he had a bit of bad luck. Bad debt,' she explained.

'Hard cheese,' murmured Jamieson. He looked round. 'Any pets?' Not that it made any difference if they kept a cheetah in the cellar, but people got suspicious if you didn't mention animals.

'Well, not a dog because of the exercise, and cats destroy the furniture, but we've got a budgie called Percy that Maureen's teaching to talk. Mind you, at present all it can say is "Hands off" and "See you later."'

'A bird of imagination,' Jamieson suggested.

'At least, that's what Maureen says it says. I can't make out a word myself.'

There was a framed photograph on the chimneypiece, the kind you automatically associate with weddings, though there was no white dress or orange blossom. 'That him?' asked Jamieson.

'That's right. My wedding-day.' She laughed, a rich cheerful sound. 'Sam's always at me to put it away, but I tell him every woman likes to have something around to remind her of her wedding-day. Sam says "Aren't a husband and three kids enough?"

but I keep it there just the same.'

Sam Hoggett had changed a good deal since he took the ill-starred Ruby to church, but there could be no doubt the bridegroom in this picture was the same man as Jamieson had seen in Ruby Hoggett's wedding photograph—older, graver, a bit less cocksure, but the same chap beyond a shadow of a doubt.

Cathie had gone out to the kitchen and now returned with a cup of instant coffee and some biscuits.

'Inquisition over?' she asked.

'Just the luxury section,' said Jamieson. 'TV. We've dealt with that. Holidays ditto. Oh—does your husband run a car?'

'Well, no, he doesn't, but that's the next item on the list. If it hadn't been for this bad debt last year he was going to get one and take us all away. Bobby—that's the boy—was as pleased as Punch, started telling his gang about it. Still, next year p'raps. Don't they say lightning never strikes twice in the same place?'

'So I've heard,' agreed Jamieson, swallowing his coffee, and standing up. 'You don't have to believe it, of course.'

And certainly in this case it wasn't true. Jamieson hadn't the smallest doubt where the car money had gone or that Ruby had plunked down her second demand shortly before her death.

*   *   *

'Jamieson always turns out a nice job,' said Crook approvingly, handing the detailed report to Paul French.

Paul looked less congratulatory. 'I can't quite see how Hoggett's skill as an amateur decorator or his disapproval of hire-purchase can make much difference in solving the mystery of his wife's death,' he replied in discouraging tones.

'You're forgetting the bit about the car,' Crook reproved him. 'Money saved about a year ago, car more or less selected, and then bing! everything vanished into thin air. Yes, I know he told his ever-loving it was a firm defaulting, but it's news to me that a chap operating on Hoggett's scale lets an account run as high as that.'

'Do we know how high?'

'There was three hundred pounds in notes paid into Mrs. R. Hoggett's account about a year before she died. It didn't come from you and it didn't come from Mrs. Luke of Canada, and we know that the late unlamented dug something out of her old man. Wouldn't you say three hundred was a pretty fair figure for a second-hand family car? And, of course, there was the holiday they were going to have ... I think I'll contrive to rub up against him and see what he'll spill. He may be a bit of a tightwad, but it's wonderful the things chaps 'ull tell you without realising they've even opened their mouths. And when you go back,' he added encouragingly, jumping to his feet and snatching at his horrible brown bowler, 'you tell my client to keep her chin up, because here,' and he brought his great hand down with a slap on Jamieson's report, 'we've got as nice a motive for murder as ever passed through my hands.'

★ ★ ★

Hoggett's Ironmongery Store was in Hartley Street, sandwiched between a wireless shop and a stationer's. The backs of these shops looked over a bombed site where a house had stood until Hitler's bombers flew over in 1940, since when the authorities had satisfied themselves with removing the shell and leaving the foundations as an auxiliary rubbish dump, where the locals could toss their tins, empty bottles and flotsam and jetsam that the dust collectors, who knew their rights nowadays, refused to accept. On the opposite corner stood a public-house, The

White Goat, and here Crook betook himself soon after opening time on that Friday night. Hoggett's, he noticed, seemed well stocked and laid out and did a fairly brisk business. Most of the customers represented small trade, he decided, but there were few occasions when the shop was wholly empty. Hoggett himself served behind the counter. Crook, who had seen the earlier photograph, could appreciate the change between Ruby's Hoggett and the far nicer Cathie's. The husband of the first had been a rather dashing young man defying the world with his expansive moustache and long chin, but Sam Hoggett nearly 30 years later was a Mr. Sobersides, an odd husband for the lively young woman Jamieson had interviewed.

At six Hoggett locked the shop, and about fifteen minutes later he came out, and turned in the direction of Hunt Street. Crook ordered a pint and got into desultory conversation with the chap behind the bar.

'Bit risky that open space behind the houses, ain't it?' he murmured.

The barman shrugged. 'Can't do anything, not unless they decide to rebuild. They put up a wire fence with barbed wire on the top at one time, but there was such a hullabaloo because of the kids—they tried to climb over, see, and one of them tore his hand badly, so down that came. Then the kids started pulling up the wire at the bottom and skulking underneath, and the old ladies taking their dogs out of a night-time helped the good work, because it was easier letting Ponto or Fido jump down into the crater than lug them round the square on a lead. Oh yes, the wireless shop's been broken into three times—I saw them once myself. Happened to be restless and got up to get myself a glass of water, about one o'clock this 'ud be, and I saw a light in the basement of Preston's. I dialled the police and they were here in under four minutes. When one of the chaps saw them he took a flying dive through the window, must have cut himself to ribbons, but he got away. They've put that unbreakable glass in now . . .'

Crook got the conversation round to Hoggett. Oh yes, they knew him, hard-working chap, nice wife a lot younger than himself, two kids, no, three, there'd been a new baby in the spring. Came in most evenings for a pint but never stopped long. If he was typical of The Goat's customers they'd shut down in a month. Not talkative, never took a hand at darts or anything, stayed at home with the missus most evenings. No, they didn't come together, because of the kids, see?

'Was he here to-night?' asked Crook, knowing very well he hadn't been.

'Oh, this is Friday. That's the night he works late at the books. Doesn't come in till nine or thereabouts. Might not even come at all.'

'You mean, there are Fridays when he gives you a miss?'

'That's what I said, didn't I? Lumme, you're curious. Like to know about Saturday, too, p'raps. Never comes in at week-ends. Goes out with the missus and the kids. Don't blame him either,' he added, candidly. 'I'd do the same if I was married to Cathie Hoggett.'

'Thanks, George,' said Crook. 'Ever hear of behaviourism?'

'I could guess,' said the barman, 'but we'll keep it clean if you don't mind.'

Crook grinned and moved along the bar and leaned against it, reflecting on what he'd learned. Ruby Hoggett had been killed on a Friday, between 8.30 and 9. Sam was always in his shop on Friday from, say, 7.30 till 9. After that, sometimes he came to The Goat and sometimes he didn't. The night Ruby died could have been one of the nights that he stayed away. Friday was usually pretty full at any pub and Hoggett wasn't the sociable sort. It wasn't likely the chaps were going to say, 'What's happened to old Sam? Why isn't he here?' A good chap, no doubt, a good husband by all accounts, but not adding greatly, in

Crook's guess, to the gaiety of nations. A formidable chap if appearances were anything to go by, and one who'd already served his apprenticeship with the unappetising Ruby.

Very interesting, reflected Crook, going out to get himself a meal at a nearby café. He passed Hoggett's shop on the way and it was in darkness, but on his return he saw a light burning in the back room. Back at The Goat he took a hand at darts, always keeping a sharp look-out on the door. The nine o'clock news had just begun when Hoggett came in. He went to the bar and George drew him a pint without being asked.

''Evening, Mr. Hoggett,' he said. Not ''Evening, Sam,' Crook noted. Some of the other chaps nodded or said some formal greeting, but nobody precisely rallied round. Crook bought yet another pint, gave his man a couple of minutes to get the flavour of the beer, and the headings of the news, which was all anyone fancied, then he moved in.

'Name of Crook,' he introduced himself.

Hoggett looked surprised. 'Speaking to me?'

'Hoggett's the name, I think.'

'Anything wrong with that?'

'Been in the papers a bit lately,' Crook explained. He had lifted his tankard and didn't appear to attach any particular significance to what he said, but his eye was as keen as a razor, and he didn't miss the involuntary start, instantly controlled though it was, the slight tilting of the beer-mug, the hint of a hissing breath.

'Funny, eh?' said Hoggett, in a low unaccented voice, and Crook thought, 'Wouldn't like to meet you in a cul-de-sac on a dark night, not if you had anything against me.' It seemed possible that he was on the right track.

He suggested they might take their drinks to a table against the wall. Hoggett shook his head. 'Nothing to say. My wife's waiting.'

Crook said something unpardonable. 'Which one?'

It wasn't often he was alarmed, but the change in his companion's face gave him a jolt.

'What's that you said?'

'You heard,' said Crook grimly, 'and if you ain't careful so will everyone else. Don't be a fool. If this is nothing to do with you you've nothing to be scared about. Only don't start telling me the lady they found in Camden Grove with her head stove in hadn't been your everloving quite a while ago.'

'So that's your game,' said Hoggett (and if he looks like that in a court, Crook reflected, the jury'll bring in a verdict of guilty before you could wink). 'Ever look through the phone book to see how many Hoggetts there are? And that's just London.'

'Surprise me to know there was more than one Samuel Obadiah who married a woman called Ruby Bertha Forrest in 1928. Oh yes, we've seen all the certificates, birth, marriage, all the bundle. What we didn't see till just lately was Mrs. Samuel Obadiah Hoggett's death certificate. Now I'm no cynic, but some things are too much even for me. Come on, give.'

'Where do you come in?' Hoggett demanded.

'Holding a watching brief for Mrs. French, and don't pretend you don't know who I'm talking about.'

Hoggett picked up his glass and they moved unobtrusively away from the bar.

'All right,' he acknowledged as they settled themselves in a quiet corner. 'So I was married to Bertha once. Bertha's what I always called her, I don't hold with these fancy names for girls, enough to drive 'em wrong.' He brooded. 'Maureen,' he said. 'That's my daughter. My wife was bad when she was born so I gave her her head, but I don't approve of it.' He shook his own. 'You were talking about Bertha.'

'That's so,' said Crook. One question that had perplexed him was now answered. He had

wondered why Cathie Hoggett hadn't smelt a
rat when she saw that a woman with her
husband's surname and an unusual first name
had been found dead. But there wasn't a
reason in the world why she should
approximate poor Bertha Hoggett killed by a
bomb nearly twenty years ago with Ruby, who
had died in such sordidly dramatic
circumstances at the end of last month.

'Say I was married to her once,' demanded
Hoggett, resentfully. 'They told me she was
dead and there was no reason I shouldn't
believe them. She could have written,
couldn't she, if she'd had a mind? She wasn't
suffering from loss of memory or anything, so
if she didn't write it was because she didn't
choose.'

'Maybe she was all for a quiet life,' Crook
suggested. 'She said you drank away the
furniture.'

'Likely I did,' Hoggett agreed, 'no chap
could have stayed sober in that household.'

'How long before she bobbed up again?'

'What makes you think she ever did?'

'Because she said as much. Told us you had
a little business Fulham way and had
acknowledged your obligations to the extent
of—three hundred pounds, wasn't it?'

'Bertha always opened her mouth too wide,
that was half her trouble,' was Hoggett's

savage comment.

'So it was good-bye to the little car for another twelve months, and when the time was up Ruby—pardon, Bertha to you—came round again. O.K.?'

Hoggett's face had hardened till it looked like one of those monstrosities you make out of a wish-bone and a bit of coloured wax.

'I don't know where you got that idea about the car. The fact was—I got welched by a firm that went bankrupt.'

'Is that so? Then, of course, you could give the details, if asked?'

'Who's asking?'

'Me now. Could be the police later.'

'You leave the police out of this. I've never been in trouble with them in my life.'

'If you say so. To continue—Mrs. Hoggett bought a little shop about the time you had to say good-bye to the car. Oh, she had some savings and a lady made her a present of £100, but even a little dog-hole like that 'ud cost a bit more than she had. So—where did she get it from?'

'You're barking up the wrong tree,' Hoggett told him, roughly. 'There was the husband of a woman she worked for—he coughed up. Don't ask me why. Had his reasons, no doubt.'

'So he did,' agreed Crook. 'Chap told me so

himself. Who told you?'

It's a strange thing, rather horrible really, to see a healthy complexion suddenly turn the colour of a corpse, but it didn't disturb Crook. Not that Hoggett was devoid of guts. He tried to bluff it out.

'In the papers, after Bertha was found.'

'Not mine. Which is yours?'

'One of the Sundays,' insisted Hoggett.

'I must put one of my chaps on to Fleet Street,' Crook told him, cordially. 'They'll be mad as hornets to know what they missed.'

Hoggett said nothing. 'You're out on a limb on your own,' said those dark fierce eyes. 'Get in by yourself if you can.' Crook could.

'Of course you didn't see it in any paper,' he went on. 'She told you. "He's paid up," she said. "Now it's your turn or your kiddies may find out they're just a lot of . . ." O.K., O.K., I'm only reminding you what she said.'

'What the hell's all this to do with you anyway?'

'I told you, I'm out to find out who else visited Mrs. Hoggett that night.'

'Well, it wasn't me. I worked late and went straight back home. When I saw the news in the paper next morning I thought, Well, some chap's done it for me . . .'

'Take a word from the man who knows,' offered Crook mildly. 'If you should find yourself in a witness-box, leave that bit out. That's the kind of thing that does prejudice a jury. Quite a shock to you, eh?'

'I thought it was some young thug.' Hoggett was still sullen but at least he was speaking. 'Then they took this chap.' He sighed. 'You know all that as well as me. In fact, you probably know a whole lot that isn't so.'

'That's why I'm here, to get you to help me sort things out. Where were we? Oh yes. Mrs. H. told you, "This chap, French, he's paid up and now it's your turn." French tried to play it smart with me at the start,' he added, simply, 'but he's thought better of it now. That creature that burrows its way through to Australia hasn't got anything on Arthur Crook.'

Hoggett's head came up with a jerk. 'You didn't say that Crook.'

'Heard of me?' Crook looked gratified. 'Now, if you're in the clear for that Friday night, I shall have to beetle off and think of something else. Someone here might remember you coming in, you might have played a hand at darts...'

'And if no one remembers that still doesn't prove anything, does it? I don't keep a diary...'

'Maybe you keep accounts,' suggested Crook.

'I'm a family man,' snapped Hoggett. 'Of course I keep accounts.'

'Then you'll know whether you bought a pint that night or not.'

'I might. But who's going to prove when I put it down in the little black book?'

'There'd be the week's total.'

'I don't put down every pint I have,' acknowledged Hoggett. 'More likely a total at the end of the week. Police know you're grilling me?'

'What do the police care what happens now? They've picked their bird. Now I'm out after mine.'

'You won't find him here. I can tell you that.'

'Happen you were home all that Friday evening,' suggested Crook. 'If so, you're in the clear.'

Hoggett scowled. 'I went home the way I always do,' he said, 'but Friday's my late night. I go back after I've had my tea and do the week's paper work. Books don't do themselves, and my business doesn't carry a book-keeper, nor a typist either, come to that. Yes, I was at the shop that Friday, same as I always am, and it's no use your trying to tell me anything different.'

'And afterwards you came across here?'

'I dare say.'

'Not sure?'

'I miss now and again of a Friday. Cathie, my wife, doesn't like me to be too late. It's all according. Some Fridays I do, some I don't.'

'Don't happen to remember that Friday?'

'Can't say I do. No reason why I should. How was I to know you'd be coming asking me questions?'

'Happen to remember if anyone telephoned you?'

'Why should they?' Sam looked surprised. 'Not likely anyone 'ud want me at that hour, unless it was Cathie because something had happened to one of the kids. Well, we don't have a line ourselves, not likely the price they are now, and Maureen or Bobby could come down in an emergency—accident, say, or my long-lost brother, the one nobody ever told me about—turned up from Australia with a fortune.' He widened his lips showing big powerful teeth—and no thanks to the Health Minister there, Crook reflected. A crocodile might envy him those snappers. 'No, no one telephoned.'

'How about a cleaner?'

'What for? My young chap and I keep the place decent. Once a year it's spring-cleaned. There isn't any cleaner.'

'Pity,' said Crook. 'Still, if you *were* in the shop that night, it has to be someone else, doesn't it? Did the lady never open up at all, give you any idea of some chap (or dame) who might have it in for her?'

Hoggett thought. 'She had it in for this chap, Robinson. According to her he led her right up the garden—hanging was too good for him—'

'In that case you'd expect the corpse to be his not hers,' commented Crook, regretfully. 'Anyone else?'

'Some smash-and-grab raider,' Hoggett suggested.

'That won't wash. It was someone she recognised, and anyway it was after closing hours. And the shop wasn't raided, and, if it had been, her body would have been found there, not in the parlour.'

'Let's get this straight,' said Hoggett dangerously. 'I can't swear where I was at half-past eight the night Bertha was killed. I might have been here—or working late—or been on my way home. I don't keep a diary so I couldn't be certain; only thing I do know is I wasn't at Camden Grove.'

'Nice little place she's got there, hasn't she?' Crook asked in casual tones.

'I don't know, because I never saw it.'

'What?' repeated Crook. 'Put down money for a joint you didn't frisk in advance?'

'I didn't care what she did with the money,'

said Sam explosively. 'It was enough for me that I paid it over. She came to my place twice. That's all I've seen of her in nigh twenty years.'

'First time you gave her three hundred pounds. Was that right away?'

'No. That was a Tuesday she came; I had the money for her on the Friday night.'

'And never saw her no more? You said it was just the twice.'

'I'm wrong,' said Hoggett stiffly. 'It was three times. She came again early that last week, the week she died, I mean, walked into the shop like any ordinary customer, lunch-hour it was, same as before. "Doing well, I hope," she said. Not well enough to support more'n one business, I told her. "Pity," she said. "Folks 'ud think it queer if my own husband let me get into the bankruptcy court." And then a lot of stuff about this chap, Robinson.'

'That the last you saw of her?'

'That's the last.'

'Did she—er—take anything away with her?'

'I told you, same as I told her, I hadn't got it. All I could do to keep square. The cost of things these days. Why, just to get the boy's shoes soled . . .'

He stopped abruptly, realising Crook was

unlikely to be interested in Bobby's shoes.

'What foxes me,' said Crook, 'is why you ever paid her anything in the first place.'

'I told you, she was going to tell Cath . . .'

'Suppose she had? Would the young lady have left you?'

'With three kids? Of course not.'

'That bein' so, why not tell Bertha to publish and be damned?'

'Because kids don't want to be known as little bastards, even if their daddy did marry their mum in good faith. Nothing 'ull change that. I know it and I can take it. Maybe Cath can too. But the children themselves—I wouldn't do that to them, have 'em pointed at . . .'

'O.K., O.K. That's the way I thought it was. So you paid over three hundred smackers in cash . . .'

'Know a lot, don't you?' exclaimed Sam, and Crook said well yes, that was his job. 'Came here for them, did she?' he went on.

'That's right. Place has never seemed quite the same since.'

'And then she makes a second demand and you can't meet it and she dies not from natural causes on a Friday night when you can't show where you were. Just working late, you say. Well, what do you suppose the police would make of that?'

'Nothing,' said Hoggett, stolidly. 'Suppose I can't prove I wasn't there, they can't show I was, and they never will, because I never was at Camden Grove.'

'You do know your own mind,' Crook commented.

'Why don't you get after one of the others? This chap, French—he could have done it just as soon as me.'

'Only by remote control,' said Crook. 'He was on a train.'

'That's what he says.'

'Found the taxi-driver who picked him up and brought him from Euston,' Crook offered.

'Well then—it could have been a smash-and-grab raider. Or this woman, after all. She's the only one who admits she was there.'

'Not her,' said Crook, firmly. 'She's my client, and I only work for the innocent. Well, sorry you can't help me.'

He was rising when an enormous hand caught his arm. 'Not thinking of calling on my wife, I take it?' suggested Hoggett.

'I would, if I thought it 'ud tell me anything,' Crook assured him, candid as a May morning, 'but I'm pretty sure it wouldn't pay off. And me, I'm old-fashioned. I like being alive, and when I die it's going to be in my bed, not strangled by an indignant husband. These ads. they put out in the Town Hall about special cheap crematorium rates for residents simply don't register with me.'

CHAPTER SIXTEEN

'HOW ARE WE GOING?' asked Miles Gordon of Arthur Crook. 'I see the police haven't made another arrest yet.'

'Why should they, with Arthur Crook on the warpath? They know I don't waste my time, ergo, they'll argue I must be on to something, so—let them sit back and later gather where they have not strawed.'

Miles grinned. 'How the police must love you!'

'About as much as the average person loves stinging-nettles. Fact is, my boy, it could still be any one of 'em. Hoggett works late on a Friday, some Fridays later than others. Some Fridays he goes into The Goat, some Fridays he don't. If he don't it's because the accounts have taken him longer than usual. No one ever telephones after the shop's shut, he hasn't got an instrument at home. In an emergency one of the kids can run down. No one ran down that night.'

'How about the light in the shop?' inquired Miles, sensibly. 'Can it be seen from outside?'

'I dare say it can, but you know as well as me that a light in a window don't mean the room's occupied. People put 'em on after dark quite a

264

lot in London to give that impression. And what's more, it works—like leaving your front door on the latch. I know a dame who leaves it that way whenever she goes out—don't ask me what the insurance company would say—but she says sneak thieves imagine she's only gone down to the post. Well, if there was a light there it wouldn't prove anything about Hoggett's whereabouts; of course if there wasn't, on that particular night that could help us, but who's going to remember on oath—with Hoggett swearing on oath the other way?'

'No one remembers anything the other end?'

'No one even remembers seeing Mrs. French, except the lady making a beeline for The Mitre, and no one's going to swear to identity on a night like that—someone they've never seen before. Time's the main factor now—sooner or later the police are going to take the easy way out and pick up Mrs. French.'

'Wouldn't care to be in their shoes when they do, not with Paul French breathing blood and slaughter every time they so much as look in her direction,' was Miles's trenchant comment.

'Then let him do something about it,' said Crook, rather sharply.

'If it was just the one man he probably

would, but even French can't dispose of the entire police force. Come to think of it, what can he do?'

They were soon to learn.

*   *   *

Coming in one day after a foray for evidence the police didn't believe existed and concerning which Mr. Crook had his own private doubts—not, as it happened, anything to do with the Frenchs—he found Paul French walking up and down the office in a state of exhaustion. His face was haggard, but his manner was both excited and defiant.

'Thank Heaven you're back,' he exclaimed, and his voice and general bearing were so much changed that Crook was prepared for almost any revelation. 'Look here, Crook, this has got to end. We've had the police round again to-day badgering Helen into making an admission . . .'

'Hold it,' Crook warned him. 'We don't have third degree here.'

'We don't call it third degree,' Paul acknowledged, 'but what's the idea in pestering her without warning unless they're hoping she'll break?'

'How can she break if she don't know any more about Mrs. Hoggett's death than she's said already?' inquired Crook, simply, slamming his brown bowler on to a hook and dropping into his chair.

'You know the one about constant dripping wearing away a stone? If they don't let up we shall get Helen on the borderline where she begins to wonder if she really did hit the old woman over the head in a state of trauma.'

'Now that's a funny thing,' said Crook, not turning a hair. 'Mrs. French didn't give me the idea she was the sort to panic easily.'

'She isn't; but—have you ever been suspected of murder without being able to prove your innocence?'

Crook shook his head.

'I thought not. I tell you, the time comes when you begin to ask yourself if you can possibly be right and everyone else can be wrong. I don't say Helen's reached that stage yet, but they're driving her half out of her wits. And even if she could stand much more of this, I can't.'

'Have to remember their point of view,' mumbled Crook. 'Their job's to get a scapegoat.'

'Exactly.' Paul's manner became wilder than before. Crook sent him a sharp glance, but the momentary suspicion that his man had been at the bottle died stillborn. This man might be intoxicated, but not with strong waters. 'I've come to put you in the picture,' Paul went on. 'If they do actually bring a charge against Helen I'm going to swear it was I who killed Ruby Hoggett, and even the mutton-headed police won't dare take her then.'

'I wouldn't be too sure,' Crook warned him. 'Always a chance the police wouldn't believe you.'

Paul looked like Lord Tennyson's greyhound that, checked in mid-leap, brought his owner crashing to ruin.

'What do you mean? Is it likely I'd confess to a murder I hadn't committed?'

'Oh,' said Crook, 'I didn't understand. That you really had done it, I mean. I thought you were on a train.'

'Well, so I was. But, listen, Crook.' He dropped into a chair, straddling it and folding his arms over the back. 'There's no absolute proof which train I caught that night. I've gone over this again and again.'

'Don't be too sure,' Crook warned him. 'There's the taxi-driver, remember.'

'The . . .?'

'The one who brought you back. He remembers it, though I dare say he wouldn't swear to your face, but it was late, and you happened to remark that you'd left the north in fine weather and a bit of a shock to emerge into rain or words to that effect.'

'Yes. It started about ten, didn't it? or that's what the driver told me. So the police have even dug him up, have they? Still, that needn't spoil things. I've said to date that I caught the slow train south, which was late, and instead of arriving at eleven, didn't get in till nearly 11.25. Which happens to be the truth only there's nothing to sustain it, beyond my word, and if I withdraw that . . .' He threw back his head in a gesture of defiance that his clients would have recognised. 'Listen, Crook. When I left the Twemlows I had every intention of catching the earlier fast train that would have got me down to London about eight o'clock. And if the Twemlows had had a thought in their heads beyond themselves I should have caught it,' he added with some resentment. 'But the fact is, they were so furious about the will, which in their heart of hearts they know perfectly well can't be upset, they'd have watched me drop dead without turning a hair. Two of the Twemlow brothers had come in their own cars; either of them could have run me down to the station in under ten minutes. But were they going to offer? Not they. I asked if it was possible to get a taxi and they said there was a garage, they believed, they never used it themselves . . . I asked Miss Tite if she knew the number, but she didn't. I found it, though, and got through—at least I could hear the bell ringing but no one answered. Well, I thought I could just make it on foot. We were a bare mile and I had the better part of half an hour. There was no question of asking me to stay to dinner and catch the early morning train, which was what I'd originally planned—anyway, I hadn't got a very heavy case, so I set out. But I don't know the neighbourhood, and, where the road forked, some playboy had turned the arms of the signpost, so that I went in the wrong direction. After a bit it occurred to me I was simply walking away from the town, so I retraced my steps. I could see the train coming in from a bit of a rise, and I had my ticket, so I thought I'd just make it, but it was farther than I anticipated and I missed it by a few minutes. I looked up the time-table and saw I could get a train to Buzzards Cross and change there for London. It meant a half-hour's wait and another twenty-five minutes at Buzzards Cross where we had to change, but it was that or spending the night in the neighbourhood, and if I'd gone back to the house I should probably have found the bolts up, so I made the best of a bad job and hung about till the slow train came in. That was 4.32. We were late at Buzzards Cross, thanks to having to pick up mails, and I was reminded of the story of the chap who got out of the carriage to sow a packet of seeds in the station bed and was able to pick the flowers before the train went on again.' He laughed grimly. 'The connection was late, too. By this time it was getting dark, naturally the refreshment bar was closed; I hung about with the rest till at last the train arrived and we limped back. We should have been in just before eleven but actually it was nearly 11.30. There were very few passengers—nobody was in the least likely to pay any attention to me—it was a hideous night down here, the rain had started about ten. I waited about a few minutes until a taxi arrived and came home. The house was dark which wasn't surprising. Since Helen wasn't expecting me she might have decided to get an early night. Miss Margetts generally goes up as soon as she comes in which is round about eleven. I rang and while I waited—Miss Margetts had bolted the front door—I noticed Helen's scarf in the area and went down to fetch it. That should have warned me there was something in the wind.'

'Why?' asked Mr. Crook, obtusely.

'When you live in your boxes, as nurses do, you become as neat as the proverbial pin. You have to. And I'd often seen Helen come in, put away her hat, put away her shoes, gloves, scarf—everything. I didn't believe she could have forgotten she was wearing it, yet there it was in the area. Well, Miss Margetts came along and I stuffed the scarf in my pocket and explained about the train; she offered to get me something to eat, but I said I'd look after myself. There hadn't been a dining-car on the train, of course. I mixed myself a drink and found some cold stuff in the larder and, as it was so late and there wasn't a sound from my wife's room, I went off to the dressing-room. You see?'

'Yes,' said Crook, stolid as yesterday's rice pudding.

'Yes, but do you?' Paul insisted. 'That's the story I've told the police. It happens to be the truth. But *supposing it wasn't*? Supposing I was the one they were persecuting? Don't you see I couldn't prove a word of it? The Twemlows would say I'd started off in time to catch the train—if I had caught the quick one and then gone on to see Mrs. Hoggett, with the consequences of which we're both aware, that's precisely the story I should tell. I should know that in a stopping train no one's going to pay any attention to a stranger. There weren't a great many people travelling, so most of the journey I had the carriage to myself. Of course, people passed to and fro along the corridor but if they saw the carriage was occupied that's about all they would see. I didn't find anyone, on the wrong road I took,

to ask the way, in fact I didn't see anyone at all.
Say I had caught the 8 o'clock and it was in to
time—you don't happen to know whether it
was or not?'

'Shouldn't be difficult to find out,' said
Crook.

'I could have put my bag in the Left
Luggage Office, because naturally I wouldn't
want to take it to Camden Grove—gone by bus
to that neighbourhood—it takes just the half
hour, I tried it out yesterday—and been there
by half-past eight.'

'And spent two and a half hours polishing
the old woman off?' asked Crook, dryly.

'Two and a half...? Oh, I see. Well, I'd
know it was too risky to go back before the late
train was in, if I was going to stick to my story
of travelling on it. I'd hang about, go into a
News Reel perhaps, or any cinema, there are
always plenty round a station, and then go
back and get my bag out of the Left Luggage
Office. That would be my one dangerous
moment, in case anyone remembered me, but
on a Friday there's a fair amount of night
traffic, probably there'd be quite a lot of
people collecting bags. It *could* have happened
that way, Crook. I've thought it over detail by
detail.'

'It's not me you've got to convince,' Crook
assured him unmoved. 'It's the police. How

would you know about the delay at Kings Cross for example?'

'I could have heard a passenger explaining to someone who'd come to meet him why the train was late. Actually I did, which is very helpful. So?'

'So you've only got to make the police believe that's the true version.' Crook looked about as credulous himself as a gorilla.

'The police? But they can't think I'd come forward to confess to a murder I hadn't committed?' Paul objected for the second time.

'Come off it,' said Crook. 'You're in the legal racket same as me, you know that whenever there's a juicy murder the local station's assailed by crackpots, all anxious to assure the authorities they were responsible. They write in from all over the country, even the bedridden join in the fun, and chaps who must know that five minutes inquiry will prove they haven't been out of the neighbourhood for the past three months. And when a fellow has a motive for making this statement—well, me and the police don't always see eye to eye, but they ain't such young birds that a tiny pinch of salt will bring 'em in.'

'But I'm not a crackpot, and I haven't spent the last six months in Lyme Regis or the

Channel Islands,' Paul insisted. 'I'm involved through Helen—well, I'm involved on my own account—and my story *could* be the truth. If I go down and tell it at least they'll have to make investigations. That'll take time and time is what we want. Unless, of course,' he added his voice changing completely, 'you've got Hoggett served up with gravy and bread-sauce.'

'Not yet,' acknowledged Crook. 'But he's in the same boat with you. He can't prove he wasn't there that night, he can't prove he was at the shop. All we know is he wasn't at home and he wasn't at The Goat.'

'Then how do you propose to bring him in?' Paul's voice sounded bleak with dismay.

'Give him rope. That's the only way, the more rope the better. After all, you can always charge it to expenses. It's always the same. Sooner or later the criminal says the one thing that betrays him, shows he knows something he couldn't have known if he hadn't been there. Some like you,' he added more grimly still, 'will fall at the first fence by proving you couldn't have been there.'

'But I could. I tell you . . .'

'I didn't mean that. Say the police start asking uncomfy questions. Ever been inside the house?'

'No, but I've gone all round it from the

outside. They won't fault me there. I went up the back way, too, the way Helen must have gone that night.'

'But you've never actually been inside the shop?'

'N-no, but . . .'

'And, of course, you've never seen the room where the body was found?'

'There was a photograph,' said Paul, eagerly.

'I didn't see one in colour,' was Crook's dry comment.

'Well, no, but—is that important?'

'What was the colour of the carpet?'

'I didn't notice. Helen would tell you I'm not naturally observant in that way. I don't think most men are. You know how women can tell you the colour of another woman's dress and hat—why, I hardly even notice the colour of their eyes.'

'You must be popular.' Crook sounded as dry as a war-time egg. 'Wall-paper?'

Paul hesitated, then shook his head. 'No. Just a general drab effect, I'd say.'

'As it happens, the walls were distempered, a particularly arsenical shade of green.'

'Thanks for the tip.' Paul actually grinned. He was looking happier now that he was contemplating something active.

'No need to look so damned pleased with

yourself,' Crook warned him. 'The police don't like being fooled any more than anyone else. What coloured dress was the deceased wearing?'

'I never saw her in anything but black.'

'That ain't what I asked.'

'I could ask Helen. She'd remember. As I said, women always notice that kind of thing.'

'How about the poker?'

'That was by the fireplace; the fire was lighted; Mrs. Hoggett actually poked it.'

'Helen told you that too?'

'Yes. It's in her statement.'

'What sort of a handle did it have?'

'Handle?'

'Yes. Brass knob? Steel knob? Flat steel handle?'

Paul considered. 'Flat steel handle, I think.'

'What makes you say that?'

'Well, it was referred to in the early reports as an iron bar. If it had had a brass knob surely it would have been called a poker?'

'You're right there.' Crook sounded grudging. 'They didn't find any of your finger-prints, you know. That might seem odd.'

'Of course not. Naturally I'd go round rubbing them off any surface I might have touched.' He frowned. 'Did they find any finger-prints at all?'

'Hers—on the mantelshelf.'

'Oh well, I wouldn't have touched the mantelshelf, would I?'

'Got it all worked out, haven't you?'

'As you've just pointed out, being in the same racket as yourself, though I don't think Phillips would appreciate that description of our work . . .'

Crook scowled. 'You ain't bringing Phillips into this? I mean, he wasn't with you? You didn't ring him up?'

'No, of course not.'

'Then keep him right out. You don't want to go confusing the police. They can get confused enough without our help. I still think you're crazy,' he added in a cool voice. 'You'll never pull it off.'

'I don't agree. I've shown I could have been there, naturally I never had murder in mind, but she said something that suddenly drove me to frenzy and I snatched up . . .'

'What?' interrupted Crook.

Paul looked puzzled. 'The poker, of course.'

'I didn't mean that. I meant—what did she say?'

'Oh.' He considered a moment. 'It had better be something to do with Helen. Mrs. Hoggett's story was (though we've managed to keep it pretty quiet to date) that Helen and I were intriguing under my wife's roof. It wasn't true, of course; Helen had only just recognised our situation and was making plans to move on within the week. Well, Mrs. Hoggett was saying we were partners in her murder—how would that do?'

'If you tell the police that or any other yarn wearing that expression they're likely to pull you in without asking any more questions,' Crook agreed. 'All right. Now you've switched suspicion, you've made it inevitable that they pull you in. I take it you don't mean to carry the thing through to its bitter end? I mean, it ain't going to help your wife much to have a husband doing a life stretch. That's all you'd get, seeing there was no intent to rob.'

'But'—Paul looked dismayed again—'we agreed that time is the essential factor. Before it comes to trial you'll have done your stuff— or wrecked your reputation.'

'Sure, sure,' agreed Crook hurriedly. 'But say the luck breaks for once—I could get bowled over by a car—or X might see his chance and make certain I wasn't there to interfere with the processes of the law. One way and another it could come to trial. No sense blinking that fact. What then?'

'I should recant my confession, of course. Can't you see, that's the strength of my position?' Once again eagerness informed the mobile face. 'There's no evidence whatever of my guilt *except my own story*; and if I withdraw that, why, it cuts the ground from under their feet. I admit it doesn't prove it couldn't have been true, but since we know it wasn't, they can't find any evidence at the eleventh hour to gaol me. That's the strength of my position,' he repeated.

'So you said before. If you ask me, you're taking an almighty risk. You may say it's circumstantial evidence, but it wouldn't be the first time circumstantial evidence had condemned a man. Or say the invisible witness turns up who could prove that you did travel by the late train?'

'He doesn't exist,' proclaimed Paul, impatiently.

'Any proof?' murmured Crook.

'Well, no, but—oh well, that's the risk you take.'

'What put such a crazy idea into your head in the first place? I've known chaps lie themselves black in the face to escape conviction, but, barring lunatics, and I take it you ain't that, this is the first time I've known a fellow try to get himself arrested for murder.'

'I love my wife, that's why.' At the change of tone Crook looked up, startled. He had heard such statements before, but always with an accompanying deepening of colour, the natural embarrassment of the Anglo-Saxon at declaring his heart. But here, he perceived, was a man who was a fanatic in love. He could even have hit the old woman over the head and felt perfectly justified. It was an unusual experience and it gave him, in his own colloquial speech, quite a turn.

'O.K.,' he said. 'No arguing with you. I see that. Just so long as you know where you're going. Only—get yourself primed. You're going to look no end of an ass if they flunk you right away.'

'Look here,' cried Paul, whose thoughts seem to have been running ahead of his companion's, 'can't you make something out of that? I mean, treat the process in reverse, as it were? If you think the police can fault me by asking me something I must have known if I'd been on the spot, can't you do the same by Hoggett or whoever the actual criminal is by getting him to tell you something he couldn't have known unless he'd actually been there? You see?'

Crook nodded. 'I see,' he said, a shade grimly. 'What exactly had you in mind?'

'I don't know,' Paul confessed. 'But there must be something. You know as well as I do that murderers generally dig their own graves, and not necessarily with the weapons they used to dispose of their victims—or tyrants. You're an adept at getting your evidence the hard way—all London knows your reputation—can't you think of something, some trifle perhaps . . .?'

'Maybe I'll have a few more words with Mr. Hoggett,' Crook agreed. 'I might drop along to The Goat presently—this is his late night—and needle him a bit. Meantime I'll drop the rozzers a hint I'm still on the warpath and that may persuade 'em to hold their hands, at least over the weekend. Don't you go letting any cats out of bags either,' he added severely. 'And—famous last words—don't ask me what I'm going to say to this chap because *I don't know*.'

CHAPTER SEVENTEEN

THAT WAS FRIDAY, by Saturday the balloon went up with a vengeance. Readers of the Sunday press had their best moneysworth for months.

It was a day of encounters. First of all came the stranger to Cathie's place, a tallish man with a dark red thatch and a moustache; he limped a little in his walk, and asked for Sam.

'He's at the shop at this hour,' said Cathie looking surprised. 'What was it you wanted?'

'Just making a few inquiries,' said the visitor airily.

'What about?'

'Nothing to upset him,' the stranger soothed her. 'Wondering if he's seen anything of a young fellow with red hair who's been going round calling at neighbouring houses and threatening women.'

'The only redhead I've seen in a month of Sundays is yourself,' said Cathie. 'And even if this chap has been going around how could Sam—Mr. Hoggett—help? He's not a woman living alone. In fact,' her chuckle became infectious, 'you can take it from me he's not a woman at all.'

'Indeed no,' agreed the visitor politely and

she suddenly felt silly.

'Are you the police?'

'Now, there's no need to take on. We have to ask these questions. It isn't every woman has a husband to look after her. At his shop, you said? What time does he get back?'

'Lunch-time on Saturdays. It's half-day. And we generally go out a bit together—If you're the police,' she went on, 'Mr. Hoggett 'ud probably sooner you went there. Hartley Street it is—you've an hour before he shuts—though why you have to badger him—'

'Just a routine inquiry,' repeated the man soothingly. 'You haven't heard any talk?'

'I don't have much time,' Cathie explained. After the man had gone she felt worried. Sam hadn't been pleased when she told him about Jamieson. 'Our affairs are our own concern,' he had said. 'We don't want these chaps nosing into them.' Still, she reflected, she hadn't told him a thing. When she went out presently she ran across a neighbour, and mentioned the fellow who had called.

'Didn't come to me,' said the other.

'P'raps you were out.'

'Not me.' She nudged Cathie with a sharp elbow. 'Sam putting the bulls on you,' she said.

Cathie was suddenly racked with fury. 'Never say a thing like that to me again,' she said. She found she was trembling from head to foot as she walked away. All the same, she didn't like it.

*　　　*　　　*

When the story finally broke, a number of people who had met Hoggett that morning said it was clear the guv'nor had something on his mind. He was never what you might call the life and soul of the party, but this was different. Not that he was less efficient than usual; he had the answer to all his customers' queries on the tip of his tongue, knew where fresh supplies of goods were stored, moved as competently about the place as always; but somewhere behind those unsmiling green eyes sat his secret self, occupied with something far more urgent than a set of ovenproof glass dishes or a new steel bottomed pan. Twice during the morning the telephone rang and each time he took the call himself. As a rule, he was indulgent on a Saturday, served a customer who came in as the clock struck one, but to-day he was ushering out his clients just before the hour and had the catch up and blind down before the clock hand moved. 'Blimey, he can't have got himself a new girl or anything,' thought his assistant. Then he went off, thankful to get away so promptly, and took his wife to the pictures. Until the news broke that evening he didn't give another thought to Sam Hoggett and his affairs.

*   *   *

'Did that chap come along to the shop this morning?' Cathie asked Sam at dinner.

'What chap?'

'Asking about some young fellow who's been scaring women.'

'Didn't come to us. What d'you tell him, Cathie?'

'Just that I hadn't heard anything about it, of course.'

'Say he was coming to the shop?'

Cathie thought. 'Asked if this was early closing day—no, asked when you'd be back.'

'I told you not to encourage strangers.'

'No need to bite my head off, Sam. I just said if he was anything to do with the police . . . you'd as lief he called there as here.'

Up came Sam's head. 'Is that what he told you? that he was the police I mean.'

'I told you, I asked if he was and he said it was all right and they had to make these inquiries, and everyone hadn't got a husband to look out for them.'

'I don't like it,' said Sam bluntly. 'Ask anywhere else?'

'Well, I met Mrs. Arthur; he hadn't been there . . .'

'Talk about an Englishman's house being his castle,' grumbled Sam. 'What a hope.'

'I thought we might see if May 'ud come in for a while this afternoon,' offered Cathie a bit later, 'then we could take in a picture. Long time since we went to a picture together.'

May was May Friend, a neighbour who, being unmarried but devoted to children, never minded being asked.

'Bobby 'ull be out with his gang,' Cathie went on. 'And Maureen's only seven . . .'

But Sam said not to bother. He'd got to go over and see a chap Bethnal Green way, something about an account to be settled. Cathie didn't like it. Just about a year ago it had been the same, and that time it had cost them the car; she hadn't thought much about it, anyone can be caught once, but Sam wasn't a mug, and a second crisis in twelve months did seem overdoing it. But, thinking thus, she was a million miles from the truth.

'It's too bad,' said Cathie, but there was no condemnation in her voice. She had far too much sense to urge him to change his plans. She could see he was worried about something—money most like—and when he wanted her to know he'd tell her. Some wives, she knew, boasted they were in their husbands' confidence all along the line, and a few really believed it. But Sam was old-fashioned, didn't approve of women interfering in business, which was a man's job; if they looked after the home and the kids properly that took all their time and a chap had enough of business where he worked, didn't want to come back and go on discussing it.

'You won't be back late?' she suggested.

He smiled then, a difficult smile but at least it broke up the harsh rigidity of his face.

'Should be home to tea,' he said.

'I'll toss up some of those honey-scones you like,' Cathie promised.

He put his arm round her shoulders. 'You're a good girl, Cath. Don't know what you saw in me, but . . .'

'Never look in the glass?' Cathie asked. 'Get away, Sam, here come the children. Don't want them to see us canoodling. You know what kids are.'

It was disappointing that he couldn't come out with her round the shops—it gave a bit of entertainment to the monotonous round, having him to carry the parcels and he never tried to oil out of it, saying 'How about my football or cricket or what-have-you?' the way most men did. A real home-lover. For once she thought about that first wife, what had she been like? A nagger, so much was certain. Sam had said once, 'What I like about you, Cath, is that you don't nag and you don't preach.' She'd remembered that throughout the years. It wasn't as if either ever got you anywhere, any road.

'Bobby 'ull stand in for me this afternoon,' continued Sam firmly, disregarding his son's, 'But the gang's meeting at Albery Street, Dad.' 'Can't start learning too young, son. Plenty of time for your gang after you've given your mother a hand.'

It was an age when children mustn't be thwarted under pain of fearful retribution in the years ahead, but either Sam had never heard of modern theories or, if he had, he didn't give a toss for them. Bobby knew too much to try and argue.

'We shan't be long,' promised Cathie.

'You take your time,' said Sam.

'What's biting Dad?' asked Bobby as they set out.

'Nothing to what'll bite you if he hears you,' Cathie warned him, but she felt a bit disturbed herself. Sam had been changed these last few days, got something on his mind. Still, they'd weathered trouble before, they'd do it again. They flew round the shops, and as soon as they were back, Bobby vanished to rejoin his gang and Maureen helped to unpack the basket. Cathie knocked up the scones and Maureen

ANTHONY GILBERT

set the table. By four o'clock everything was ready. Saturdays they had a sitdown tea at four and supper at seven.

But Sam didn't come; nothing came except the rain that had been such a persistent and unwelcome visitor all that year. He wasn't back by five; at half-past there was a step and Cathie sprang up, but it was May Friend, who had been at the Parish Jumble Sale and had brought something for the baby.

No, she said, she wouldn't come in, Sam liked his home to himself of a Saturday, she knew.

'Sam's not back,' said Cathie.

'Not back? You should tell him all work and no play makes Jack a dull boy. You'd think he saw enough of the shop all the week to stay away from it on Saturday afternoon.'

'He isn't at the shop. He's gone to Bethnal Green.'

May Friend was no actress; she had one of those round candid faces that all wives should have and so many don't. Cathie, no fool, saw she knew something, and her heart sank. Being married to Sam hadn't been all honey, he had moods like anyone else, and she'd guessed there were things in the past he didn't want talked about, but so long as they stopped in the past that was O.K. by her. But now for the first time she felt afraid.

290

'What is it, May?' she asked.

'Well, I don't want to speak out of my turn, but when I went past the shop after lunch Sam was there, leastways the light was on in the office at the back. Oh, it's gone now,' she added. 'That's what made me think he must be home.'

'I suppose he had to get some papers or something before he went to Bethnal Green,' surmised Cathie. 'It's funny, though, he said he'd be in to tea. Stop and have a cup, May. Scones are all spoiling and the rain's coming down heavier than ever.'

May agreed. Cathie looked distraught, and that was out of the ordinary. So she came in and tried to cheer Cathie, telling little stories about the jumble and what somebody had bought and what somebody else had worn and Cathie began to laugh and ask questions and the clock said six before they realised how time was getting on. And still there was no sign of Sam. It was ten minutes past the hour when a policeman came to the door asking for Mrs. Hoggett. It wasn't Dick Pryce, the one they knew on the beat, but a constable from the big station on the corner. There'd been an accident, he said.

Cathie turned as white as paper.

'Sam? Mr. Hoggett?'

'He must ha' slipped on something,' said

the copper evasively.

'What's happened?' Cathie insisted.

'You'd best come along right away,' the policeman said. He was a stranger to them, and somehow that made it worse.

'Go on,' said outspoken May, 'you ought to have been on the Inquisition. Why can't you tell us outright what it is? Can't you see you're giving Mrs. Hoggett kittens?'

So reluctantly he told them. A courting couple (and they must be in the very wrath of love to be courting out of doors in this weather, his manner implied) had been in the Park, walking along by the lake, what the Council fussily called the ornamental water, and, glancing down, they'd seen what looked like a great bundle caught among the reeds on the edge. So they'd gone down and it was a man. They kept their heads commendably, in spite of the shock, one of them stopped by him while the other legged it for the police station. A card in the sodden pocket had given Sam's name and address—'Good old Sam,' thought Cathie, 'always on about people too selfish to carry marks of identification about with them' (he never could understand why they called in identity cards, pandering to criminals and breakout men, he said). Cathie listened and put on her hat with quite steady hands, said 'Thanks ever so,' to May who told her she'd stop along with the kids all night, if need be (though, mind you, she knew that wasn't going to be necessary. No sense hanging round a mortuary and that, unless she missed her guess, was where Cathie was bound as of now).

'I'll just see to the children's supper,' said Cathie—wanting a minute to herself, May decided sensibly. And while she was in the kitchen May mentioned to the officer about Sam being in the shop that afternoon, which had never happened before, and that was how they came to find the letter.

It was in one of Sam's commercial envelopes addressed in typewriting to the coroner, and it ran:

'You could call this the last will and testament of me, Samuel Obadiah Hoggett. By the time anyone finds this I'll be finished. I've thought about it quite a while and I don't want any verdict of suicide while of unsound mind. I was never saner. When I was out of my sense was when I did for my wife, Ruby. Mind you, she only had herself to blame. She'd wrecked my existence for twelve years till the war separated us, and the best thing she ever did for me was to get herself killed in that bomb explosion. When she walked into my shop more than a year ago you could have

293

downed me with a feather. She got the price of my car, all I had, and I warned her then it was no good coming again. But Ruby never had any sense. Back she came with her hand out. Next thing she'd have been round at the house, I dare say, so I went over that Friday, like Mr. Crook supposed. She got me riled right away, telling me I couldn't go into the inner room. When I did break through, of course there was no one there; she started to say things about my wife—"I'm your wife," she said—and she went on to tell me what Cathie was. She got me so mad, and my eye happening to fall on that poker, before I knew what had happened I'd got it in my hand and she was lying there on the floor. I was flummoxed, I didn't even remember hitting her. Still, there it was and no sense telling that yarn to the police. I put the poker down, remembering to wipe off my finger-prints, I went round rubbing everything I might have touched—I didn't think about the light that was still burning in the shop and if I had I dare say I'd have left it; you can't ever be sure who might be passing—then I came out the back way and back like light, back to sanity and goodness ... I didn't see why anyone should pick me up, there'd never been any letters between us, the money I gave Ruby was in cash; I hadn't even talked to her on the telephone, she didn't have a line. No, I thought I'd be in the clear. But—I reckoned without Mr. Crook. If I've got to go I'll choose my own way out. It's better for my children like this. If anyone's interested in where I am they can look in the big lake in Barneys Park. There won't be anybody there to come interfering in this weather. Maybe when they're older the children might think it was an accident, I slipped—the bridge 'ud be slippery enough in weather like this and leaning over the way we used to, watching the ducks ... Cathie never guessed—how should she? I never meant her to know, but she'll take care of the kids, trust her. The goodwill of the shop should be worth something. The best thing she can do is forget me, she's a young woman still...' And then, as though, with death standing at his shoulder, he was shaken already by that chill hold, there was a scrawled signature—and that was all.

* * *

'Wasn't there anything for me?' Cathie asked when they told her.

They shook their heads.

'It doesn't seem like Sam.'

'Posted you a letter perhaps,' said one of the policemen. 'Get it in the morning—well,

Monday, of course.'

'I'll be back to tea, he said.' She paused a moment, then suddenly grief had its way with her. 'He should ha' told me. Did he think we couldn't face it out together? No, I never thought this one could be anything to do with him. He hardly spoke of her all our time together, and then he called her Bertha, so when I saw a Ruby Hoggett was dead—and him a widower eight years before we went to church together—how should I guess it was the same one?'

*   *   *

It was the detective-inspector who remembered Arthur Crook. 'Watch out for developments this week-end,' he'd told them, and that was out of character. When Crook started confiding in the rozzers it seemed a sure sign he was beginning to break up.

'Wonder if he expected this?' said the policeman grimly. And he called Crook at his home address.

'Good grief!' said Crook, when he heard. He came rushing round to the station as though the bears were after him, and they let him see the letter.

'Well, that tells us everything,' he said in grim tones. 'I always knew it wasn't Mrs. F.'

He stopped on a little while talking and putting his point of view. Then he said he thought he'd go round to South Square.

'She'll have to hear the truth and I'd better be the one to tell her,' he said. 'You can dot the i's and cross the t's in due course.'

And off he went like the wind.

*   *   *

Helen had spent the afternoon at a matinee with her friend, Althea Butts, while Paul said he might as well go to a cinema. Afterwards they had tea at Althea's club and stayed talking till it was time for her train. Paul was back when Helen arrived, putting out the drinks.

'How was the play?' he asked.

'A whodunnit. They all seem to be these days.'

'Good?'

'Well, if you can believe people behave like that. I couldn't help thinking our story makes a better one. Oh Paul! When is it all going to end?'

He put his arms round her.

'It's going to be all right, darling. I swear it is.'

'How can you be so sure?'

'Crook's got this in hand, and if he hasn't

found his man by Monday we've got a plan.'

'What is it?'

'I'll tell you on Monday. It may be we shall never have to put it into operation.'

'Paul, you're hiding something from me. It—I don't like it.'

'Can't you take my word for it it's going to be all right?' he mocked her softly. 'Come and have your drink.'

They were still drinking when the bell rang and Crook came bursting in.

CHAPTER EIGHTEEN

HE TOLD THEM the news. 'Have they found him?' asked Paul.

'You're not doing yourself justice,' said Crook. 'It was the courting couple that found him—remember what I told you about the invisible witness? Well, here you've got him and it's Siamese twins. Then they found this letter . . .'

'Have you seen it?'

'At the station. Typed on that old machine of his in the back office.'

'What made them look for it, I wonder?' Paul reflected.

'Some woman remembered seeing a light there during the afternoon and thought it was rum, seeing Sam was always walking round the Supermarket with his wife of a Saturday. So they got in the back way—there's been work on the bomb site at last and the wire was down, so all they had to do was put their great ham-hands through a convenient hole some chap had knocked in the window with a pole or a spade or something—the workmen were storin' their tools in a shed just outside Sam's back door—and in they went and there it was, all nice and neat, ready for the coroner.'

ANTHONY GILBERT

'Well, that really does tie up the ends,' said Paul. 'Oh darling.' He turned to Helen. 'It's such a relief'—he shook her arm gently—'well, isn't it?'

'Well, of course.' She smiled at him but her manner was still dazed.

'Just a little enthusiasm,' Paul pleaded. 'I was on the verge of—still, never mind. All that matters now is that you're safe. Safe.'

'Yes. But with you and Mr. Crook I've felt safe from the start. You see, I knew I hadn't done it. I'm not ungrateful, don't think that,' she turned warmly to Crook, 'but I can't help thinking of that girl Hoggett married and her children; how awful it must be for her. Did she have any suspicions?'

'Nary a one. Thought her husband was all to the harps and haloes.'

'Beats me why she never connected the dead woman with his first wife,' Paul speculated.

'Because he always referred to her by her second name of Bertha, when he spoke of her at all which wasn't often. It was only in the letter that he called her Ruby. Mrs. French is right. It's been a big shock for her.'

'On the whole Bertha suits her better,' Helen agreed. 'I remember Blanche used to say—oh, darling, I'm sorry, I think I'm a little light-headed. Reaction or something.'

'It's been a shock to you both,' Crook

300

agreed sympathetically. 'You and Mrs. H. From all accounts she took it very hard.'

'You mean she was in love with him? Even though he was a murderer.'

'It beats me,' said Crook, 'how it never seems to occur to the ordinary man or woman that murderers are the same as themselves most of the time, like watching football and helping the kid to sail his boat on the pond of a Saturday, go to the pictures with the missus. There's just that minute when they're different . . . I'd say it was just as easy to love a murderer as anyone else.'

'Of course, so long as you didn't know. And I suppose you could say he did it for her.'

'You could, but that wouldn't be a lot of help in court,' Crook agreed grimly.

'What will she do?'

'Change her name and leave the neighbourhood if she has any sense,' said Paul at once. 'At all events leave the neighbourhood.' She saw he was thinking of his own ordeal and its solution. 'Stop breaking your heart for her, my darling. I take it the shop 'ull be hers and the goodwill must be worth something; it was a tidy little business. Besides, this is the sort of story that'll latch on to the public imagination. People will be writing in from all over the country, wanting to start a Catherine Hoggett fund . . .'

'Don't, Paul.' Helen shivered. 'Can't you see it from her point of view?'

'Perhaps I shall presently,' Paul agreed. 'But don't expect too much of me all at once. I can't think of anything at this moment except that you're safe. It's been hanging over me like the sword of Damocles, the fear that I'd come in one evening and find you gone. I'd have gone to any lengths.'

'Fact,' Crook confirmed. 'Did he tell you what he was planning, sugar?'

'He said he had a plan. He wouldn't tell me what it was.'

'Crook never thought much of it from the start,' amended Paul hurriedly. 'But it was the best I could think of. Still, from a purely selfish standpoint, this is much better.'

'Want I shall tell her?' Crook asked. 'O.K. He was goin' to tell the rozzers it was him polished off the late unlamented. Now, don't look at me like that, sugar. I warned him it was bughouse from the start.'

'It was an absurd idea,' Helen exclaimed, looking exasperated rather than moved by her husband's intended quixotry. 'They'd know he couldn't be guilty. He was in a train coming south when Mrs. Hoggett was killed.'

'That's what he told them. But, as he pointed out to me, if he chose to withdraw that statement, there was no proof his first story was the true one. He'd gone into it like the lawyer he is. It was his unsupported word either way, and the police are such an unbelieving lot they always want their statements confirmed. Mind you, I warned him that when he came to withdraw the confession, it mightn't be such plain sailing as he seemed to imagine, but he said that was a risk he was prepared to take.' He grinned suddenly. 'Occupational risk of any good husband.'

'How on earth could it help me, your being arrested?' Helen demanded.

Crook thanked his stars he was a bachelor; it seemed you couldn't please a woman any road.

'You've never been tacitly accused of a murder you didn't commit, have you?' suggested Paul, in rather grim tones. 'Well, I've had first-hand evidence, and believe me, I didn't intend *you* to go through that hoop.'

'But what did you think would happen?' Helen persisted.

'That I left to Mr. Crook. What he needed was time to get his case together—I was buying it for him.'

Helen shook her head. 'I still don't understand. Time can't alter facts.'

'Maybe,' suggested Crook, 'we hadn't got all the facts.'

'And now you have.'

'I guess so.' But he didn't look as happy about it as you'd expect. There's an old proverb about not being able to make an omelette without breaking eggs, and sometimes, irrationally, your sympathy was with the eggs.

'You mean, Hoggett's letter . . .'

'Precisely. Fills in all the gaps. If only criminals wouldn't play for safety, they could even get away with murder. But they won't learn. They see the holes in the story and rush out to block 'em, and while they're blocking 'em the police—or outsiders like me—come strolling up and catch 'em red-handed.'

'Had you got your case against Sam Hoggett?' asked Helen. 'A case you could have brought into court?'

Crook shook his head. 'Not a sausage. He said he never saw the shop and I couldn't prove he had. Even our enterprisin' police can't arrest a man without evidence, however strong their suspicions may be.'

'At least they've got that now,' said Paul. 'The evidence, I mean. I'll try and take you away for a few days,' he told Helen. 'This 'ull only be a nine-days-wonder.'

Helen shivered. 'It just occurred to me—while Althea and I were tucked up cosily in the theatre watching a fictitious murder, he was in his shop writing out his last letter, and then going out—why did he choose the lake in such weather?'

'He couldn't swim,' said Crook.

'There were easier ways out surely.'

'Such as?'

'Well—poison . . .'

'Not so easy to come by, not now you have to sign a register. You can't even lay hands on arsenic in your weedkiller, everything in life gets more and more difficult, and that's a fact. There used to be cleaning fluids, girls in trouble took them when I was a boy—salts of lemon, say—no notion what they were letting themselves in for, of course. Besides, take it by and large, poison's a woman's weapon. Men go for guns, hanging, even jumping out of a window, though that's a selfish sort of thing to do. Railway stations, too,' he went on, 'though that 'ud take more nerve than I possess—and he wouldn't have wanted her to be the one to find him. No, if he had got self-murder in mind this was as good a way as any. Just luck he was found to-night at all,' he commented. 'No one could suppose there'd be this couple of duffering lovers mooning round the edge of the lake. Kind of a shock for them, if you come to think of it.'

Helen was watching him carefully. 'You don't like this any better than we do, Mr. Crook.'

'Well, no. Not what I anticipated, not at all.'

'Then what did you think he would do?' Paul demanded. 'You must have given him the impression you knew something fatal, whether you actually did or not. What was the 64,000 dollar question, after all?'

'I told you last night I didn't know. I still don't know.'

'Then what *did* you say to him that drove him to this?'

'Don't go pinning it on me,' said Crook, indignantly. 'I never saw Hoggett last night. I was at The Goat as arranged, but Hoggett never turned up.'

There was a minute's silence. Then Paul said, 'If it wasn't you who made him throw up the sponge, who was it?'

'Little God Conscience, perhaps,' said Crook. 'But no, I don't think so. It seems some chap went calling on Mrs. H. this morning—gave her the idea he'd come from the police.'

'And had he?'

'If he had they don't know anything about it.'

'What did he want?'

'Well, that's a funny thing. He didn't seem to want anything special. Spun some yarn about looking out for a chap who'd been frightening women—but he didn't call anywhere else. Mrs. H. told Sam and he said he'd got a date that afternoon—just like that.'

'You mean, he put two and two together?'

'I feel as though I were at Hampton Court Maze,' cried Helen.

'I don't blame you,' said Crook. 'By the way, the police may be coming round later.'

'What on earth for?' asked Paul.

'Just to tie up the ends. Mrs. French was on the spot on the night, wasn't she? She heard the murderer at the door, even if she didn't see his face and can't identify his voice. By the way, sugar,' he turned to Helen, 'that scarf on the chair there, that the one you were wearing on the night?'

'Yes,' said Helen, picking it up and shaking it out. 'We bought it in Paris on my honeymoon, an original design, and I put in my monogram.' She showed it to him on one corner.

'Neat as a daisy,' Crook approved. 'Just back from the cleaners, I take it.'

'Cleaners?' Helen looked puzzled. 'No. It hasn't been to the cleaners.'

'Not? Oh, I see. Dare say you washed it yourself. The ladies get up to every kind of caper these days.'

'I wouldn't dare. The girl explained it must be dry-cleaned, it's hand-painted, you see.'

'So it's just the way it was the night your husband brought it in?'

'Yes. Oh, I pressed it with a warm iron. It was very creased.' She was laughing at him, but there was no laughter in his face.

'Like as if it had been in someone's pocket?'

'Well, yes . . .'

'It had been in someone's pocket,' put in Paul rather impatiently. 'I stuffed it there when I rescued it from the basement.'

'What made you look for it there?' asked Crook curiously.

'I didn't. I was waiting for Miss Margetts to open the door and I happened to see it.'

'Luminous paint, maybe?' guessed Crook, intelligently.

'No. Well, that explains why it was so creased.'

'There's a lot of things it don't explain,' observed Crook with sudden severity. 'It don't explain why, having picked it up, you shoved it into your pocket, instead of carrying it in where Miss Margetts could see you had it. No reason to hide it from her, was there?'

'Of course not.'

'And it don't explain how, on a wet night—it had been raining for the better part of two hours, remember—it still was just creased. I'd have expected it to be in no end of a mess.'

'I didn't think of that,' said Helen. 'It

wasn't even damp. How extraordinary.'

'Extraordinary if it had been there all that while,' Crook agreed. 'Of course, if it had been under cover all the time . . . I'll tell you another funny thing, that woman, that Mrs. Peacock, that saw you coming away from Mrs. Hoggett's place, she gave a pretty detailed description, height, colouring, hat, costume—no mention of a scarf though. And it's a sizeable article.' He picked it up thoughtfully and bunched it in his hand. 'You'd think she'd notice that.'

'Well, perhaps I wasn't actually wearing it. I picked it up in a fearful hurry and dashed for the door. It could have been in my hand.'

'Why didn't she say so? And, last question coming up, how come you didn't notice you'd dropped it over the parapet that night?'

'I was in such a state about the whole thing, discovering that Mrs. Hoggett was blackmailing Paul and meant to ruin our lives if she could. I hadn't much thought for anything else. And when I found I hadn't got it I thought, "How horrible, I'll have to go back and see her again." It may sound ridiculous to you, Mr. Crook, but the very notion gave me cold shivers down my spine. It wasn't just that she was quite, quite hideous, but—Paul, you understand.'

He took her hand in a simple and reassuring

gesture. 'I know. All the same, I suppose she felt fate owed her something giving her a face like that. And worse than ever since she took to spectacles. It's a funny thing, you look for a *femme fatale* to be in the Helen of Troy tradition, but this one was just the reverse. It's no wonder you lost your head and took to your heels.'

'And left the scarf behind you?' Crook suggested.

'That's what I thought I'd done,' Helen corrected him. 'Now we know I dropped it while I was fumbling for a latch-key, I suppose. Paul found it in the area.'

'Unless he was looking for it . . .'

'I told you, I saw it quite by chance.'

'So you mentioned when you were explaining your great plan for being the Big Hero and acceptin' responsibility, only—Bill and me made an experiment, using a white scarf on a night when it wasn't even raining, and when we looked over the top we couldn't see a thing, the basement was as dark as a coal cellar.'

'What does that prove?' asked Helen.

'Why, that your first suspicion was right. You had left the scarf in Mrs. Hoggett's room, and that's where your husband found it when he went calling on the late unlamented at 8.30 that night.'

The silence went on and on. At last Helen said, 'Paul, what does he mean? You couldn't have been in Camden Grove that night, you were on the train.'

'Precisely. And I found your scarf in the area when I came back.'

'Funny thing,' observed Crook, 'that taxi-driver that brought you back, he waited a minute counting his change, he says he saw the door open, never saw you go down into the area. And Miss M., she didn't see the scarf, because it was in your pocket, where you'd shoved it after despatching Mrs. Hoggett— Ruby to you—mark that.'

'I don't know what on earth you're driving at,' cried Paul. There was contempt but no fear in his voice.

'Sam Hoggett never called his wife Ruby, didn't hold with it. She was Bertha to him start to finish. And yet when he comes to write out a confession for the police, she's Ruby all along the line.'

'That makes sense to me,' remarked Paul. 'Bertha Hoggett wouldn't mean a thing to them.'

'If he said at the beginning, the way he did when he talked to me, "I always called her Bertha," even the rozzers would have tumbled to what he meant. Besides, that letter was written in a whale of a hurry. He hadn't bothered to read it through, typing errors and so forth, but he never once even started to call her Bertha.'

'What does it mean?' Helen asked again.

'That it's all Lombard Street to a china orange against Hoggett having written that letter.'

'Then who . . .?'

'The chap who really killed Ruby, of course, the chap who, on his own admission, was there that night, a chap called Paul French.'

Helen's sudden laugh had a note of hysteria in it. Paul said, looking amused and cool, 'So you are accepting my second version, I see.'

'Only because you've just proved you had to be there that night.'

'Proved . . .?'

'That's what I said. You told us that Ruby looked more hideous than ever in spectacles. But she only got those giglamps the day before she died, *so how come you knew she wore them,* if you weren't there Friday night?'

'I know because Helen told me, of course.'

'That ain't what you said just now. You said she looked more hideous than ever.'

'It wouldn't require much imagination to realise that glasses would scarcely improve her appearance, so when Helen said . . .'

'Did you, Mrs. French? Come back and

say, "I've just seen Mrs. Hoggett, she's taken to spectacles, she's more repulsive than before." Is that what you said?'

Helen was staring from one to the other in a shocked amazement; she felt like someone who has suddenly walked over a straight path and finds herself in a riverbed with the water rising steadily.

'I don't remember. Yes, if Paul says so. Yes.'

'But when?' Crook urged. 'You didn't happen to mention Mrs. Hoggett till this boy, Alfie Savage, was picked up by the police. And you didn't mention spectacles in your statement . . .'

'Perhaps there was a picture in the papers,' suggested Helen, weakly.

'The only picture anyone could find was the wedding group; and seeing the glasses were smashed when she fell, there was no hope of getting a snap after death.'

'Then I must have told Paul. There's no other answer.'

'Except mine. That he was there that night and found your scarf and brought it along . . .'

'And then got into Hoggett's shop and typed the letter?' Paul looked openly amused. 'Is that what you're saying?'

'Why not?'

'Oh, but that's absurd,' said Helen. 'Paul

was at the cinema this afternoon.'

'I don't doubt it. Well, an afternoon's quite a period, and it don't take more than half an hour say to type a letter sending another man to his death. Of course, there are quicker ways, like shooting—or drowning—'

'And I walked through a locked door, I suppose? I can't believe a careful chap like Hoggett wouldn't lock the place up for the week-end.'

'Like I told you, the police got in the back way. There was a nice convenient hole someone had made in a window. It could have been the chaps when they put their ladders away at twelve o'clock, but in that case it's funny Sam didn't notice it and at least block it with a bit of wood or something, if only for the sake of the insurance. Makes you wonder if the hole was there when he locked up at one o'clock.'

'And I suppose,' said Paul elaborately, 'I had a story all ready in case Hoggett came in, attracted by the light, say, and found me there?'

'The chap who typed that letter knew darn well that Hoggett was in the lake at Barneys Park, he wasn't taking any more chances than he need.'

'And how did he know?'

'Them as hides know where to find. I

suppose when you rang him up at the shop that morning you passed yourself off as me.' His voice changed uncannily. 'Is that Hoggett? Crook here, Arthur Crook. Like a word with you. Understand from your lady wife you'll be home this afternoon (You'd had a word with Mrs. H. already, remember, being a policeman that time. Quite the actor, ain't you)? Now I could drop round... What's that? Not convenient. Well then, how about the bridge over the lake at Barneys Park? Not likely to be many chaps about a day like this, and we'd both prefer privacy, I take it. All the same,' acknowledged Crook, reverting to his own voice, 'if he hadn't been in such a stew he might have wondered why I couldn't come along to the shop, same like Ruby did. Still, that's one thing about havin' a reputation for being an eccentric, chaps don't start looking for reasons why you want to do things the hard way. But—though it's a bit late in the day for this—I'll give you some advice. There's a lot of truth in the old proverbs, remember, and one of them says "More haste less speed." If you hadn't been in such an all-fired hurry to get back and get that letter typed and then beetle along to your cinema, you'd have stopped another minute after pushing Hoggett off the bridge, and then you'd have seen the boat that had been dislodged by the storm, come floating by. Came from the boathouse farther up the lake and he must have snatched at it, and it floated him to the edge and that's where the young couple found him. Lucky for him they did, another hour even and the medicos say it would have been all U.P. with him. As it is, he'll live to give evidence against his murderer—would-be murderer, that is—look out, sugar.'

In a trice, bulky though he was, he had his arm about Helen and had whirled her into a corner of the room. The atmosphere, sultry enough in all conscience, now suddenly flamed into melodrama. Helen looked over Crook's shoulder in stupefaction to see her husband facing them, a pistol in his hand.

'Well, I'll be shot,' murmured Crook more appositely than he intended. 'Mean to say the court let you keep that thing after you'd done for your first wife?'

'No,' whispered Helen, 'not Blanche. He swore to me—it was an accident. And Ruby was an accident, too; I mean, she hit her head when she fell . . .'

'Only because someone had hit her with a poker first. Difficult to explain that away as an accident.'

'You mightn't feel responsible all the same,' Helen insisted. 'And Blanche shot herself.'

'And Hoggett? I suppose he chucked himself off the bridge. Never taught you any arithmetic at your school, sugar? Why should he? Got as nice a little wife as you'd find in the three kingdoms, a rising family, a snug little business—and the knowledge that he hadn't killed the woman he called Bertha and no one living, not even Arthur Crook, could prove he had.'

'I don't understand,' Helen confessed, 'but I know Paul wouldn't do that, get an innocent man condemned.'

'Not with me in the picture he wouldn't,' Crook agreed. 'But—wait till you've heard Hoggett's own story. Now, sugar, stop shaking to pieces like that. You're a brave girl and you've got to take it on the chin. Don't go fooling yourself any longer. You were wonderin' a while back how anyone could be in love with a murderer. Well, now you know. Fact is, you've married a natural killer. They come every so often, and it's part of their power that women fall in love with them. Anyone who gets in their way has to be liquidated. Right now he's wondering how he can put me out and get away with it, before any witnesses put in an appearance. Self-defence, maybe.'

'But I . . .'

'You're a wife, sugar. Wives don't have to

give evidence against their husbands, even when it's murder.'

'But—Hoggett was a man, too. It's not possible.' She spoke like someone in a daze, or coming round from an anaesthetic.

'What's Hoggett to him? Or Cathie Hoggett either?' For the first time Helen realised that Crook was furiously angry, and though his manner remained unchanged and offered no gesture to support his attitude, he was at once immensely formidable; against all reason, he made the pistol in Paul's hand look no more use than a toy.

Crook, of course, had the good sense to realise he was never likely to be nearer death than he was at this moment. A man who has lost the rubber can afford to play ducks and drakes with his life, since it is forfeit in any case.

'I don't understand anything,' said Helen. 'I feel like someone caught in the octopus of a nightmare. Any minute I'm going to wake up. Paul, put that down. Or give it to me. It may still be loaded.'

'Five bullets,' agreed Paul, 'Blanche had the sixth.'

'Your attitude only lends colour to Mr. Crook's story,' she besought him. 'Put it away, tell him it isn't true . . .'

'He wouldn't believe me. He's on your

side.'

'Then he must be with us. Because I'm on your side.'

'How can you be? You're on Hoggett's side. You can't support us both. Oh Helen'—warmth came back into his voice—'try and see this thing straight. It is expedient that one man shall die for the people. Only in this case you were the people. What was Hoggett's life to me compared with yours? Don't you understand, everything I've done, all the risks I've taken have been for you, to preserve you from losing what you valued, to save love for you . . . Some women would envy you. There can't be so many wives whose husbands have taken such risks, not once but three times, for their sakes.'

He looked at her with a new confidence, but she stepped back. 'Did you never ask yourself if I wanted you to take those risks and involve me in the consequences? If you're not mad, surely you can see you've simply slung these three bodies round my neck, like the albatross round the neck of the Ancient Mariner. Oh, I loved you, I loved you, but no love has the right to cost that much. You wouldn't steal a man's purse to buy me a necklace, you'd wait till you could afford to give it me yourself, or I'd do without it. Life's bigger than a necklace. I feel,' she cried desperately, 'as though I were talking to a stranger . . .'

'You're the reverse of the Victorian heroine who in chapter 21 turned to the hero with shining eyes, crying, "Oh Humphrey, I believe I have loved you all along and I never knew." Why, you've never known me at all. I could have been any husband. And that goes for me, too. I'm like the man in the Bible upon whom a great light suddenly shone, seeing you for the first time. The fact is, Helen my dear, you weren't worth one of those deaths, let alone three—counting mine. All my planning and suspense and walking into danger with my eyes open were for nothing. I believed our love was something beyond the limits of convention and the law. I thought it was its own justification. And I was wrong. You're no different from the rest, just the little suburban housewife of the woman's magazine, as alarmed by the thought of scandal and possible retribution and what the neighbours will think as any little scullery-maid. I feel like a man who's given a fortune for what he thinks is the Koh-i-noor diamond only to learn it's something he could have had for half-a-crown from any chain store.'

'But you must have known you couldn't get away with it,' cried Helen. 'Mr. Crook, he's mad.'

'Not within the limits of the McNaughton

rules,' Crook assured her.

'Get away where?' asked Paul. 'Don't you understand what you've done? Destroyed my last refuge. You were that refuge from the first instant I set eyes on you. I never had a thought to spare for anyone else. It was just you and me in a world of ghosts. It's no crime to kill a ghost, is it, and that's all Blanche had become to me? Mrs. Hoggett too . . . but I can see I'm wasting my time. I might as well be talking Choctaw . . .'

'Paul,' cried Helen, 'take care. Behind you.'

He laughed. 'My dear, that trick went out of date when Crook here was in the school-room.'

His laughter hadn't died away when there was a crash of glass as a stone was banged against the long window, then a police officer came charging in and caught Paul's arms from behind. The weapon fell to the floor whence a second officer retrieved it. The front-door bell rang furiously, steps sounded in the hall. A minute later the room door opened. The housekeeper, incurious as a marble statue, announced, 'The police would like a word with Mr. French.'

She saw the pistol on the carpet at her feet and stooped to pick it up.

'You shouldn't have touched that,' said one of the officers sharply.

'It's news to me to be told what to do in my own house,' retorted Miss Margetts. 'I was always one to believe there's a place for everything and everything in its place; and the place for lethal weapons isn't the drawing-room carpet. Excuse me, I'm sure.' Stiffly she walked out of the room.

Helen began to laugh, she laughed and laughed till Miles Gordon, following the police, took her from Crook's unresisting hold.

'I'll be getting along,' said Crook gratefully, 'now that you chaps have taken over. I've got other fish to fry, and you know where you can find me if I'm wanted.'

It was symptomatic of their attitude towards him that no one begged him to stay.

CHAPTER NINETEEN

THE NAME of his alternative fish was Cathie Hoggett. He found her sitting on a chair in a corridor when he got back to the hospital. When she saw Crook she struggled to her feet, and he saw that she had scarcely strength to remain erect.

'They wouldn't let me stay with him, my own husband,' she said indignantly. 'There's a policeman there, who never set eyes on him before, but his wife mayn't stay with him, even though he may be dying.'

'He ain't going to die,' Crook assured her, taking the cold hands in his. 'He's got too much sense of duty. Besides it's to everyone's interest to keep him alive.'

'Except his own.' There was so much bitterness in the voice that he was startled—that made twice in one day. 'Why couldn't they let him take his own way out?' she went on. 'He did wrong—of course he did. I know you can't take the law into your own hands. That Bertha deserved to die if anyone did, but he shouldn't have killed her. And I'll never believe he meant it; if she'd kept her tongue off me she'd still be alive. In a way you could call it suicide, but of course the judge won't see that.'

He had never heard her so voluble, he saw that even her control was broken, she couldn't stop. He pushed her back into the chair from which she had risen. He had hands like hams but now they touched her with an exquisite gentleness.

'Take it easy, honey,' he said, 'take it easy. Of course you want him to get well, we all do. Even the authorities. So that he can tell them what really happened.'

'We know what's happened,' she said bitterly. 'He's told them already. He went to see her . . .'

'Who says?'

That stopped her. 'Why, Sam himself. In that letter.'

'You haven't got it right yet. Remember that poet everyone went mad about when I was a boy? No, of course not. You're much too young. Ella Wheeler Wilcox, that was her name, and I've often thought the name helped. Sorts of trips off the tongue doesn't it? Ella Wheeler Wilcox.' His voice was having a gentling effect; already she looked calmer. '*No question is ever settled until it is settled right*. All we know so far is that the writer of that letter burst into Ruby Hoggett's house and killed her. What ain't proved yet is who wrote the letter.'

'But Sam—Sam—we do know . . .'

'We'll know that when he tells us.'

She shook her head as if she should shake away the mists of disbelief.

'Who else would write it?'

'The chap who murdered Ruby Hoggett, of course, and my guess is his first name wasn't Sam.'

He began to explain.

'You mean, someone rang him up pretending to be you and suggesting he should come to Barneys Park. It doesn't make sense, Mr. Crook. What was wrong with the shop?'

'There wasn't any water there,' said Crook simply. 'Remember, he knew Sam couldn't swim. He'd seen Jamieson's report.'

He had to digress again to explain who Jamieson was.

'Sam always thought there was something phony about that,' she agreed.

'Mind you, I don't say he couldn't have polished Sam off in the shop, but it 'ud be a different cup of tea making it look like suicide. I did know a case once where a chap suffocated his victim and then tied him up to a beam, but I don't think our man would have been a match for your Mr. Hoggett. And then it takes a lot of nerve to sit down and type a confession with his victim swinging—O.K., honey, now take it easy. Just get it into your head everything's going to be all right.'

Women were funny, he thought. She hadn't even asked the name of the real murderer; he saw that for her no one but Sam existed—her children, perhaps, as extensions of Sam, and himself, the bringer of good news. But that was all. The singlemindedness of women sometimes quite frightened him. It made them such desperate characters if they took a yen against you. No logic, no thought of consequences. 'You have to admit he put a lot of work into the job,' he went on. 'Must have thought he'd covered everything, but it's like what the old song says—"It's the little things that matter, don't you see?" Little things like not knowing Sam called his first wife Bertha— believe me, he didn't even know she had another name—forgetting about the spectacles, trying to trim it up with his silly story about finding the scarf in the basement on a wet night without a mark on it—he only had to drop it in the gutter and that 'ud have franked him. I don't blame him for not thinking of the courting couple, because only lunatics would have been wandering round the Park on such an afternoon. Now, why don't you take your Uncle Arthur's advice and go home and have a bit of shut-eye? Stop worrying about your precious Sam. I'll hold the fort, and I need him, even if you don't.'

He had a fatherly arm round her shoulders, but as he said that he felt her stiffen and draw away.

'You don't know what you're saying. Not need him? Why, he's the breath of life to me.'

That made two of them, thought Crook. He hadn't a ghost of a doubt that Paul had had Helen in mind all through his murderous campaign, and, if he had an odd way of showing his devotion, there was no question he'd been demented about the girl. And demented, reflected Crook grimly, is just about right.

'I'll run you back,' he went on soothingly. 'I had a word with matron on the way in. There's no chance of your being able to see hubby for hours to come, and when you do you don't want to be asleep on your feet. Kind of discouraging for a man who's just come back from the gates of death. Besides, the kiddies 'ull be wondering what's happened to Mum. You can't make an orphan of that baby...' So gently he persuaded her.

'He might ask for me,' whispered Cathie, but she was weakening.

'I'll be on the trail,' Crook promised, 'and I'm like the hedgehog, I always feel widest awake after dark. I'll come right round for you in the Superb the minute he opens an eye and get you here like winking.'

So, at last, she nodded and went.

May was waiting up when they arrived, the children were all asleep.

'I'll stay here,' she told Mr. Crook confidentially, after Cathie had been persuaded to take off her clothes and go properly to bed. 'I can make up a shakedown. Then Cathie'll be able to sleep. Of course, it's all dreadful,' she went on, 'but there's no getting away from it, it is dramatic, isn't it? I always say there's nothing so exciting as people, and with life being so monotonous nowadays with bombs and everything, it does put a bit of colour into the days.'

Crook went back to the hospital, his head singing. Life being so monotonous what with bombs and so on, he thought. No wonder you never got tired of life. He thought that if there was an eternity he could spend it in bliss just watching the world go by. There's nought so queer as folk and it was the queerness that held him in perpetual thrall.

*　　*　　*

Sam had recovered sufficiently to make his statement the following afternoon, and it proved to be much on the lines Crook had anticipated. It hadn't occurred to him, he said, that when a man's voice announced over

the telephone that the speaker was Arthur
Crook it might not *be* Arthur Crook. He'd
made his way to the bridge, and a nasty dark
afternoon it was, with nobody about; he
hadn't been there long when a fellow came up,
wearing a big moustache and trailing one foot
a little.

'Mr. Hoggett?' he'd said. 'I'm Parsons,
Crook's right hand man. He'll be along quite
soon, but he got held up and he sent me to let
you know it wasn't a practical joke.'

They'd stood for a minute looking at the
pewter-coloured water and then the wind
must have blown the chap's hat off. Anyway,
there it was on the ground and his stick was
hampering him, so Sam stooped, but before
he could get his fingers on it something struck
him on the back of the head, and he supposed
he'd passed out, because the next thing he
knew he was in twelve feet of icy water. He
might have called out, he couldn't remember,
but there wasn't anyone so far as he could see.
He had thought he was done for, but the love
of life is strong and there was Cathie and the
kids, and fate was playing the ace of trumps on
his behalf that afternoon. Because a boat, that
had been moored by the boathouse farther up
was adrift and floated under the bridge, and
he'd grabbed at it and presumably it had
floated him to the edge where the young

couple had found him; but he was out all right
by then, didn't remember a thing till he woke
up and found himself in a hospital bed with a
copper on guard. 'Where's Cathie?' he'd
asked. She was the only one he had thought
for, not the man who'd tried to murder him,
not the dauntless young couple who hadn't
given a tiddley-push for the weather, just
Cathie. Maybe it wasn't only women who were
single-minded, Crook told himself.

'Know why I never committed a murder?'
he asked Miles Gordon who came drifting
round to Earls Court the next day. 'It's too
damned dangerous, loaded dice, all the
bundle. You could say French asked for it,
legging it before he made dead sure his chap
had gone under for the third time, but he
naturally didn't want to be seen there, leaving
a man to drown without making any sort of
effort to get him out. He never saw the
courting couple. Maybe they were hidden
behind a gooseberry bush; but that's the kind
of thing that happens time out of number,
something you can't be expected to anticipate,
like rain when the Queen goes to the Trooping
of the Colour. And that's why I play safe. I
wouldn't say I was exactly a mollycoddle, but I
have to draw the line somewhere.'

'You should tell the police that,' said Miles
nastily. 'And see how many of them believe

you.'

*　　　*　　　*

'What'll happen to French?' he asked later on.

'What do you suppose? He can't get out of the murder of Ruby Hoggett, too many witnesses; there was a chap under the window, as well as me and Mrs. F. Mind you, she can't be made to give evidence, but it won't be necessary.'

'How about the first Mrs. French?'

'We-ell, he practically told us he did for her. Whether we could prove it's a moot point, but I doubt if we shall have to. My own feeling is he'll give the world the truth. Well, what has he got to lose? He'd get a life sentence for Mrs. H., and there's his murder attempt on Hoggett—why, he'd spend the rest of his days in gaol, and that 'ud reduce him to the squalid little murderer he's never appeared to himself. Chaps like that spend half their time looking into distorting mirrors, which double their height, so that they see themselves as giants. He won't want to carry on as a number in a prison working squad. No, he's the hero who thought the world well lost for love, and he may as well go down with his colours flying. And, you see, he'll justify what he did right up to the end.'

Crook proved a true prophet. Against all legal advice, Paul insisted on pleading guilty not only to Ruby Hoggett's murder but also to that of his first wife. In the short time remaining to him after sentence had been passed—the country still maintained capital punishment for death by shooting as well as for multiple murder—he sat unbowed in his cell writing articles for the 'Foot of the Scaffold' series run by the *Sunday Gossip*.

'Is Paul French the greatest lover of the year?' screamed the *Gossip* all over the country.

'What's the sense?' asked Miles. 'If he's being paid £1,000 a word it won't do him any good. Helen wouldn't touch the money . . .'

'He isn't thinking about the money. He ain't even thinking about his wife. No, this is the last chance he's ever going to have to be in the limelight. He's always been a great man to himself, now he's going to share that opinion with all the *Gossip's* readers and I leave you to guess how many million that's likely to be.'

One of the consequences of this 'stupendous scoop' was that car-loads of depraved sight-seers came to gawp at the house in South Square, hanging about half the day in the hopes of catching a glimpse of the Mystery Woman for whom these crimes had been committed. Helen scarcely dared look out of the window.

'Dress up a bolster with a wig and the pink scarf and stick it in the window,' Crook advised. 'Then go to Brighton for a change. Brighton's like London, so big no one worries about you.'

* * *

After the execution Phillips insisted on settling Crook's bill. 'I feel I owe it to you,' he explained candidly. 'I might have been the next obstacle in French's path, and the chap seems to have had no more conscience than a cyclone.'

* * *

Sam Hoggett went through a second wedding ceremony with Cathie—'to make sure they don't do you out of the widow's pension one of these days,' he remarked grimly. He left the shop in Bernie's charge and took the whole family away for a fortnight to the seaside. After he came back he made no references to what had occurred; no one threw

ANTHONY GILBERT

any stones, verbal or actual, and there was no
question of pressing a bigamy charge. Hoggett
had had official notification of his wife's death
and in any case had waited more than the
statutory seven years before re-marrying.

* * *

'There's still one point not quite cleared
up,' Miles Gordon pointed out. 'Was there a
first bell before the shot?'

Crook shook his head. 'Only Mrs. H. could
tell you that. My bet 'ud be no, or she'd have
brought it up at the inquest. But afterwards—
she was no fool—she realised that even the
suggestion that she'd been mistaken would
put him in a sweat. Y'see, he was guilty and
when you know a thing like that about
yourself it's hard to realise it ain't so obvious to
other people. And the fact was, he couldn't
afford to let that rumour circulate. What
matters in the last resort is less the truth,' said
that amiable cynic, Arthur Crook, 'than what
you can persuade people to believe.'

But he wasn't paying much attention to the
French case any more. He'd got something
else on his plate, a honey of a puzzler, and he
was after it like a poodle puppy after its own
tail.

334

*   *   *

The house in South Square was closed for a while, then handed over to the agents to sell lock, stock and barrel.

'I never want to set eyes on it again,' shuddered Helen. 'I want to forget that chapter of my life altogether.'

Crook said nothing. He knew she was after the impossible, you can no more obliterate a chapter of your life than you can jump from page 20 to page 50 in a book and pretend the intervening 30 pages had never been written. Life's like a patchwork quilt, everything has to be worked into the pattern. Helen herself had resumed her maiden name and once more gone abroad nursing.

'Good thing, too,' said Crook, heartily. 'She'll soon realise what a small potato even Britain's most famous widow is outside this right little, tight little island.'

'Anyone ever try to murder you?' asked Miles dryly.

'Plenty,' said Crook, 'starting with Jerry back in 1916. And they're still hoping.'

'There are times,' said Miles, 'when they have my sympathy.'

And he slammed out of the office.

*   *   *

About a year later he came strolling back. 'I'm thinking of making a trip to the States,' he announced blandly. 'Have a look at the architecture there. Doesn't do to get into a rut.'

'So you've run her to earth,' said Crook. 'Yes, of course I knew where she was. She sent me a picture postcard of the Statue of Liberty. Symbolic or something, whatever that means. Now, Gordon, don't you go upsetting her. Might be the best thing could happen to her if she married out there—a nice girl like that shouldn't have any difficulty—and they say that often the best cure is a hair of the dog that bit you. Could be she's consoled herself already,' he added.

'You've got about as much heart as a dried pea,' Miles accused him, but this time there was no heat in his voice. Crook deduced he'd had something more than a picture postcard. 'In my opinion we've already ceded too much to the Yanks. We may not be a first-class power any longer, but we still have some rights, and one of them is the right to hang on to our own nationals.'

'Some ladies seem to stir up the dust wherever they go,' Crook commented. 'Don't go getting mixed up in a duel—you know how romantic Americans are. O.K., O.K., I'm not blaming her. She can't help being born a *femme fatale*, I suppose, any more than I can help being born with red hair. And when you've simmered down,' he added, 'and we've had a drink to the future Mrs. Gordon, I'll show you how you can get your whole trip, including the wedding cake, on your expenses sheet. And as a wedding present,' he gave Miles a thump on the back that nearly sent him sprawling—'I'd say that's more than somewhat.'

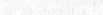